SHERLOCK HO
OTHER WOMAN

BY

GERI SCHEAR

To Nigel, Heather & family -
Thanks for reading.

Geri Schear

1

Paperback ISBN 978-1-78092-832-6
ePub ISBN 978-1-78092-833-3
PDF ISBN 978-1-78092-834-0

Published in the UK by MX Publishing
335 Princess Park Manor, Royal Drive,
London, N11 3GX
www.mxpublishing.co.uk
Cover design by www.staunch.com

Grateful acknowledgment to Conan Doyle Estate Ltd. for the use of the Sherlock Holmes characters created by Sir Arthur Conan Doyle.

2

1

Doctor John H. Watson is a man of many remarkable talents, something readers of his semi-fictional accounts of my cases might not guess, and one of the most precious of these is silence.

Usually.

As I am, by nature, a more solitary individual than most, I find it comforting to share my accommodation and a great portion of my life with such an individual.

Usually.

However, it is irksome when one wishes to engage in conversation only to find one's closest companion relentlessly... silent.

Watson did not speak when I trudged up the stairs with my suitcases, nor did he offer to help as I creaked my way into my bedroom and clattered all my belongings onto the floor.

After many vexed exclamations, at last my arms were free and I was able to sink into my customary chair beside the hearth. Still the wretched man did not look up nor acknowledge my presence in any way. Wounded, I spluttered, "Well, I'm home!"

He glanced up at me indifferently and said, "Oh, hullo. Toss some more coal on the fire if you would, Holmes."

I did so in no happy temper and sank back in my seat with my coat wrapped around me. I might as well go back out if this was all the welcome I was to receive in my own home after ten weeks abroad.

Before I could remonstrate, there was a knock on the door and Mrs Hudson entered carrying a heavily laden tray. "You might help me with this, if you please, Mr Holmes," she said, all but tossing the object at me. I had no option but to take it. I placed it on the table and made to return to my seat by the fire, but the woman said, "Come, now, Mr Holmes. You must be thirsty after your long journey. Sit there and have a nice hot cup of coffee."

There was more than coffee: several dishes of hot food were there for my pleasure. I glanced up at my housekeeper and she tittered. "There now, you didn't think we'd let you come home without some sort of a welcome, did you?"

Watson grinned and sat at the table beside me.

"You knew when I'd be returning?" I said.

"We had a telegram from Paris," Watson said. "We've been keeping a close watch for your arrival for over an hour."

"I shall leave you to your breakfast, Mr Holmes," Mrs Hudson said, patting me on the shoulder. "It is very good to have you home again." At which point she kissed my forehead and I had that extraordinary sensation of feeling like a very small child again. That, in turn, compounded a quite ridiculous sense of gratitude that threatened to engulf me. Can there be a greater joy than to return home after a long absence and to be warmly greeted by dear old friends?

I waved the woman away, "Yes, yes," I said. "This was a splendid thought. Thank you, Mrs Hudson."

Watson laughed loudly. "I had you going, didn't I?"

I sipped my coffee and said, "I cannot imagine what you mean."

"Fibber."

I joined in his laughter and admitted, "Well, I did think it was a bit much that a man's closest companion doesn't greet him with even a hullo when he returns home after a long absence."

4

He brushed a non-existent speck from his trouser leg and said much too casually, "You're home sooner than I expected. Is everything all right?"

"Yes," I said. I handed him a telegram. "I received this from Mycroft."

"*Zugzwang?*" he said. "Who is that?"

"Not who; what. It is a term used by German chess players. It means one is compelled to move when one wishes not to."

He stared at me in bewilderment.

"It's Mycroft's way of telling me I must come home, whether I will or no."

"Whatever for?"

"There is insufficient data for me to speculate. I suggest, my dear fellow, we finish breakfast and make our way to Whitehall to see what is on my brother's mind. I need to talk to him, in any case."

Watson sipped his coffee and said, again too casually, "It must be important if you had to cut short your holiday. Still, it is a shame. I'm sure Beatrice wasn't happy about having to return after just a few short weeks."

"Hmm? Oh, B didn't come back."

"What? Good grief, Holmes, you cannot mean you left her alone on the Continent?"

I bit into a piece of buttered toast and swallowed it before saying, "She is not alone; she's with friends in Paris."

"Paris?" he spluttered. "You cannot be serious. Do you know what is happening all over France right now? Riots and who knows what sort of outrages. This 'Dreyfus Affair' has become even more violent since Zola's arrest."

"Of course I know; I just came from there. I do not understand why you are in such a lather, my dear fellow. B is no fool and she's perfectly capable of looking after herself."

"In London, perhaps; under civilised conditions. But for goodness sake, Holmes, leaving a woman alone in Paris during such turmoil: Is it wise? Is it safe?"

"It's not some 'woman alone in France,' Watson. It's B. She is as capable as any man I know. In fact, it was her idea that I should return and speak to Mycroft."

"Why? What does she expect him to do?"

"Mycroft is a man of considerable influence. B thinks, and I agree, that he might be able to prevail upon the cooler heads in the French government to find some peaceful solution to this situation."

My friend seemed prepared to argue further but I forestalled him. "My wife and I have an agreement, Watson: the terms of our marriage are that we live our separate lives without infringing upon each other's freedom. We even wrote up a formal contract stating the terms. I cannot say I am entirely happy with her decision, but I am honour-bound to support it. Now, if you have quite finished those eggs we really should be off."

Half an hour later—nothing can hurry Watson through a meal—my friend and I made our way through the streets of London to Whitehall. The weather was typically English: cold, wet, and blustery, but there is something in the British air, particularly London air, which I usually find sweeter than all the perfumes of Lombardy.

Mycroft's aide Gillespie greeted me warmly, as always. "A great pleasure to see you again, Mr Holmes," he said. "It's been a while. Last time I saw you was when you and the doctor took me to lunch at the Devereux during the last day of court."

"Excellent food," Watson said. "Dreadful case."

"Yes, indeed. Still, that villain is dead now, along with all his cutthroat conspirators, thanks to you and Mr Holmes. Don't think I've ever met a villain to equal that Porlock fellow, not in all my years."

"And you've had more years than most, Mr Gillespie," Watson said, laughing.

"I have at that. I still find it hard to believe that an Englishman should be so corrupt."

"An Englishman he was, nonetheless," I said. "With a pretty English wife and pretty English children. I suppose we are as capable of villainy as any other nation."

"We are at that. By the way, Mr Holmes, I must congratulate you on being awarded the Royal Victorian Order. It is a great honour and richly deserved, if I may say so."

"Hear, hear," Watson said.

"And congratulations to you too, Doctor," Gillespie said. "Her Majesty was very taken with you, yes, very taken. She speaks of you often with great affection."

"Does she indeed? May I ask how you know?"

The old man lay a long index finger to the side of his nose. He keeps his secrets close to his breast.

There is no doubt Watson would have stood chatting if I had indulged him. Gillespie fascinates him. "The things he has done, Holmes. The life he has lived." I hear the same exaltations every time we come here. Then he repeats the old man's stories word for word and declares them "quite charming." It is almost enough to make me want to stop bringing him with me to Mycroft's office. Instead, I have encouraged him to write down some of man's exploits. At least that keeps him (mostly) quiet.

To be fair, few have seen as much as that old man has. Years of service to the Queen, a combat veteran of extraordinary experience, and one of Mycroft's most trusted assistants: he's privy to more secrets than the Prime Minister. It is not that I do not understand Watson's admiration. I just wish I were not subjected to it with such regularity.

I was in no mood for chatter this afternoon, however. We had work to do and I was anxious to get on with it.

Mycroft barely glanced up when we entered his office. Watson and I sat by the roaring fire and took off our coats while my brother continued to work at the papers on his desk. I caught a glimpse of a familiar seal on the document in his hand.

At length he returned the papers to his drawer, locked it, and came to join us.

"Welcome home, Sherlock," he said. "I am sorry you had so rough a crossing from Calais."

"How did you know the crossing was rough?" Watson said.

"Come, Watson," I said. "I realise my brother is a busy man but even he must be able to find the time to read the shipping forecast telegrams."

Mycroft smirked. "True," he said. He sat down heavily in his large armchair, eased his foot up on a stool, and winced. Watson leaned forward and was on the point of donning his medical hat when my brother pre-empted him by saying, "We have gathered up almost the last of Porlock's nest of vipers. A few remain at large, of course, and there are a couple whose complicity remains in doubt, but I am confident we have identified the most dangerous."

"Identified? But not arrested?" Watson said.

"Sometimes it is wiser to watch from a distance. Vipers have a talent for finding other vipers."

"Just make sure you do not lose sight of them, Mycroft," I said. "We do not want another Moriarty or a Porlock arising from the ranks."

"I know," he said, rubbing his calf. He stretched his leg out, winced, and said, "You missed the hanging."

"I saw no reason to attend. Execution is necessary, I suppose, but I find no pleasure in seeing a man, even a man like Porlock, being hanged."

"I understand he went bravely enough. Kissed his wife and children as if he were merely going to his club. He made some dire prediction that England's fall is inevitable and died a 'good soldier', as he put it."

"Monstrous," Watson said.

"Unquestionably," I said. "But we have more pressing matters to discuss. You sent me a telegram. Zugzwang?"

"Yes." My brother frowned and I saw his face set into its most implacable expression. "You know as well as I, Sherlock, the situation in France is volatile in the extreme."

I said, "It is a dreadful situation. There is a deplorable injustice being perpetrated, Mycroft. First upon Dreyfus and now on Zola. We must prevail upon the government—"

"Absolutely not!" he cried. "It is out of the question. I was horrified to learn that you went to Paris in January. Lord only knows what damage you might have done. And as if that wasn't bad enough, you return there this week? I declare you have lost what little wits you possessed. Sit down!"

I remained standing and glowered at him, meeting his fury with ice.

"What on earth were you doing there, anyway?" he thundered. "The entire country stands on the brink of utter chaos and you decide to take a holiday? We have towers in England, Sherlock. No need to rush across the Channel to see their *Tour Eiffel.*"

"We stopped on our way to Italy because Zola was a friend of Beatrice's late father and she was concerned about him. There was no sightseeing."

"And your return?"

"Word reached us in Milan of Zola's arrest."

My brother released a long slow breath and sank back in his chair. "It is an extremely dangerous situation. Believe me, Sherlock; I am as outraged as you are, but there is a great deal at stake, far more than the lives of a foolhardy novelist and a disgraced Jewish captain." He held up his hand, anticipating my argument. "I am not unsympathetic to Dreyfus's plight. Devil's Island is a terrible place even for a guilty man."

"You acknowledge the man's innocence, then?" Watson said.

"Of course. Only a fool would believe otherwise. There are sensible men in Paris who know this and whose approach is far more temperate than Zola's impassioned *J'Accuse.* Why, even the title is provocative. I have contacts among the more sober members of the government. I shall do what I can, but privately. Discreetly."

He sighed and his eyes flickered with pain. I caught Watson's look of concern and shook my head slightly. Not yet.

"If you and I were private citizens it would be different," Mycroft said. "But whether we like it or not we are public figures, as is Beatrice to a lesser extent. Still you're both home now so possibly there's no harm done."

"Beatrice is still in Paris," I said.

"What? Sherlock, I hope this is a jest. You cannot mean you left the woman alone in the middle of the riots?"

"She's not alone; she has friends in Paris, some of them influential. She's not a fool, Mycroft." I sat back in my chair and said, "I think her loyalty is admirable."

"It is admirable," Mycroft said. "But it is also exceedingly dangerous. Not only has she put herself at risk, but her presence could cause some serious difficulties for the government if she is noticed by the wrong people."

Silence fell on the room. The only sound was the crackle of the fire and the ticking of my brother's clock. Mycroft shifted uncomfortably in his seat and then in a weary voice he said, "I can only advise. And my advice, Sherlock, is you get Beatrice out of there. Now. Today. The situation is a powder keg and may explode at any moment. There have already been riots and I fear worse is yet to come. If you value the woman, you must tell her to come home. While she still can."

I was shaken by the degree of his alarm. He is right. Of course he is. It is unfair to blame him when I am the one at fault.

"It may not be easy," I admitted. "She's not a woman who takes kindly to being told what to do, but I shall do what I can to persuade her."

"I doubt you'll need to do much, Holmes," Watson said. "Just tell her you wish it. I think you'll be surprised how effective that will be."

I changed the subject: "Was there anything else you wanted to discuss, Mycroft?"

"Primarily I wanted to get you out of France. I did not anticipate you would be fool enough to leave your wife there… However, yes, there are a few things. To begin with the mundane,

I received a communiqué from the Pinkerton Agency in America regarding an old friend of yours."

He handed me the report and I read it without much surprise. I passed it to Watson.

"This is the fiend who murdered that entire family?" Watson said. "Mundane? This man is void of all humanity, and he's living like a prince in New York. It's unconscionable."

"Calm yourself, doctor," Mycroft said in his most unperturbed voice.

"Michel Watteau?" said I. "Well, well… That name is not familiar to me but I shall review my archive. We know him well enough by another alias, eh, Watson?"

"We do. A blacker villain never lived."

"He is capable of any monstrosity," I agreed. "You have asked Pinkertons to keep an eye on the creature, Mycroft?"

Watson spluttered, "Keep an eye…? But can we not do something? Extradite him?"

"With what evidence?" I said. "The murders did not take place in these islands. From this report, it appears the Canadians have done a credible job, but our friend here was very careful not to leave any traces that might incriminate himself. We can only suppose it was he who committed the dreadful crime."

Watson made a noise like a growl. Never did a man more resemble the English bulldog. "'Only suppose…'" he said. "Who else could it have been?"

"We have no way of knowing. That family—more specifically the men of that slaughtered family—had a knack for antagonising people. While Watteau is very probably the killer, he will not face justice without evidence. The Canadians are still working on the case and I see they have instituted proceedings to have our old friend returned to their authority for questioning."

"That's something, I suppose," Watson admitted.

"Thank you for the update, Mycroft. You will keep me informed?"

"Naturally."

"Anything else?"

"There are several matters that concern me at present: France, Spain, South Africa... However, there is one other thing. This one is rather odd, Sherlock. I must admit I vacillated about whether or not to refer the matter to you, but under the circumstances, I think I must." He rang the bell and said, "This may take some time. We may as well have some coffee and cake."

I rolled my eyes. Watson, ever the oil to soothe troubled waters, said, "That's an excellent idea. Don't you agree, Holmes?"

"You will not get my brother to concede, Doctor," Mycroft said. "He has no interest in the social niceties."

"Ha!" I said.

Mycroft, with an unsubtle attempt to distract me, said, "How did you enjoy Italy once you actually got there?"

"It was a delight. The opera was particularly excellent." I paused remembering the brush of silk, the warmth of soft fingers touching my cheek, a tantalising fragrance...

"And Beatrice?" Mycroft continued. "It was her first time there, I think?"

"Yes, she enjoyed it very much," I said. "Particularly the music, but she also appreciated the art. She has very refined tastes."

Silence fell and I was aware of a peculiar non-verbal communication between my friend and my brother.

"Well?" I demanded, but before either could reply the door opened and Gillespie entered with a tray of food and steaming coffee.

"Come and join us, Gillespie," Mycroft said. "I thought it wise that my brother hear the strange tale from your own lips."

"Very good, Mr Holmes," said the old man. He finished pouring the coffee then sat in an armchair and proceeded to tell his story.

2

"My youngest daughter is the most reliable and sensible of women," Gillespie said. "Her name is Alice and she is married to a railwayman by the name of George Prentiss.

"George drives the train from London to Scotland and so is gone for days at a time, leaving Alice alone with their three children. She is an intelligent, sensible woman, Mr Holmes, and not the sort to imagine things."

He took a sip of his coffee, his worn face looking deeply troubled. The man had evidently planned his narrative for he continued his tale in a coherent and unhurried manner.

"Alice and George have been married for fifteen years. In addition to keeping house and rearing their children, my daughter translates documents for Brahms Antiquities. Alice is fluent in French, German, and Italian and she has a reasonable knowledge of Greek and Russian, so she is much in demand. She works at home after the children go to bed, so she is often up until after midnight. I should add that the Prentisses have a very comfortable home in Camden Town, and have kept the same two servants for many years."

"Thank you," I said, "that is very clear. Pray continue."

"Over the past several weeks, Alice has been hearing noises in the house after everyone retires. It started with a scraping sound. It seemed to come from everywhere and nowhere. At first she thought it was rats."

"Has anyone else heard these noises?" Watson asked.

"Not at first, but about a week ago the two maids said they'd begun to hear them, too."

"And had your daughter mentioned these sounds to the servants beforehand?" Watson asked. "Sometimes people can imagine things if they are made to expect them. It's not unusual."

"My daughter only questioned them about the cleaning. She asked if the servants had seen rats or mice because she thought she'd heard a scraping sound. At the time the girls denied it, but since then Connie has said she's heard the noises early in the morning when she starts her duties and Agnes says she has too."

"It is by no means definitive," Watson said.

I said, "But you believe, Mr Gillespie, that there is something tangible causing these sounds? Something other than London's vast numbers of rodents?"

"I do, Mr Holmes. To be sure if it were any other woman I'd put it down to nerves, but that's not Alice."

"There is more to your story, I perceive," said I. "You would not be consulting my brother and he, in his turn, would not be seeking my input were it merely a matter of unexplained scratching noises."

"There now, Mr Holmes, I always said you and your brother are the smartest men in the Empire. You're right, of course.

"Alice first noticed these noises at the beginning of February, but a couple of weeks ago she began to notice things in the house were being moved or even disappearing. Initially she blamed the children though they stoutly denied the charge. Eventually, she came to believe there must be some other explanation."

"What sort of things are being moved?" Watson asked. He was, as is his habit, making careful notes in his journal.

"Very strange things, Doctor," said Gillespie. "The broom went missing, aye, missing, for three whole days. It reappeared in a cupboard in the cellar, of all places. Then a block of cheese vanished. Other things have been moved. Coats have been taken from racks and thrown onto the floor; one of Agnes's petticoats was hung outside on the front door; a small brass figurine that sits on the mantle turned up in the back garden."

"It sounds as if someone is playing silly games," Watson said. "How old are the children?"

"Margaret is twelve and she's a solid young girl, very serious, like her mother. Peter is ten. He's a bit of a handful, to be sure, but he's devoted to his mama, and would never play games like this to upset her. The youngest is William. He is six and always has his head in a book. I really cannot believe any of the children would have a hand in something like this."

"No," I said. "This matter has been going on since early February, you said? Generally, children's attention span is not so enduring. There are exceptions, of course. Since the servants have been with her for many years it seems unlikely to be one of them, unless something happened to precipitate some mischief."

I was not convinced of the innocence of any party, but I thought then and think now that there is nothing to be gained by distressing the old man until I had investigated.

"It must be very hard on your daughter," Watson said.

"Well, it is." For the first time, the depth of Gillespie's anxiety rose to the surface. "She's at her wit's end and no mistake."

"She's fearful of her safety?" I asked.

Gillespie stared at me. "I don't think so… Mr Holmes, you do not think she and her children may be at risk?"

"My brother is simply trying to understand the circumstances of the case," Mycroft said. He shot me a look of caution and I reined in my unease.

"I meant what is it in particular that worries her?" I said. "On the surface, moved or even missing objects do not seem particularly alarming. Yet she was obviously concerned enough to confide the matter to her father."

"I think her greatest concern is that she may lose her servants. The younger, Connie, tends to histrionics. She is quite superstitious and has become convinced that the house is haunted. It's not that I don't believe in ghosts, Mr Holmes. I've seen any number of strange things when I worked for Her Majesty; I could tell you tales about Balmoral that would freeze your bones, but Alice does not believe in such things. As for Connie, well, she has become very close to a young man and Alice is afraid that the girl will leave."

"There are other servants."

"Yes, but Connie has been with her for eight years, and the children are fond of her."

I met Mycroft's eyes. There was concern there; I read all the doubts and apprehensions I also felt. As he himself often says, we are not brothers for nothing.

"I shall go and see your daughter, Gillespie. If you would be so kind as to give me her address."

Mrs Prentiss lives in modest three-story terraced house in Harrington Square at the Lidlington Place end.

Camden Town is a curious district. Where else can one find the comfortable middle-class living cheek by jowl with the disadvantaged? While Harrington Square retains an air of middle-class gentility, not more than a few yards away is Mornington Crescent, a place of working class tenants and aspiring artists.

"An elegant address for the wife of a railwayman, Holmes," Watson said as we alighted from our hansom.

"Yes, indeed. I believe Mrs Prentiss inherited the house from her late aunt, Gillespie's sister."

I paid the cabby and climbed the steps but I did not immediately knock. I stood and looked out at the scene before me. "Odd that they call this a square," I said.

"Odd?" Watson, though he saw exactly what I did, seemed to have missed the obvious.

"The park here would be more accurately described as a triangle. Not a true triangle, of course. The northmost angle is slightly rounded. Still, if I recall my Euclidean geometry correctly, the park is far closer to an isosceles triangle than a square."

"They don't call places triangles, Holmes."

"Why not? We have squares, circles—what do city planners have against the unfortunate triangle?"

Watson had no answer to that. He made to knock on the door but I forestalled him.

"Stand here beside me, Watson. Look around. Tell me what you see."

He joined me and took a moment to study the landscape.

"Well," he said, "I see that all of the houses face the square— or triangle, if you prefer—and overlook each other."

"A salient point," I said. "Even the top flats at the end of Mornington Crescent yonder probably have a good view of this house, too."

"Meaning people can see what's going on in their neighbour's lives?" Watson said, grasping the inference at once. "So if some stranger is making those noises he probably isn't entering through the front door."

"Not during the daylight hours, anyway," I said. "Even late at night it would be a risk, particularly with that lamppost no more than ten feet from the front door."

"Which means…" he thought a moment then said, "It's probably someone inside the house who is up to mischief. Unless," he added, grinning, "It is actually an evil spirit."

I ignored his attempt to tease.

"Possibly. I mean your first supposition, of course. Or perhaps the culprit has found another means of entrance. At this point, I am less interested in how than in why… Well, we shall not learn anything by standing in the cold discussing the matter. Let us see what the good woman can tell us."

The door opened almost the instant we knocked by a burly, middle-aged woman with brassy red hair. The apron and the size of her biceps identified her as one of the labouring classes.

"Mr Holmes and Doctor Watson?" she said. "Come in. The mistress is expecting you."

The house was immaculate and well ordered. From somewhere at the rear I could hear a young girl reciting German verbs. Her accent was excellent. Presumably young Miss Prentiss inherited her mother's linguistic skills.

The housekeeper led us into a small study. The mistress, a slender young woman with her father's bright eyes and genteel air, greeted us warmly.

"Some coffee for our guests, please, Agnes," she said. The housekeeper bustled away and left us alone with our new client.

"Thank you so much for coming to see me, Mr Holmes," the woman said when we were settled by the fire with our hot drinks in our hands. "My father holds you and your brother in the very highest esteem. Indeed, there can hardly be a person in this whole land who has not heard of your extraordinary accomplishments."

"Thank you," I said. "I am sorry you have need of help, but I will serve you to the best of my ability. Perhaps you would be kind enough to review the events in as much detail as you can recall. It is important you be as specific as possible. You may speak freely before my friend and colleague, Doctor Watson."

"I can be perfectly precise, Mr Holmes. I prepared a record of the events as they occurred. I had them noted in my diary, you see, and it was a simple matter to track back."

"Excellent," I said taking the book. "I wish all my clients were so exacting. You are a credit to your father, Mrs Prentiss."

I read the items carefully.

"Now," I said. "I see the first instance of the scratching sound came at the very end of January, on Monday the thirty-first, in fact. You are quite certain there had been no such noises prior to that date?"

"It is possible," said she, "that there had been some noise that I did not hear. I think it unlikely, however."

"And why is that?"

"Because I stay up very late working on my translations. It is difficult to concentrate when the children are up. They are good children but boisterous, as you can expect from that age. If there had been noises at night prior to the date I noted, I think I would have heard them. Of course, I cannot be certain. My husband was home for a few days at the end of January and I do not stay up late when he is here."

"I understand." I reviewed her list of dates and events again. "I see there was a week-long break in the middle of February. There were no disturbances at all during that period?"

"None."

"Can you recall what else had been happening in your household at that time?"

"Very clearly. My husband was ill and had to take a week off work."

"Ah," Watson said, leaning forward. "And can you remember if the noises and so forth ever occurred while your husband was home?"

"They did not."

"You are certain?" I said.

"Positive. I have spoken to him about these matters and I may say received a little gentle teasing from him on the subject. I hoped he would witness these occurrences for himself but, alas, that has not been the case."

"Ah, that is helpful. Tell us about the objects that were moved."

"Well, the first thing to go missing was the bell. It's a little brass figurine like a crinoline lady. We keep it on the mantle and one day I noticed it wasn't there. We searched everywhere and I questioned the children, but there was no sign of it. Then several days later it showed up in the back garden."

"Do you use the garden often?"

"During the summer we do. It's small but pleasant enough when the weather's good. We tend not to use it at all during the bad weather. Connie hasn't even been able to hang the washing outside because it's been so wet these past few weeks. But Agnes went out one afternoon to tidy up and she found it lying there."

"And the other items?"

"Well, there was the cheese. A fresh block of good cheddar went missing. We never did find it. And the children's coats one day were flung all over the hallway. Then there was the broom.

That was exceedingly odd: it just vanished one day and then reappeared in a cupboard in the cellar. Another thing was Agnes's petticoat mysteriously moved from her drawer and we found it hanging outside on the front door. Oh, she was embarrassed."

"Naturally," I said. "Please tell us about the household. I understand your maids have been with you a long time?"

"Yes, Agnes worked in this house for my late aunt Esmerelda. When we inherited the building, it made sense to keep Agnes on. She's such a good worker and very devoted to me and to the children.

"Connie came to us about eight years ago when she was fourteen. It was her first position and it took her a little while to adjust, but she's come along very well. She's particularly good with the children."

"Do you employ anyone else? A gardener or tradesman?"

"I take care of the garden myself. The only tradesmen are people like the butcher or the milkman who deliver every day. We have the chimney sweep in every year in October, and I had a man come and look at the basement last September. We have a problem with mould. There has been no one since."

"I believe this is a pretty settled district. Do you get many newcomers here?"

"To live, you mean? Now and then, I suppose, although not so many in the past year or so."

"Who are the newest neighbours in the Square?"

"Well, there's an African man moved in around Christmas. He's just a few doors down."

"Anyone else?"

She thought for a moment. "There's more transition in the Crescent. Artists and people of that sort. I don't know them, I'm afraid. The only one I know of is a widow woman. I see her walking in the square sometimes."

"How well do you know the rest of your neighbours?"

"I know most of the people on this side of the square. We visit each other from time to time but we are all very busy people."

"I assume they are good enough neighbours who would tell you if they saw someone prowling around the house?"

"Certainly. Good heavens, Mr Holmes, do you really think that is the case?"

"Holmes is merely exploring all the possibilities, Mrs Prentiss," Watson said.

"Yes, of course," I said, taking my cue. "I must have all the facts if I am to get to the bottom of this matter."

My client looked sceptical. "Come, Mr Holmes, I am not a child. I do not need to be protected from the truth. You have a theory about this situation, I can tell."

"I have formed six theories so far," I said. "But I must investigate further before I can come to any conclusions. I must ask you to be patient a little longer, Mrs Prentiss. I am confident we shall resolve this matter."

"I know my children and I are in safe hands. You may be sure of my complete cooperation, Mr Holmes."

"Excellent," I said. "I have only a few more questions. Do you have any valuables on the premises?"

"Some jewellery but nothing of any great value. There are other people in the Square who are far wealthier than we."

"Quite. Tell me about your work. I know you translate documents. What is their nature?"

"It varies. Sometimes I translate letters for private individuals. The bulk of my work is for Brahms Antiquities.

They deal in *objets d'art*, acquiring and selling. They also authenticate rare and valuable artefacts."

"Yes, I am familiar with their reputation," I said. "Mr Brahms is renowned in the field of antiquities. But I interrupted you. Pray continue."

"Most of the documents I receive are queries about pieces that would-be sellers hope the company will authenticate or sell. Now and then, I am required to translate a response to a client. These tend to be in Russian or Greek."

"Why those languages in particular?"

"Because the company has standard documents to address queries in French, German, and Italian."

"A form reply, you mean?"

"Yes, exactly."

There was a sound of laughter from the back of the house. I could hear a young woman's voice and a boy's.

"My son Peter and Connie. She's very good with the children but she does get a bit noisy sometimes."

Mrs Prentiss rose and went to the door. "Peter, have you finished your verbs?"

There was a muffled response and silence resumed.

"I can see why you work late at night," Watson said, sympathetically. "It must be difficult to stay up late after a long day."

"It is," she replied. "But I enjoy it. I like being able to use my brain."

I suspected the additional income was welcome, too. Even with an inheritance, this house must be costly to run, a stretch for a railwayman.

"You were saying there are standard documents in French, German, and Italian. I assume there is none such for Russian or Greek?"

"No. The cost of typesetting would be considerable because of the different alphabets, you see, and these queries are infrequent, no more than two or three a year. It's cheaper to have me translate them."

"And the documents are always related to art works?"

"The great bulk of them, yes. Now and then if the correspondent is acquainted with Mr Brahms or has conducted business with him before there may be the odd personal comment. 'I hope you're feeling better' sort of thing."

"I see. Now, when you work on your translations, which room do you use?"

"This one, the study. I keep all my papers in here and it is one place I can be sure the children will never come."

"Because?"

"Because I always keep the room locked."

"And the window too?"

"Yes."

"And you use the gaslight when you are working?"

"I prefer the table lamp. It is less expensive and I only need to throw light on the papers I am working on. I find it focuses my attention, too. There is plenty of ambient light from the streetlamp outside."

I rose and went to the window and examined it. The lock was a standard bolt. The heavy velvet drapes were purely decorative.

"You have a charming view of the park," I said. "And you have no sense of being overlooked, though you have houses all around you."

"No, indeed," she agreed, "particularly not during the summer when the trees are full of foliage. It's really only at this time of year that I even notice the buildings on the other side of the park."

"Quite. Now, when you are working, do you ever leave this room for any period of time?"

"Yes, but never for more than a few minutes. Sometimes I will go into the kitchen and make some coffee if I am tired. Now and then I check on the children but I'm seldom gone more than a few minutes."

"And do you lock the study door behind you when you leave the room for these brief periods?"

"No, of course not."

"Ha! Tell me, Mrs Prentiss, with all the strange things that have happened in the house, have you ever noticed anything moved from this study?"

"No, never."

I clapped my hands. "Thank you," I said. "Now, with your permission, I would like to examine the house."

3

Before I began my examination of the house, I scrutinised the door to the study. The mortise lock was standard. There were a great many fine scratches on the metal, some of which were at least a week old. The chalky brown substance that filled the grooves was fresh.

"Your maids polish the brasses how often?"

"Every Monday and Thursday."

"May I ask you to lock the door?"

She gave me a puzzled look and did as I asked. The key slid easily into the lock and turned.

"You see, Watson," I said. "Mrs Prentiss is so well used to performing this action she does not have to think about it. I imagine you could easily secure this door in the dark and have no difficulty finding the lock?"

"No difficulty at all," the woman replied.

We followed our hostess up the stairs to the top of the house. The servants' room was under the eaves. It was clean, pleasant, and bright, even in the fading light. The two big windows overlook the tidy back garden and the house that abuts the Prentisses' home to the rear.

There is a rag-rug on the floor, floral curtains, a desk, a wardrobe, and a chest of drawers. The two narrow beds have a folding screen between them to allow for some measure of privacy.

"This is charming," Watson said. "Your servants are very fortunate, Mrs Prentiss, to have such a welcoming room."

"They're good girls, both of them, and have been with me a long time. This is their home after all and I want them to be comfortable."

"Quite. I understand the younger of the maids has recently become, ah, attached to a young man?"

"Connie. Yes, she met him one night a few weeks ago."

"What is he like? Have you met him?"

"No, I haven't, though I have inquired, of course. Connie says he's a gentleman from South America."

"You sound sceptical," Watson said.

"Do I? I suppose I am rather. Connie's a bit flighty and given to nerves but she has a good heart. Unfortunately she's not... well, not to put too fine a point on it, she's not exactly comely. I am responsible for her and I wouldn't like anyone to take advantage of her good nature."

"Or take advantage in any other sort of way," Watson said.

"Precisely. Not that there's much fear of that. I don't have many rules, but gentlemen callers are forbidden and the girls must be in their beds by nine o'clock."

We made our way systematically through the house but found nothing remarkable in any of the rooms. Everything was clean and well-ordered.

The ground floor proved more interesting. There was a long narrow hallway with the study and the breakfast room in the front, overlooking the so-called square; there was a comfortable sitting room, not large but well appointed; a good-sized dining room; a walk-in pantry; an airing room, and the kitchen.

The two maids were busy but glanced at us curiously. Agnes, who had admitted us to the house, was at the stove. The younger woman, Connie, was setting the table in the dining room.

At the end of the hallway was the door to the garden.

"No, there's no need to follow me," I said to our hostess. "Please stay where it is warm and dry, Mrs Prentiss, we shall not be long."

Watson and I pulled up our collars and stepped out into the drizzle.

"What are your impressions, Watson?" I said.

"A pretty garden, if a bit small. Overlooked by the other houses not only on either side but at the rear as well."

"Precisely."

"Mrs Prentiss," I called. She came to the door. I said, "I beg you do not get wet. Can you tell us where the missing bell was found?"

"Over there to your right, Mr Holmes."

I went where she indicated. "Here?" I said, "By the cellar window?"

"Yes, that's right. Agnes found it."

We continued to work systematically around the garden.

"Matchsticks… you see here, Watson? This one is a day old; these two are older still…"

"Yes?"

"These are suggestive, are they not? Yes… I can think of four possible explanations. Let us go and see what the basement has to tell us."

Back in the warm, dry house I said softly, "Mrs Prentiss, can you find some task to occupy your younger maid upstairs?"

She looked puzzled but complied at once. "Connie," she said. "Would you be so good as to sort the laundry for tomorrow morning?"

"Now, Mrs Prentiss? I'm just setting the table."

"Now, if you please."

With a scowl, the unhandsome girl left the dining room and clomped up the stairs.

"Excellent," I said. "Now, can you show me the cellar?"

Mrs Prentiss opened the door that led down into the dark, unwelcoming area beneath the building. The smell of dankness was repellent.

"Do you use it at all?" I asked.

"No, never. It is a most unpleasant place, and none of us likes to go down. We do not even use it to store coal."

"Does anyone ever go down there?"

"I did, that night I first heard the scratching. I thought we had rats. Agnes is the only one who is not bothered by the place. She goes down from time to time. She hides the children's Christmas and birthday gifts down there because she knows it's the last place any of them will go."

She spoke softly with an eye on the parlour where the children were occupied with their schoolwork.

"What of your younger maid?"

"Connie? No, she's a very superstitious sort, I'm afraid. These recent events have all but convinced her that the house is haunted."

"But you do not think so?" Watson asked.

"I do not believe in such things," she replied.

"I wonder if we may trouble you for a lamp or a candle," I said. "I assume there is no gas laid on in that part of the house?"

"No, there is not. I shall fetch a lantern."

Thus armed with a serviceable railwayman's lamp, Watson and I made our way down the steep, old steps into the cellar. Watson pulled his scarf up over his nose and mouth. "It really is a most unwholesome atmosphere down here, Holmes," he said.

"You need not come with me, you know," I pointed out. "I can certainly examine the area on my own."

"Will my presence assist you?"

"Always."

He said no more but continued to follow me down the steps, just as I knew he would. I know my Watson!

"Take the lamp, if you'd be so kind, my dear fellow," I said. "And direct the light upon the floor."

I knelt down and examined the ground carefully. Then, taking care of my clothing—the floor was covered with the most fetid sort of mould—I tracked back to the corner.

"Shine the light up here, if you please."

The thin greenish beam picked out the window that sat at street level. It was about a six inches above my head. There was an old chair immediately under this window and after a quick examination of it and the floor beneath, I climbed up and took a closer look.

"This glass was changed recently," I said. "The putty is fresh, and there are still shards on the floor. Yes... You see the scuff marks upon the wall? It all fits. Well, almost all."

"So this is how our 'poltergeist' has been getting into the house," Watson said, following my reasoning.

"He is a tall man, our nightly visitor. Slender, too. It cannot be easy to get through that window, particularly in the dark. His first attempt was clumsy, I surmise, and he broke the glass."

"Thoughtful of him to fix it," Watson said. He was shivering with cold and his words stuttered.

"Almost done, old man," I said, taking the lamp from his freezing hands. "Thoughtful? No, I suspect he was merely trying to avoid drawing attention to his activities. The chair shows his footprint clearly. He has used it to facilitate his climb. I could not climb in and out without some effort, though I suppose it is easier with practice."

I shone the lantern around the room and examined it.

"That cupboard over there must be where the broom was discovered. Yes, a grown man could easily hide in here."

"Hide?"

"Mrs Prentiss came down here, remember? She was looking for rats, not a grown man. I doubt her examination was more than cursory."

Watson said, "Thank goodness she did not discover him or who knows what might have happened. What have you learned about this villain, Holmes?"

"Well," I said, "he is tall, as I already observed. I should put his height at around six foot three or four. He is right-handed, forgetful, has a gentleman's education, is possibly of Nordic descent, and he is not a smoker."

"I should be used to these analyses by now, Holmes, but I admit I still find them astounding. I follow your reasoning regarding the height, and I suppose you can determine which hand is dominant by the way he fixed the window, but the rest? How do you deduce he is forgetful?"

"Because he twice knocked his head on the low beam. See here." I directed the lantern's beam at the marks that were clearly visible on the wood. "Any tall man might bang his head once, but to do so twice in almost exactly the same spot demonstrates forgetfulness."

"Or preoccupation with something else," Watson pointed out. "How do you determine he is not good with his hands?"

"Because of the shoddy job he did with the window repair. It is really very badly done. Even a schoolboy could do better. This also suggests he had a gentleman's education: most working-class boys learn pragmatic skills such as rudimentary repair work. Their fathers or brothers teach them. It is only the gentleman who is so ham-fisted.

"Also, on the ceiling beam where he bashed his head I find two hairs…" I showed them to him.

"Very fair," Watson said. "So you guess he's Nordic."

"Guess? Watson, you know me better than that. But yes, these hairs lead me to conclude that the fellow may have some Nordic blood."

"Hmm, yes, I see. I'm not sure how any of this helps us find him, but at least it will help us recognise him when we do. Oh, wait, how to you know he does not smoke? We saw matches outside. Doesn't that suggest he is a smoker?"

"Yes, we did, and when we examined the garden I thought perhaps he lit a cigarette before climbing down here, but if you recall we found no butts or tobacco, not outside and not in here. You can clearly see the marks on the floor where the man paced, no doubt waiting for all the family to go to bed. A smoker would have lit his cigarette or pipe."

"Not all smokers suffer your degree of addiction, Holmes."

"Ha! That is a good point, Watson. Still, I think you'd agree a man would need some sort of comfort standing in a place like this in the middle of the night. It could make even a non-smoker take up the habit."

"That's certainly true." He looked around with distaste and shuddered. "All the same, Holmes, it's a serious enough business that a man is breaking into this house with some frequency."

"It is, indeed."

We reconvened in the study and I asked to speak with the servants. Agnes, as the senior, came in first. She bobbed slightly and took the seat as I directed her, then with her hands folded on her lap answered all my questions.

"Your full name, if you please?"

"Agnes Mary Dearing, sir."

"You need not be concerned," Watson said gently. "We're just trying to get to the bottom of this strange business."

"I understand, sir. It's very distressing, especially for the children."

"You have been with Mrs Prentiss for how long, Agnes?"

"A little over twelve years, sir. She kept me on when she first moved into this house. I was with her aunt, Miss Gillespie, for eight years before her death, poor woman. I've been with Mrs Prentiss ever since."

"She is a good mistress, I take it."

"The best there ever was and no mistake. She doesn't treat me and Connie like servants, not like some. She sends us to bed at a Christian hour while she stays up and does her work, though I'd gladly stay up with her. She calls for the doctor when we get sick and she makes sure we have as much time off as we need. When my mother was ill a year ago, Mrs Prentiss paid for a train ticket herself so I could go and visit. I ended having to stay a month, but there was never any question my job was waiting for me when I returned. Not many mistresses would be half as accommodating."

"No, indeed," Watson said. "You are very fortunate. Does Connie share your high opinion of Mrs Prentiss?"

"Indeed she does, sir. But, there, I can't imagine where she'd find herself so well off."

Something in the woman's manner belied her words. There was a defensiveness in her demeanour that was at odds with the rest of her testimony. I said, "Perhaps Connie doesn't care for service as well as you do, Agnes?"

"Well, there's no denying that, Mr Holmes. I don't know what's happening to the young people nowadays. When I started out as a twelve-year-old for the late Mr and Mrs Chandler I was just glad to have a wage and a roof over my head. There are far worse ways for a woman to earn a living."

"That is true," Watson said. "It can be exceedingly difficult for a single woman to support herself."

"The Chandlers were good people, I must say, but always ready to point out the difference in rank between them and the servants. Mrs Prentiss never makes such a distinction... Though I flatter myself I know my place."

"I suppose," I said, "Connie doesn't have your range of experience to know how well off she is?"

"That's a fact, Mr Holmes." She leaned forward and expounded on a theme she had, I thought, given a great many thoughts and, probably, words to. "She's never worked for anyone else. She came to Mrs Prentiss when she was fourteen and she has no idea how hard it can be for servants in other houses. I could tell you stories, indeed I could. But no, she thinks she's too good to wait upon a fine family. Miss Constance Kidwell, Lady Muck."

"Perhaps she has hopes to be married," Watson said.

"Aye, she does at that. She's been seeing this young chap since January and she's convinced he's going to whisk her away to South Africa with him."

"South Africa?" I said.

"Yes, he's a, what do you call them? A Boer. Connie said she thought he was German when she first met him because of his accent. He told her he gets that a lot but he's from Capetown."

"What is his name, this young gentleman?"

"Avery Rickman."

"You haven't met him, I take it?"

"No, sir. She keeps him pretty much to herself. A bit embarrassed of us, I'd say. No doubt she's given herself all sorts of airs and graces to impress the fellow."

"Well, thank you, Agnes, for all your help. Would you ask Connie to come and see us?"

A moment later, the pudgy young woman with greasy hair and badly blemished skin joined us. Her air was a curious mixture of apprehension and excitement.

"Hullo, Connie, please make yourself comfortable," Watson said, displaying his most charming manners.

She flushed and said with a certain brio, "I'd prefer Constance, if you would be so kind, sir."

"Please, sit down, Constance. I am Doctor Watson and this is Sherlock Holmes."

"Cor," she said.

Watson bit his lip to suppress a smile. After all these years, he never fails to be amused by the public's reaction to me. I sat back and let him get on with it. He has a talent for dealing with truculent maids and this one was as surly as any I've ever seen.

"Now, what can you tell us about the strange goings on in this house, Constance?"

She flushed. "I think it's haunted," she said in a breathless tone. I wasn't convinced. Her voice sounded awed enough but her features never altered. It is a mistake all bad liars make: they put all their effort into sounding convincing and forget that how they appear is just as important.

(*Note*: I should write a monograph about the many ways people betray themselves through their body movements and facial expressions.)

This girl was anything but a good liar. I decided to let Watson's interrogation run its course.

"Now, Constance," he said sternly. "You know that's not true, don't you?"

She shifted in her seat and picked at the hem of her apron. "How else do you explain it then?" she demanded. "Strange sounds in the middle of the night; things being moved about. I reckon we've got one of them polt... pot..."

"Poltergeist?" Watson said. He glanced at me and we know each other well enough to read very small signals. He was as sceptical of this young woman's tale as I was.

"That's it," the maid exclaimed. "One of them evil ghosts that makes things move about."

"I have always believed," Watson said. "That the simplest explanations are the best. And, you know, once you've eliminated the impossible, whatever remains must be true."

I smothered a guffaw by burying my face in my scarf.

"What does that mean?" Connie said.

"It means that you're not being honest with us. Come on, my girl, out with it."

For an exceedingly kind man, Watson can be quite terrifying when he chooses to be. Seldom does he unleash this harsh side of himself, and very rarely upon a woman, but it was exactly the right approach. The girl burst into tears and cried, "Oh, sir, please don't tell the mistress. She'll dismiss me for certain and then what will become of me?"

"You should have thought of that before you started playing these silly games," my friend said. "Do you know how much anxiety you have caused your mistress? She's a very charitable woman and has always treated you and Agnes with great generosity. This is how you choose to repay her?"

The maid was sobbing now; even so, I was not quite convinced. I had a feeling this woman could turn on tears as easily as a tap.

"Stop that nonsense at once," I said. She did so and gaped at me. "Now, tell us about this man that you have been letting into the house."

Her mouth fell open and she stared at me. "Why you're the devil himself," she hissed. "Who told you?"

"You told me by your behaviour. Who is this supposedly South African fellow—I really cannot call him a gentleman— that you have let into this house repeatedly?"

"'Ere," she cried, all pretence of dignity forgotten. "You don't know 'im. You don't know nothin' about 'im. Just 'cos 'e don't wear fancy clothes and speak like a toff don't mean 'e's no gentleman."

"He has encouraged you to deceive your mistress, to engage with him in premarital intercourse underneath your mistress's roof, and to play the hussy. No, no gentleman."

She flushed and began to rise.

"I don't 'ave to listen to this," she said.

"Yes, you do. Sit down."

She did so, now shaking, more with anger, I thought, than fear. Foolish girl probably thought this man would come to her rescue. He'd marry her and give her a home after she was dismissed.

"Well?" I said. "Your only hope is to tell me everything."

"His name is Avery Rickman. He's a diamond merchant from Capetown."

"A diamond merchant. Indeed? And where did you meet him?"

"At the pub. I went out one night with my friend, Miss Patricia Quinn. It's not something I'd do as a rule, but it was a special occasion, like, being her birthday. Anyway, it wasn't much fun; there were so many people and the snug was noisy and smoky. I told Patsy I was leaving. I came outside and knocked into this gentleman."

"Mr Rickman?"

"Yes, sir. He was very kind and asked me if I was all right. Then he said he knew another pub just down the street and he thought it would be quieter. So we went there but it wasn't much better. All the same, we had a drink together and then he walked me home and he asked if he might see me again."

"And how long before you began to have relations with him?"

"That's none of your business," she cried. The tears threatened to start again.

"Everything is my business."

"Well, it was a couple of weeks later." She flushed deeply and said, "I never did before like… but he's a gentleman, like I said, and he loves me."

"Why the cellar?" Watson asked. He seemed anxious to move on from the distasteful subject of Connie's love life. I cannot say I blame him.

"Because the risk of being caught by Mrs Prentiss was too great in any of the other rooms," I said. "Her nocturnal employment must have incommoded you considerably."

"We managed. I mean, it wasn't ideal, but he wanted me so badly…" She shot me a triumphant look that was wholly unpleasant to see.

"But not so much that he would take you to his lodgings, nor even to a cheap hotel," I pointed out. "Tell us about the objects that got moved."

"Well, the broom was because he'd broken the windowpane in the basement getting in one night. He was afraid that if someone saw the glass they might put two and two together. He didn't want me to get into trouble. Anyway, I fetched the broom and cleaned it up, but I was so tired I forgot and left the bloomin' thing down there. Still, at least I didn't have to sweep for three days." She smirked.

"And the brass figurine?"

"That's really a bell. She looks like a crinoline lady but she has a bell hammer under her skirt. Avery borrowed it so he could ring to let me know he had arrived. It was a good idea, but we worried at waking people up. Anyway, there was such a fuss when I left it outside and that dopey Agnes found it. After that..."

"After that, he took to lighting a match as a signal. And you decided to cover up the reason for moving the bell by moving other objects, too. Then you started to enjoy yourself."

"Well, she's no better than me, is she? That Mrs Prentiss. I mean, she's a good sort, but she's so dull with her letters and her books... After all, what's George Prentiss but a railwayman? Just because her aunt left her some money and her father rubs shoulders with them toffs..."

"And the cheese?" Watson asked.

"Well, Avery was hungry one night—he does work up an appetite. What's a little bit of cheese, after all?"

"Very well. That will do."

She left with her head held high.

Watson and I sat in silence for several minutes. Eventually he cleared his throat and said, "I don't know about you, Holmes, but I feel like I need a bath."

"Yes indeed," I replied. "What a wholly unpleasant and unrepentant creature she is. Well, I hope the adventure was worth the price. She has destroyed her life and is too stupid to realise it."

"She will soon enough. I don't suppose there's any chance this fellow Rickman could have any genuine regard for the girl?"

I gave him a look and he flushed. "Yes, well," he said. "It was just a thought."

It is after midnight, but I am too restless to sleep. What a bitter night it is. The wind is howling down Baker Street and the windows rattle with rain and sleet. All of London is awash.

I hope it is not so wretched in Paris.

4

Saturday 26 March 1898
This morning brought a letter from B:

My dear Sherlock,
It is less than a day since you left and already I feel your absence. For all that the Zolas are good people, they lack your refinement, your wit, and your sensibility. Almost I wish I had not been so stubborn in insisting upon staying here, but how am I to abandon my father's old friend when he is in such straits? I know these straits are almost entirely of his own making, yet I cannot help but sympathise. For all its folly, there is something noble in his thirst for justice. He has an artist's fascination with the tragic and there is surely no more 'beautiful tragedy', as he calls it, than the plight of an honourable military officer publically disgraced and forced to spend the rest of his days on Devil's Island.
Jean Jaurès called in about half an hour ago and joined the rest of the Dreyfusards in the salon pouring oil on Zola's embers. Now there are a dozen of them making a commotion. I retired to my bedroom but it is not tranquil. Despite two floors between us, I can hear them plainly. Jaurès is shouting that if the good captain were Christian, the case against him would have been exposed as a sham, but because he is a Jew, he is assumed to be guilty.
I have spoken to people on both sides of the argument and even among the Dreyfusards there are those who say that Zola has inflamed the passions of the public. I must concede their point. Zola insists that passions are of little use if they are not inflamed. He is a man who thrives on turmoil; where none exists,

he must create it. He polarises where he ought to seek compromise. Will you think me a disloyal friend if I confess he makes me weary?

Now that he has been given the maximum sentence— imprisonment and a fine of 3000 francs—I think he may have begun to realise the folly of his actions, not that he'd admit it. His poor wife is terrified but stands behind him. I suppose she has no choice.

In the meantime, poor France descends into madness. The Jews are sorely pressed and subject to beatings and other outrages. I hear that along the coast men are removing their garments to prove they are not 'guilty' of circumcision. The violence escalates daily and the Dreyfusards insist on escorting me when I need to go out. This is burdensome to them and to me, but a necessity at present, alas.

While his conviction is awaiting appeal, Zola has spoken of fleeing the country if seems things go against him. Do you think England might offer Zola a safe haven if he must flee?

Have you had an opportunity to ask for British intervention in the Dreyfus case? I know it is exceedingly unlikely, but perhaps a quiet word in the right quarters might prove sufficient.

I must go. Please write soon.
Your troublesome wife,
B.

I replied by return post. I copy my letter here:

My dear troublesome wife,
I should not find you half so entertaining if you were docile and meek. It is greatly to your credit that you should want to

support your father's old friend, particularly as he can be irksome at times.

I confess I am alarmed at the increase of violence in France. Mycroft asks that I plead with you to return. He points out, with some justification, that you are not a nonentity who might blend into the background. You are the Queen's goddaughter and you are my wife. While the latter remains a close secret, the former is significant enough that it must lend weight to everything you do, even if you do very little—and I know you too well to suspect you would ever do very little.

Would you despise me if I implored you to return to England?

I shall ask Mycroft about offering Zola a safe haven, should it prove necessary.

In the meantime, please take no unnecessary risks. Who else can play Mozart like you?

S.

Watson looks rather smug and I've discovered it is because Mrs Prentiss sent a joint of beef by way of a thank you for our work in resolving the Camden Town 'hauntings'. We shall have it for dinner.

I went downstairs to use the telephone and after some minutes was connected with Mycroft's office. Gillespie assured me he would have my brother return my call as soon as he is free. While I await his response, I have written up my notes on the Camden Town incident. Watson is engaged in writing another of his tales about my exploits. He promises not to pen this most recent case for the moment. Is it merely my bewilderment that a man could form a romantic attachment to the likes of Connie

Kidwell that makes me uneasy? Watson points out that for all my many talents an understanding of romance is utterly beyond my ken. Still, something tells me the business is not yet done.

Half-seven

Mycroft just returned my call. ("Talking to you twice in as many days, Sherlock? Isn't that carrying familial affection too far?")

"I had a letter from B," I said. I told him the gist and he heard me out in silence.

"I hope you told her to leave well enough alone and come home."

"Yes, I did, but I'm sure you must realise the impossibility of persuading her to do anything she does not wish."

"If she insists on staying, I hope she can keep out of harm's way. I wish she were not there, Sherlock. The situation is volatile and worsens daily. I hope your letter was persuasive."

So do I, but I did not admit it.

"What of her query about Zola?" I asked.

"Unofficially, I think we would be delighted to have him, but obviously we cannot extend an official invitation."

As I hung up the receiver, I ruminated that the problem with older brothers is they can never forget they are older and one's brother. Mycroft and I get on well enough most of the time – we have come a long way since our often-tempestuous childhood – but now and then there are frissons of memory. Tonight was one such occasion.

I must not go to Paris. I gave my word to B that I would never try to manage her. Am I to sit with my hands folded and do nothing?

Midnight.

I have written an update to B telling her of my conversation with Mycroft and his prognostications. I have told her to do whatever she thinks is wise and I shall support her, come what may. To my own surprise, I found myself writing the words, "Do, please, be careful." For a moment, I contemplated striking out the sentence but ultimately decided to let it stand. It is not as if it will influence her in any way.

Monday 28 March 1989

Despite my fatigue, I had a wretched night. It was considerably after the clock chimed three before I fell asleep. Watson would have his readers believe such nights are due to what he calls my bohemian lifestyle. The truth is I am worried. I cannot turn off my mind and in the middle of the night all my mistakes and failings gnaw at me. When I did at last fall asleep I was haunted by dreams of terrible things.

This morning Watson said nothing but poured me a cup of very strong coffee. I pushed away my kippers and he pushed the plate back in front of me.

"She will be no safer for your starvation, Holmes," he said. "Just eat one kipper and I will be satisfied."

I forced myself to comply. When I finished and had my second cup of coffee, I said, "It's not Beatrice, you know. That is, it's not only Beatrice that worries me."

"What then?"

"Avery Rickman."

He took a moment to reflect on the case. "No," he said at last. "I'm sorry, Holmes, but I'm afraid I don't follow."

"Does that Camden Town case not seem too easy? Too obvious?"

Another silence as he mused. "Is it possible, my dear fellow, you are merely repulsed by the sordidness of the solution? After all, housemaids do have illicit love affairs, and often with contemptible cads."

"I know," I said. "I know. But something gnaws at me, Watson."

"What?"

"I do not know. Something does not sit right."

"Then we missed something."

I chuckled. "My dear fellow, how can you have such faith in me?"

"Because I know you," he said. He buttered a slice of toast and put it on my plate. To humour him, I ate it.

"If something is nagging at you, then there probably is something we've overlooked. You will not be satisfied until we've met this Rickman fellow and questioned him."

It sounded absurdly easy once he said it.

"What a fool I am that I did not question Connie about the fellow when I had the opportunity," I said. "If only I had not let the matter drop so easily."

"She would have dissembled in any case, Holmes," he said. "And that's assuming she knew anything to begin with. If this Rickman fellow is like other cads, he probably lied about everything, including his name. He's probably really Charlie Snout, a pig-farmer from Somerset who already has two wives."

We laughed heartily at the idea. I think the laugh benefited me at least as much as the kippers.

Watson and I took a cab to Scotland Yard. I spoke with Lestrade and Tavistock Hill. They will keep close watch for

Rickman. Even in a city the size of London there cannot be many very tall men with fair hair. A shame, they pointed out, that I have nothing more to tell them about the fellow. I cannot imagine they will devote much time and attention to the search in any case. It is not as if Rickman can be arrested or charged with anything. His crime is against decency. Well, as far as we know.

We returned to Baker Street around three o'clock. I have instructed the Irregulars to keep watch for Rickman, too. Billy and Tommy have sent word to their eyes all over the city. I have more faith in these boys than I do in all of London's official force combined.

Watson and I went to the Savoy to attend the revival of Gilbert and Sullivan's *Gondoliers*. It's not exactly Mozart but pleasant enough and a welcome distraction from irksome maidservants and Paris.

Dinner at Simpson's.

Tuesday 29 March 1898

Around four o'clock I was lying upon the sofa reading the newspapers when I was interrupted by a knock at the door. After a moment, Mrs Hudson came in and said there was a young woman who wished to consult with me. It was apparent from her air of distaste that the client did not meet my housekeeper's minimum standard of ladylike behaviour.

A moment later, I discovered why. Connie Kidwell came sailing into the room in a state of high dudgeon.

"Here," she said. "What you done with my Avery?"

I stared at her for several seconds, waiting for her to control her emotions. Even Watson, kind and gentlemanly though he is, did not so much as offer her a seat.

She stood before us, her coat wet and muddy, her hair wilting under a ridiculous black hat, and her cheeks flushed with deep anger and resentment.

"I am afraid, Miss Kidwell," I said. "I cannot talk to you when you behave in so uncivilised a fashion. Govern your manners or I shall escort you off the premises."

She stared at me, caught between fury and desperation. The latter won, as it always must.

"I'm sorry," she said in a manner that utterly belied her words. "I'm that worried about Avery. About Mr Rickman."

"Ah, done a bunk has he?" I said. "You do astonish me."

"Holmes," Watson said. He shook his head and I assume he felt my sarcasm was misplaced. "What happened, Miss Kidwell?" he asked in his most soothing voice.

I rolled my eyes, flopped back on the sofa, and listened.

"After that old cow—I mean, after Mrs Prentiss dismissed me I went to my friend Patsy. She hid me for a couple of days… Their basement isn't bad. Not like the one at the Prentiss house. But her missus, Miss Fellows, found me and kicked me out.

"I tried to find Mr Rickman, but I… I can't. I'm that worried… I went and stayed with my mum only she gave me the old heave-ho an' all.

"I went to Mrs Prentiss and apologised all sincere-like, but she wouldn't take me back. She said I was a wicked girl for playing games. I think it's that Agnes's fault. If she hadn't been so mean to me I'd never have hung her petticoat up for the world to see. Only a bit of fun it were…"

"You didn't have an address for Mr Rickman?" Watson said, cutting off this barrage.

The girl shuffled. "I never needed it, did I?" she said. "I mean, 'e always came to me. He said he lived in Holborn. I've been all over that stinking place... I mean, I should say, I've searched but I can't find him or anyone who knows him."

For the first time her voice cracked and I felt almost sorry for her.

"I found a pub that I was told is a haunt for men from South Africa but they say they've never heard of him nor know anyone who looks like him. Did you make them say that just to put the wind up me, Mr Holmes? Because that's as low a trick—"

"I did no such thing, I assure you. So, I think we can safely deduce that Avery Rickman is not who he claimed to be."

"But..." I could see tears were not far from the surface as the enormity of her folly hit her. To her credit, she did not weep.

"Tell me what you do know of him," I said. "I should be very interested in learning what Mr Rickman's business really is."

"He said he loved me."

"Yes, well... I think we cannot discount the possibility that this fellow's intent was to gain access to your mistress's home rather than for any of your allurements. Such as they are."

"Holmes," Watson hissed.

"No, it's all right," she said. "Perhaps I've been a fool. I know I'm no oil painting, and a man like that, a gentleman... But I love him." The tears came at last, silent and without any attempt to wipe them away. They ran down her coarse red cheeks and plopped onto her cheap black coat. I confess, in that moment I did feel sorry for her.

Watson said, "I think you should sit down, Miss Kidwell. I shall ask Mrs Hudson to bring some coffee." He went downstairs to speak to our housekeeper, leaving me alone with the unfortunate young woman.

"You must think me a fool," she said.

"I believe people in love are often fools, Miss Kidwell. You were deceived by a very clever trickster. However, I shall make every effort to find him, if I can. Now, what can you tell me about him?"

"I don't know how much is true. He said he was from Capetown and had been in England for six months. He definitely had an accent and that never changed."

"Do you think his accent really was South African?"

"I thought he was German, but I don't know. I don't know what a South African is supposed to sound like."

"And his appearance?"

"Well, he's very tall, perhaps taller than you, but not by much. He has very fair hair, like pale gold, and bright blue eyes. He dresses well, but not really like a toff, now I think about it."

"How so?" I rose to get a cigarette from the Turkish slipper and stood by the mantle watching her. There was no doubt she was making an effort to be truthful and cooperative.

"Well, his suit was made of good stuff but it was old. It had been taken in and mended a few times but I could do a better job of the sewing and I'm no seamstress. You'd think a man like that could afford a proper tailor. I offered to mend it for him."

"Hmm. Yes. Go on."

"And the coat was heavy, suede with silk lining and a nice fur collar, but that was old, too. The cuffs were frayed." She forced back more tears. "I can't believe I let him fool me like that…"

"He claimed to be a diamond merchant?"

"Yes, he did. He knew an awful lot about jewels. He told me about the cut of diamonds and how gems just look like little bits of stone when they're mined and it takes craftsmanship to make them look the way they do in a piece of jewellery. He said when he gave me a ring it would be the best of all the Cs. I thought he meant like the seven seas, but he explained that diamonds, well gemstones, have a standard of carat, cut, clarity and oh, I know there's another..."

"Colour. Well, it may mean nothing, but on the other hand it suggests he took time to study the subject, or at perhaps had worked for a jeweller at one time. I understand Mrs Prentiss owns no expensive jewellery?"

"No, Mr Holmes. I mean, she has her wedding ring and some nice earrings, but nothing out of the ordinary. Nothing anyone would go to any length to steal."

Watson returned with a tray. He poured a cup of coffee for each of us.

"Drink that, Miss Kidwell," he said. "I am sure you'll feel better for having something hot inside you."

"Thank you, sir," she said. She drank the coffee too quickly and coughed. Then she took one of the cheese sandwiches my friend offered her. I suspect she'd had nothing to eat or drink for some time.

After she'd eaten, she said, "He said he was going to be rich. That he knew where there was treasure for the taking and there would be no harm in it because it they were no Christians who hoarded it."

"No Christians?" Watson said. He glanced at me. "What an odd way of saying it. I assume he meant scoundrels."

"You're certain of his words, Miss Kidwell?"

53

"Yes, Mr Holmes, absolutely certain. I worried over them, you see. I mean, hoarding sounds like something a thief might do. I was afraid he'd get hurt."

I glanced at Watson and saw my concern reflected on his face.

At length there was nothing more she could tell me. She rose to leave but stood, undecided. "I know what a fool you must think me, Mr Holmes, but a woman knows when she is loved. Avery would not stay away from me by choice. Something's happened to him or someone is keeping him from me. He does love me."

There was nothing to say to that. For a moment we all stood together in silence, then suddenly she wailed, "Where am I to go? What am I to do? I have no money, nowhere to live, my family want nothing to do with me. Oh Lord, what's to become of me? I might as well just throw myself in the river."

Watson wrote something on one of his cards and handed it to her. "Hush, now," he said. "Go to this address and explain your situation. They will look after you until the baby is born. You may tell them I sent you. Here's a little money to tide you over for a day or two."

He placed a few coins in her palm and closed her fingers over them.

"You're a proper gent, sir, and no mistake. Thank you." She turned to leave then, facing me, said, "If you see Mrs Prentiss will you please tell her I'm so very, very sorry for all the trouble I've caused. I know she'll never employ me again, but I want her to know I understand now what I've done. Please will you tell her?"

"Yes," I said. "I'll tell her. And if I find any news of your Avery Rickman I shall let you know."

She left a sight happier than she had arrived. I stood at the window and watched her waddle down the street.

"Baby?" I asked Watson.

"Oh yes, no doubt about it. Wretched girl. I don't know what's to become of her, Holmes, I really don't."

5

Wednesday 30 March 1898

I slept better last night and woke feeling refreshed. There has been no word from Beatrice; I can only hope she is on her way home. I telephoned Lestrade and gave him a more complete description of Avery Rickman.

After breakfast, I made my way to Holborn. I decided to start in the Hatton Garden area. It is quite an extraordinary place, a perfect replica of a shtetl right in the heart of London. Most of the diamond merchants here are Jews. The ultra-religious hurry by wearing long ringlets, full beards, and black frock coats. The locals call them 'Whitechapel cowboys', I suppose because of the big hats they wear.

Lestrade was able to help me in one area. He suggested that if I want information about the locals I should speak to Inspector Glaser. The man has been assigned to this district for the past five years. He seems to be well liked and trusted by the community. No easy task in an environment as suspicious as this.

"It's because I'm Jewish, too," he told me when I met him. "I'm not a true insider, of course. I am not in the jewellery business, and I'm not from Russia or central Europe as so many of the merchants are. I'm a Londoner through and through. Nor am I particularly religious and, more to the point, I am a policeman. However, the people here trust me well enough because they know I will keep the peace and protect them as best I can. But I won't stand for any monkey business either. If a man commits a crime I will find him and lock him up and I don't care if he's a gentile or a rabbi."

His eyes flashed as he looked at me and I found myself smiling. "You are a man after my own heart, Inspector Glaser."

We sat in a kosher café that has a clear view of Hatton Garden. Even as he sipped his Turkish coffee, Glaser's eyes never left the street. Little, I believe, escapes his notice. Though I seldom have much regard for the official police force, there is so vital a sense of intelligence and honour in the fellow's demeanour, I found myself instinctively trusting him. He is a strongly built man though some three or four inches shorter than I. His hair is thick and curly. Unlike many of his coreligionists, he goes bareheaded. His profile tends more to the Roman than to the Jewish. From the glances that follow him, I believe he is much admired by young women.

"The people in this area have a reputation for insularity," I said, watching the endless stream of black-coated men hurrying down the street outside. "They are not welcoming of strangers."

Glaser's eyes flicked from the street to my face. "Can you blame them? They have been hounded from every place they've ever lived and suffered unspeakable cruelties and atrocities. No, trust does not come readily. That said, once you have gained their acceptance they will show you extraordinary loyalty."

"So if a stranger were to show up he would stand out?"

"Unquestionably." He leaned towards the window suddenly. Out on the street an urchin, following close on the heels of one of the 'cowboys', stopped and turned. Glaser tapped on the glass. The boy turned, gave a cheeky grin, waved, and ran off.

"Young Weiss. One of the best pickpockets in the city, but he knows better than to try something with me watching him."

"Do you need to go after him?"

"No, I shall talk to his mother. Believe me, she's worse than a month in Pentonville." He grinned.

"What else do you know about this Rickman fellow, Mr Holmes?" he said. "Other than his claims to be a diamond merchant?"

"Well, he purports to be South African, but might be German, or anything else, for that matter. I am told he speaks with an accent, but that could be fake. He has very fair hair and blue eyes and he is my height or a little taller."

He whistled. "Such a man would certainly stand out, and I haven't seen anyone who fits the bill. Nor have I heard of any new merchants, not for some time. As for an accent, well, most of the dealers are from Russia or Germany or Poland so an accent would not distinguish him, not here."

Glaser downed the last dregs of his coffee. The café owner came over and refilled his cup. He nodded at my own, still full cup and I shook my head. The man handed Glaser a pastry. The policeman said, "Thank you, Avram, but it's a bit early for me to eat."

"Put it in your pocket for later." The man patted Glaser on the shoulder and said to me, "Twice this past year men tried to break into my place. Both times young David caught them. He's a mensch. You know what that means? Mensch?"

"It's German for 'man'."

"Oy, German. But in Yiddish it means..." he fumbled.

"A gentleman," Glaser said. "A man worth knowing."

"That's it, that's it," said Avram.

Glaser slipped the pastry into his pocket. "Thank you, Avram," he said. "This gentleman is Mr Sherlock Holmes. You've heard of him, yes? He's looking for a stranger who might be up to no good. South African, perhaps. Very tall. Very fair. You've seen no one?"

"Sherlock Holmes? I thought you were a character in a story book." He guffawed and I found myself joining in. "I've seen no one like that, David. But I'll keep my eyes and ears open." He pronounced the policeman's name 'Da-veed'. He went away, still chuckling at my name.

After our coffee, Glaser led me through the meandering alleyways and lanes of his district. These thoroughfares are so narrow that in places neighbours can pass jugs of milk from their window to the people who live opposite. This might make for harmonious relations but the overall poverty has made this a high-crime area. Prostitution and thievery are stock in trade. There is violence, too, and the occasional murder. Still, compared with Whitechapel it is a very model of civility. Some of that, I surmise, is due to Glaser's constant vigilance.

I suggested this to him and he said, "I should like to take the credit for it, Mr Holmes, but there are enough religious Jews in this area to help keep the crime levels less than it might be. Not that a man cannot be both religious and a criminal, of course. Ah, here we are."

He led me into a dark building. There was a lad about eight years old sitting on the hall floor. He nodded at the policeman.

"Any trouble, Ari?" Glaser said.

"Only old Nancy and Liza having a bit of a barney." The boy grinned showing a mouth empty of teeth.

"Ari keeps an eye on things," Glaser said. "He's as watchful as any bloodhound and twice as savage."

"Bark's worse than me bite, though," the boy said, broadening his toothless grin.

"Have you seen any strangers about?" Glaser said. "This gentleman is Mr Sherlock Holmes. He's looking for a tall, *goyishe* fellow. Fair hair and blue eyes. You've seen no one like that?"

"Not I, but I'll keep my eyes peeled."

"Do. And pass the word on to the other lads, won't you?"

"Money in it?"

"A shilling for good information," I said. "Half a crown if we catch him."

"Cor. Right you are, sir. I'll spread the word."

Glaser led me down the long dark hallway. "Don't give him or any of the lads money before you get their information, Mr Holmes," he said softly. "They're good fellows, but they drink and then they're no use to anyone."

The hallway led to a heavy door. Glaser knocked twice and said his name. I heard three bolts being slid back, then the door opened and we stepped into another age.

The room was about fifteen foot square and dominated by an enormous oblong table, at least twelve feet by eight, around which sat twenty men who were polishing, cutting, and setting precious stones. They were all engrossed on their own task and though conversation, in Yiddish, was continuous, it seemed to have no impact upon their concentration on their tasks.

There was a big window, very dirty and barred, that let in a cold light. Thin rays slanted down onto the table and came to life amid the glittering jewels.

I breathed in a coppery odour of metal and solvent and in an adjacent room saw another half dozen men soldering precious metals.

No one looked up when we entered. No one paid any heed to us at all. Glaser led us through a series of ramshackle rooms that defy logic. Not only is there no apparent order to the layout, but the flagstoned floor is uneven and catches the unwary foot.

Nor can the visitor concentrate on his feet, for dense black beams crisscross the dingy ceiling. Some of them are low enough to bash in a careless head.

We came into a small room at the back of the building. I was vastly amused to observe that a beam here, about ten feet from the floor, was decorated with a collection of leather pouches. A closer inspection revealed that these were filled with tobacco.

Most of the main room was in semi-darkness but one thin shaft of light from a very high, barred window illuminated a square of black silk upon a wooden bench in which half a dozen diamonds glittered like a coronation crown.

At the table sat three men. All had beards and skullcaps. All were dressed entirely in black. Something about their features, the hollow cheeks and the pallor of their skin, highlighted by that slant of pale light, made me feel I had stepped into the canvas of a Caravaggio painting. Here was chiaroscuro come to life. I had a fleeting moment of regret that my ancestor's gift for painting has not come to me. My next thought was what an image this would present to a photographer of B's talent.

The three men glanced up when we entered. One beckoned with his hand and said, "David, come, see what *Reb* Schwartz has brought us."

Glaser glanced at the gems and whistled. "That's quite a haul, Mordechai. They must be worth a fortune."

"A king's ransom," the man agreed. "Uncut, a king's ransom. Cut, mounted… ransom enough for five kings."

"Five kings and an emperor," said the man sitting beside him.

"Rabbi Steinmetz, Mordechai Schwartz, and Daniel Solberg, say hullo to Mr Sherlock Holmes." With a barely perceptible nod of the head, he indicated that it was safe for them to speak to me.

"*The* Sherlock Holmes?" said Solberg, rising and shaking my hand. He was the youngest of the three, no more than forty. He, alone, was clean-shaven. "Well, well, this is an honour. It's not every day a real celebrity comes to call."

"I suppose it's an honour," Schwartz said, "And doesn't mean trouble for someone."

"Pooh, pooh," said the rabbi, and spat on the floor. "We don't look for *tsouris*, so *tsouris* should not look for us."

"Tsouris?" I asked.

"Trouble," Solberg explained.

"No trouble for any of our people, Rabbi," Glaser said. "But for a *goy* who is pretending to be a merchant."

"He is up to no good, this make-believe merchant?" Schwartz said.

"I think so," I said. "He is certainly a liar, and he has been sneaking into the home of a woman and her children late at night."

"Oy," said the rabbi. "That is not good. Not good. But why do you look for him here, Mr Sherlock Holmes? Are there no places beyond our walls where such a man might hide? Sit, please. David, sit."

Glaser and I sat at the table with the diamonds glinting in the dusty light before us. A few moments later, a young woman came in with a tray. She was about eighteen and had the brightest red hair I've ever seen. She poured the tea, spilling almost half. I surmise it is difficult to pour when your eyes are fixed upon the features of a handsome young policeman.

"Thank you, Rivkah," Solberg said, pointedly. The girl left, leaving one last lingering gaze at the young man by my side. Solberg sighed, but not with any sadness. "You must forgive my daughter, Mr Holmes," he said. "She forgets herself when our young friend comes to call."

Glaser flushed. "She's a sweet girl," he said.

"She's waiting for you," Solberg said. His long beard shook with laughter. "In the old country I would have married her off, but this is a modern world. Ay, even here we must accept new ways."

"Not too new, Daniel," the rabbi said, patting the man on his arm. "Just because something is new doesn't mean it must be better. Still, Rivkah could do worse than David. He's a good man, for all he's a policeman."

The rabbi passed around the cups and we sipped. The tea was black and flavoured with cherries. "Not quite what you're used to, I suppose, Mr Holmes," he said. "But it is our way."

"It is very good," I said.

"About this stranger Mr Holmes is looking for," Glaser said, not losing sight of our objective. "He is a tall man who claims to be from South Africa. He has fair hair and blue eyes."

"We do business with a number of South Africans," Schwartz said. "But not recently, and not so tall, as you describe."

"Have there been any strangers in your community in the last few months?" I asked.

There was a lull as they pondered. This was followed by a conversation in Yiddish, too fast for me to follow other than a familiar German word or two. Glaser, listening, shook his head at me.

"It's a small community, Mr Holmes," the rabbi said. "We know one another and strangers stand out."

"From what you've told me, Mr Holmes," Glaser said. "This man is lying about everything. Why should we trust him when he says he's a diamond merchant?"

"Your point is well made," I said. "But I think this is a very peculiar lie. He could have claimed to be involved in any number of things. Fur, wine, politics… Something suggested this particular trade to him. I think he was taken by surprise and did not have a story ready. He is also knowledgeable. He knows gemstones, or at least the language of the jeweller."

"Any man can sound like an expert," Schwartz pointed out.

"True."

"And a man can be a jeweller or work in the industry without being part of our community."

"You are concerned, Mr Holmes," the rabbi said. "Do you think my people might be in danger?"

I hesitated, torn between honesty and fear of causing alarm.

The rabbi seemed to read my indecision for he patted my arm and said, "Please just tell us, Mr Holmes. The Holy One, blessed be He, has sent you for our protection."

"I've never seen myself in that light," I said. "But if you insist, Rabbi, I shall tell you.

"This fellow claims to know something about gemstones. He told someone that he was going to be rich. He said he knew where there was treasure and there would be no harm in taking it because they 'were no Christians' who hoarded it."

"*Mein Gott,*" the rabbi said.

"He may, of course, have meant that he knew of some scoundrels who had something of value that he might steal, but I cannot rule out the possibility that he meant it literally."

Another conversation ensued, again in Yiddish, and this one was considerably longer. As it wound to a close, Glaser summarised:

"There are merchants and jewellers throughout this area and they are all vulnerable. Mordechai and the rabbi are men of influence; they will alert the others to be on particular guard. I have two constables and I've agreed to double the frequency of their patrols for the moment."

"Those are sensible precautions," I said. "Tell me, what sort of security is in place for the merchants? I observed the bolts on the door and the bars on the windows, but is there more?"

Schwartz said nothing. The rabbi leaned to him and said, "Come, Mordechai, Mr Holmes wishes to help us. We should be grateful."

"A *goy*?" Schwartz gave me a look that was neither grateful nor friendly.

Glaser explained, "A 'goy' is someone who isn't Jewish." Then, "You shame us with your suspicions, Mordechai. Who hasn't heard of Mr Holmes's reputation? Why he is as renowned for his integrity as for his wisdom."

"I understand *Reb* Schwartz's reluctance to trust a stranger," I said. "You need reveal no secrets. However, I would ask that you check all your locks and windows. I would go so far as to say check your roofs, your walls, and the walls of your neighbours. Who knows how this fellow plans to gain entry?"

"Your advice is very sound, Mr Holmes," Solberg said. "We shall do exactly as you suggest. And we shall certainly keep watch for this fair man with a dark heart. How do we get in touch with you if we spot him?"

The rabbi snorted with laughter. "Ah, Daniel, Mr Holmes's address is as famous as he is. 221B Baker Street. Please let Doctor Watson know I really like his stories. And you must feel free to visit us again, Mr Holmes. Ah, it is a shame you are not a Jew. What a Talmudic scholar you'd have made."

After leaving Hatton Garden, I returned to Camden Town. For some moments, I stood on the steps of the Prentiss home and stared at the park, the houses beyond, and the streetlamp. This was where my sense of unease began during my first visit. The same doubts recurred and I felt, feel, more certain than ever that something far more insidious than a tawdry romance is at the heart of it.

At last, I knocked on the door and Agnes opened it.

"Oh, it's you, Mr Holmes," she said, forcing her annoyance into a smile. "Do come in. I'll let Mrs Prentiss know you're here."

After a moment, Agnes showed me into the study where the mistress of the house was sewing up a pair of boy's trousers.

"Ah, Mr Holmes," she said, attempting to rise. I gestured for her to remain seated.

"Please, you will undo all your work," I said.

"I'm afraid you are right. Do please take a seat, Mr Holmes. Agnes, will you bring us some coffee?"

"Not for me, thank you," I said.

"So," said the woman once the maid left us. "What can I do for you?"

"I wanted to follow up with you. Tell me, how are things?"

"Not too bad," she said, but the strain on her face belied her words.

"I understand Miss Kidwell came to see you."

"Yes, she wanted her job back. I had to say no. It was a hard thing to do. One doesn't wish to be unchristian, and she was with us a long time. The children were fond of her. Still, she utterly betrayed my trust and I had no choice."

"None at all," I agreed.

She tried to smile but could not manage it. "I really dislike all these domestic trials. I should much prefer to focus on my work. There are days, Mr Holmes, when I truly envy my husband, or indeed, any man who gets to leave the house and need not worry about things like laundry or keeping the chimney clean. There, I am just feeling sorry for myself and, after all, it's much harder on Agnes. She's had to pick up the brunt of the chores and she's not as young as she was. She doesn't complain, but I would be heartless indeed not to notice the strain it has had."

"You have started interviewing for a new maid?"

"Yes, but I confess my experience with Connie has made me very suspicious. It's no easy thing, Mr Holmes, to open one's home to a complete stranger and trust so many intimate details of one's life to them."

"I understand." I thought about it for a moment and said, "Would you like me to ask Doctor Watson if he knows anyone who might suit? It would ease your mind, I think, if you could employ someone who came with a personal recommendation."

"Oh, that would be very kind," she said. For the first time since I arrived she looked animated. "Yes, that would be a very great help. Thank you, Mr Holmes. What a wonderful idea."

"I take it your husband is away?"

"Only for the morning. He changed his schedule so he can be at home for a few days while I get the domestic matters sorted. He took the children to the zoo, bless him, so Agnes and I can get caught up."

"He is an admirable man," I said. Though in hindsight why should I say so of a man merely because he's willing to spend a few hours with his own children?

"I wonder if I might go down to the cellar," I said. "I would like to make sure it is adequately secure so you will have no further disturbances."

"Of course. But really, Mr Holmes, surely there's no reason for that dreadful man to return, not now that Connie has gone."

"Indulge me, if you will, Mrs Prentiss. I feel I must be thorough if only for your father's sake."

"Then by all means, Mr Holmes."

"No, you need not accompany me. I can find the way on my own by now. Please, continue with your work."

There were no signs the mysterious Avery Rickman had returned to the Camden Town house since my last visit. The small precautions I had taken—a hair that would snap if the door were opened; a pan of water on the chair beneath the window—all remained intact. Was it mere happenstance that the intruder had not appeared during that period? During my last visit, I concluded that Connie Kidwell was keeping Rickman up to date on all the happenings within the house. Upon reflection, however, I suspect he was not dependent upon Connie alone for his information.

I set my safeguards back in place and climbed the steep steps to the ground floor. I carefully locked the cellar door behind me and placed a chair with its back beneath the handle. Of course, that served only to ensure that no one would enter the house via the cellar, at least, not without considerable difficulty. On the other hand, a desperate man would not let that stop him and he would be as likely to gain entry by another way.

The house was quiet with all the children away. There were sounds and aromas of cooking emanating from the kitchen and the odd sound of passers-by outside, but otherwise all was still.

I went out into the back garden. There was no question that Rickman had gained entry to the house via the basement, but why? Why get in that way? Surely he need only wait in the park and watch for the light to go out in Mrs Prentiss's study. She said she uses a lamp and ambient light; therefore, she keeps the curtains open while she works. Why wouldn't Rickman simply wait and then stand by the front door for Kidwell to open it as soon as she deemed it was safe? No, he made a production of climbing in through the basement window. Was it merely to add to the sense of mystery and excitement? But the basement is unwholesome; the back garden enclosed by six-foot-high walls. Even a tall man must strain to climb over them, particularly in inclement weather. Is Rickman mentally ill? Could it really be so simple?

What have I missed? Something. Something.

Think, man. Start again. What do I know?

Well, the garden is small and abuts onto that of the house to the rear. The house is part of a terraced set of buildings. To the front, the building is overlooked by other homes that surround the so-called Square. The Square itself, at least at this time of day, is lively with children, dogs, cats, tradespeople, nannies and Lord knows what else. It is deserted at night, of course, but there is always a chance of being observed.

Perhaps I am looking for something that is not there. Well, if the fellow does not return I can reasonably assume that his only interest was in Kidwell. However, if he does come back…

For over an hour, I examined every window and door in the building. I ascertained that both front and back doors have a bolt, though the one at the front door is at the top and difficult for anyone but a tall man to reach. The windows are of the sash variety and offer little in the way of security.

I had just finished when George Prentiss returned with his children.

"Mr Holmes," said he, shaking my hand. "I am delighted to meet you. Alice told me what a help you have been. That Connie was a bad lot, eh? Letting all and sundry into the house while my wife and children slept in their beds. Goodness knows what might have happened without your intervention."

"I am glad to be of service, Mr Prentiss," I said. "I should like to talk to you about this matter in more detail. Can you spare me half an hour?"

"By all means," he said. "Agnes, bring us some coffee. It's fierce cold outside. Not a day for the zoo really, but at least it entertained the children."

We sat in the parlour alone while their mother took the children upstairs. As soon as the coffee was served and the maid had left, I began to share my analysis of the events.

"We are still trying to trace this fellow Connie Kidwell was seeing, but it appears he was using a false name. The address he gave her does not exist."

"Scoundrel," Prentiss said. "Some men are utter cads. I am very sorry for the girl, but she made her bed."

"Indeed. I confess, Mr Prentiss, I cannot rule out the possibility that Rickman was merely using her to gain access to your house."

"Good God! But why? To what end?"

"Why, indeed. I understand you have no valuables on the premises?"

"Nothing but some jewellery but even that is of very little value. There are houses in the square that are far richer than ours. We are not wealthy people."

"What about the documents your wife translates?"

"Very ordinary things, so far as I know. Letters and so forth from the Brahms Antiquities, pretty dull stuff to my mind, though she seems to enjoy it. Alice also translates documents for individuals from time to time, but nothing out of the way. She would have told you, I am sure, if she had found anything unusual."

"She denies seeing anything of the sort. Still, it is possible she did not realise the significance of something."

"But this man, Rickman, has been coming into the house for weeks. Alice works rather quickly. It only takes her a few days to translate a box of papers and then she returns all the documents to the company or the owners."

"Yes, that is what she told me. And yet there must be some reason why this fellow should take such risks as to come into your home with such frequency."

"Could it not be as Connie said? Merely to...? Well, you know what I mean."

"Yes, it is possible. Still, I am uneasy, I confess. Why the subterfuge? Why take such elaborate precautions against being seen?

"Rickman, or whatever his name is, deceived Connie about his name and his address. He obviously had the run of this house and I believe made several attempts to gain access to your wife's study, seems to suggest a motive other than copulation."

"He tried to access my wife's study?"

"There are faint scratches around the lock. Initially I thought it was because your wife was very tired when she finished her work for the night and so sometimes missed the lock. However, I cannot rule out the possibility that Rickman was trying to gain access to the room."

"Good God!"

"Your wife would know if any of her documents had been moved, so I infer he was unsuccessful in his attempts to gain access. I suspect Kidwell did not give him much time to make these attempts."

He flushed and sipped his coffee. "Yes, I see what you mean."

I gave him a moment to consider what I told him. He seemed bright enough to see the implications and the more he thought the more anxious he became. "Mr Holmes," he said. "As you know, I am gone from home for long periods. Is my family in any danger?"

"I have been examining the security of the house," I said. "I have taken pains to secure the basement, and the back door is safe enough with its lock and the deadbolt. However, the bolt on the front door is high and it is quite stiff. I assume your wife does not use it when you are not here?"

"No, she can't reach it, nor can Agnes."

"I would recommend in the strongest terms that you get another bolt placed on the bottom of the door. You should also purchase stronger locks for the windows."

"I shall," he said. "I shall do everything you ask, Mr Holmes, and at once. Is there anything else you would suggest?"

"Yes, I wonder, would it be possible for you to take your family away for a few days and leave the house empty?"

"Empty?" He stared at me, bewildered.

"So I and Doctor Watson might keep watch. If this chap is keeping your home under surveillance, it's possible we may be able to lead him into a trap."

"It will take a day or two to organise," Prentiss said. "But we shall manage. Yes, by Jove, we shall."

6

Monday 4 April 1898

A letter from B arrived in the morning's post. At last! She writes,

Forgive the delay in my reply, my dear Sherlock. For several days I was much in demand, meeting with representatives of the Dreyfusards, trying to calm M Zola, and lending what assistance I could. In addition, going out became perilous for a short while. I was forced to remain indoors until this morning when the violence abated somewhat.

Something about this entire affair reminds me of your thorny case last year. Perhaps it is the memory of the dreadful business with Porlock that makes me imagine spies and cutthroats everywhere. I envision a puppet-master controlling the situation and observing the resulting chaos with amusement.

One of Zola's neighbours, Maurice Lachapelle, was set upon by thugs as he returned home from his work in the bakery last night. Although he is Catholic, he has a somewhat Jewish appearance. The facts of the matter were irrelevant for his assailants and they stripped him naked, cut off his hair and beard, and left him unconscious in the street.

Yesterday I was privileged to meet Émile Duclaux. What an extraordinary man he is, not merely a microbiologist and chemist of the first order, but a true logician who approaches this shameful business with exemplary rationality and courage. He is a great admirer of your work, Sherlock, and says your practical applications for science are remarkable and innovative.

I fully apprehend Mycroft's concerns and your own husbandly sense of duty. Nor am I fool enough to be unaware of the difficulties posed by my presence in France. To that end, my friends are making arrangements for my return to England. Safety is, at this stage, a greater matter than urgency, so I beg you be patient until the most prudent route may be planned. I shall let you know as soon as the details have been finalised.

Now Zola's conviction has been overturned I can leave with an easy conscience.

Fondly,

B.

My first reaction to this letter was a profound sense of relief. She is coming home, and she is taking proper precautions. Thank heaven.

I have never met Duclaux but I have certainly heard of him and have read his papers with interest. I recall he once described himself as one of those who "are devoid of any other preoccupation than the truth." These are principles I have always tried to uphold. I am deeply honoured to be esteemed by such a man.

Zola's conviction has been overturned on a technicality only, and so the whole farce begins anew. I am not optimistic of the outcome. The French military and government are too deeply embroiled to do anything but uphold his conviction. Still, it allows B to leave France with an easy conscience and that is enough from me.

This afternoon's post brought a letter from Zola himself. He urges me on no account to return to France. It is not safe, he says. Although he is greatly appreciative of B's support, he is worried for her safety. It is wise, he says, that she is coming home to

England. He outlined the plans he and his trusted supporters have made to ensure she gets safely out of the country. Thursday sees the beginning of the Jewish Passover: they anticipate a great deal of trouble. Best have her leave before then.

Zola begs me to make sure B, too, does not return to France. Her presence has been noticed. She is too visible, too outspoken. Her support for him and the beleaguered Dreyfus has excited attention in the worst possible quarters. For the sake of her safety, he begs I keep her in London.

How am I to accomplish such a thing? A woman is a woman and will do as she pleases. While I share Zola's concerns, I am, I confess, very proud of B for her courage, her tenacity, and her loyalty. Not that I have any right to be proud. I have no part in her choices or her actions. Her esteem is something to treasure. I would not dream of breaking our agreement to honour each other's freedom, and yet I would keep her safe.

Well, if all goes according to plan, B will be back in London on Thursday.

Watson looked up from his newspaper to say, "So she's coming home then?"

He looked smug, though I suppose I can hardly blame him. "Well done, Watson," I said. "You are really coming along remarkably well."

"Well, Holmes," he said, "I may not have your talent for ratiocination nor your astute observational skills, but I do know you. That smile and that relief in your shoulders can only mean one thing: Beatrice is coming home."

"I am relieved," I said. "B's passions lead her to defend the defenceless, and passion is a very dangerous thing in Paris at present."

"Yes, I've been reading the paper. New outrages every day it seems."

"B has a theory that some puppet-master may be behind the whole thing," I said, picking up my violin. I did not play it however, but lay it upon my lap.

"I knew it was a mistake not to arrest all of that Porlock gang," Watson cried.

"Calm yourself, doctor." I plucked at one of the violin strings. "Those villains are being watched. Although…"

"Although?"

"Mycroft's report from the Continent concluded there were a few fellows whose links to Porlock could not be proved. There was Casonne who vanished before the agents could talk to him, and a banker called Zeiss. He had ties to von Schwartzkoppen."

"Von Schwartzkoppen? Why do I know that name?" Watson said.

"He's the military attaché at the German Embassy in Paris."

"Ah, that's right, I remember. Those documents that got Dreyfus arrested in the first place, weren't they found in von Schwartzkoppen's wastepaper bin?"

"Yes," I said. I plucked another string and then set down the instrument. I rose, stretched, and put on my coat. "It may not signify," I added. "France is marinating in suspicion. B may simply be a victim of the prevailing mood."

"Will you pass on her suspicions to Mycroft?"

"Hmm? Not yet. I want to talk to her first and see if this is anything other than that old traitor, 'woman's intuition'. You need not look at me that way."

"It will be good to have her home, in any case," he said, mildly.

"Yes, indeed."

"So will she come here, our Queen B, or go to Wimpole Street?"

"Oh, Wimpole Street, I am sure." I sounded aloof and disinterested. Yes, I am certain I did.

I was almost out the door when Watson added, "So you shall be at Wimpole Street then, for a few nights? Just so I know that you're safe."

He grinned and then hid his head in the newspaper. I threw an apple at him.

Just after dinner, Lestrade called in. As I poured him a sherry I said, "You look well, Lestrade, but you really shouldn't let your wife make the Easter eggs so early. There's another six days to go, you know. The wretched things will stink by then."

"There, Mr Holmes, that's exactly what I did say. But we have the grandchildren staying for a few days and it's entertaining for them… Here, how did you know?"

"That curious red and green stain on your left index finger and thumb are unquestionably food dye. That particular shade of carmine exists nowhere else in nature. You would be unlikely to have a stain on those particular fingers if you were merely painting a picture, nor would you use such an odd medium as food colouring. But a right-handed man will hold the brush in his right hand and the egg in his left. The advent of the Easter holiday makes the conclusion a certainty."

"I held the egg with my thumb and forefinger. You're right, you're right! You know, it always seems so simple when you've explained it."

"So I have been told," I said. I do not believe I sighed too loudly.

Lestrade winked at Watson. Before I could remonstrate he said, "I called in to tell you a tall, fair-haired man matching the description of that Rickman fellow was spotted in Great Russell Street. One of my lads spied him and took chase but the bounder vanished somewhere near the British Museum."

"Damnation. Did your officer get a good look at him?"

"No, Mr Holmes, young Dobbs was a fair distance behind the villain, but he said it was a tall fellow with fair hair. Once the man spotted my officer chasing up the road he took off at high speed. Guilty conscience, I'd say."

"I am inclined to agree."

"I, ah, thought it would be better if I told you in person," Lestrade said.

"Holmes understands it wasn't your fault, Lestrade," Watson said, giving me the look.

Why give me the look? Do they think I would blame the man just because one of his underlings is incompetent? I am not so unjust.

"Certainly not your fault, Lestrade," I said.

He relaxed and took a gulp of his sherry.

I added, "You might train your men a little better though."

He coughed, spluttered. Sherry ran down his chin. Watson patted him on the back and gave me a heightened version of the look.

I added, "At least we have learned two important things, so that is something."

"Two things, Mr Holmes?" Lestrade said, wiping his mouth.

"We have learned that the man is still in or near the Holborn area, and that he fears being questioned by the police."

George Prentiss called a few minutes after Lestrade left to say he had spoken to his father-in-law and Mr Gillespie was happy for the family to stay with him for as long as they need.

"'If Mr Holmes says it's necessary then necessary it must be,'" Prentiss quoted. "It's a smallish house and not ideal for three young children; still, they'll be safe and that's really all that matters."

Prentiss, himself, is back to Scotland next Monday on the ten o'clock train. He is relieved to know his family will be safe in his absence.

We have agreed that at eight o'clock on Monday evening, Mrs Prentiss, her children, and servants will leave the house to stay with her father. The delay cannot be helped. Old Gillespie already has visitors and though he longs to accommodate his daughter, he can hardly evict his guests. In any case, so long as George Prentiss remains at home and the safeguards I set up in the house are observed, the family should be safe enough. It is only another handful of days, in any case.

For the next fifteen minutes we refined our plans. I regret the delay in putting it into action, but that cannot be helped.

On a slightly related note, Watson brought the daughter of one of his old patients to meet Mrs Prentiss. Bessie Turner is the oldest of five children and very level-headed, I am told. "Her father died much too young," Watson said, "and it's such a struggle for her mother to cope with so many children. Having one less mouth to feed not to mention having the girl's wages, will go a long way towards helping her family."

He tells me the meeting went well on both sides and Bessie starts work tomorrow morning. Watson, determined to harangue me with all this domestic nonsense, added, "The important thing is Agnes seems to like her. She, more than anyone, will have to work with the girl. But they hit it off right away and I think it will work out perfectly. Bessie's used to children and always looked after her brothers and sisters so she'll manage well with the young Prentisses."

"You look thoroughly pleased with yourself, Watson," I said. "It's positively indecent."

He laughed heartily and confessed I was quite correct.

Thursday 7 April 1898

Beatrice is home. I met her at the station. She was tired and pale. Not until that moment did I truly appreciate the strain she has been under these past two weeks, but she smiled when she saw me and shook my hand.

We took a cab directly to Wimpole Street and for most of the journey she was silent. Not until we were alone in her library, surrounded by books and mementoes of her father, with good English tea before us and the door shut did she at last begin to relax.

"It seems a lifetime since we said goodbye, my dear Sherlock," she said. "I hope you will not consider it a breach of our contract if I say I missed your company very much."

Another man might have flushed. I merely replied that I was not sanguine about leaving her alone in Paris, particularly under the current circumstances.

"Your continued presence, much as I would have welcomed it, would have drawn attention," she said. "While I usually find it irksome to be ignored because I am a woman, under these conditions it was helpful."

"Were you really so inconspicuous, do you think?" I asked it innocently enough but she cannot be fooled, not even by me.

"How well you know me," she said. "I suppose I may have let my thirst for justice override my good sense once or twice, but it is really a shameful state of affairs. Dreyfus was a reliable, even brilliant soldier with an excellent reputation and a great career ahead of him. But because of his religion it was easy to forge documents and charge him with treason. Treason! A man like that?" She paced the floor more and more vigorously as she spoke.

"Yes," I said mildly. "I can see how you might have allowed your passions to carry you away to imprudence."

She stopped to look at me, gave a brief laugh, and then sank back in her armchair. "You are right. I confess it. I was very foolish—but only some of the time."

"Your friend, M Zola, is a very brave man," I said.

"Yes. Isn't it curious that when a man and a woman behave exactly alike he's considered brave while she's called a fool."

"I do not think that is fair."

"Isn't it? Do not misunderstand me; I am very fond of Émile. He is indeed brave; but he rushes into this matter with no thought for the consequence. It is all the same to him if he is imprisoned. In fact, he dares the government to do their worst."

"A little reckless, perhaps," I agreed.

"If he had only himself to think of it would be a little reckless, but he has a family. He has a wife and a mistress and children. What right does he have to subject them to abuse and possible violence?"

"You think a man has an obligation to put his family before his conscience?"

Her shoulders dropped and she released a long sigh. "No. No, of course I don't… Ignore me, Sherlock. I am out of sorts and cantankerous." She stifled a yawn. "The journey home was not pleasant. Zola was very alarmed for my safety and insisted that I have an armed escort all the way back to England. It did not make for a relaxing trip."

"I am grateful to him for taking such pains," I said. "You do look very tired. Perhaps you should lie down for a while."

"I will. Later, I will. I have not seen you for so long. It feels like an age instead of just a couple of weeks. How are you? What have you been working on? You have a case, I see."

"Ha! How well you are able to read me. I vow between you and Watson I feel utterly transparent."

I told her about the events in Harrington Square. She listened in silence.

"Oh, how delicious," she exclaimed. "But I fear it will turn out to be no more than some sordid tale involving a scullery maid."

Frankly, I was a little vexed that she hit upon it so quickly.

She smiled at my chagrin and said, "Tell me, what title has Watson given it?"

"'The Case of the Camden Town Poltergeist'," I said.

"It lacks poetry."

I smiled. "It does indeed. I suspect he is attracted to the Gothic nature of the thing." I went on to tell her about the mysterious Avery Rickman, my visit to Hatton Gardens and my increasing concern for the Prentiss family. Like Watson, B has a talent for silence. She does not interrupt and when she poses a question or offers an opinion, she is always on point.

"These are deep waters, Sherlock," she said when I concluded. "From what you say, I have no doubt there is more to the matter than a mere love affair..."

She stopped and flushed. I knew she, too, was remembering that night at the opera. The glory of La Scala, the exquisite music, our journey through charming streets with her hand in mine and then later in the hotel...

Beatrice rose again. For all her weariness, she was as restless as a puppy. She stood by the window gazing out into the street. "I have missed this view, this house. I have missed speaking English," she said. She turned and smiled at me. "It is very good to be home."

"I confess I am relieved to have you back here. I have seldom seen Mycroft so concerned."

"He is right to be. There have been violent clashes and the streets are no longer safe. Jews are beaten or stoned, as is anyone who speaks for Zola or Dreyfus. There are whispers on the streets of Paris. One word, a bloody word, said in hushed in terrified tones..."

"Revolution?"

"*Exactement.*"

"Mycroft would be very interested to hear your observations," I said. "Perhaps I could arrange a meeting?"

"I would like that. Tomorrow, perhaps. Oh, and might we meet in his office? He has told me so often of the view from his window. I would love to see it for myself."

I smiled. "I shall see what I can do."

Later, as she helped me put on my coat she said, "You will keep me informed about this case, Sherlock? It sounds too benign for my comfort."

"Indeed, some of my most notorious cases have rested upon details no more extraordinary than parsley on butter."

"At least it will keep you properly entertained for a while." She smiled sweetly and I realised she was again teasing me.

"I am glad you are home, safe and sound, Beatrice," I said.

"As am I." Then, more sombrely, she said, "You will be careful, won't you?"

"You have my word, I shall take every precaution. Besides, I have Watson. He's as dangerous as a tiger and loyal as a bulldog."

"True. Please send him my regards. Good afternoon, Sherlock."

7

Mycroft was outrageously pleased to see Beatrice. Whether this was because he was relieved to have her safely home, or because of his genuine regard, I cannot say. He showed her around his prestigious building, introducing her to a few trusted colleagues, and to my astonishment, cleared an entire hour from his schedule.

Gillespie brought out the sherry—something I have never seen before except when the Prime Minister comes to call—and some of his oldest daughter's fruitcake. B bore all this attention with grace and good humour, inquired after Gillespie's family, and essentially made conquests of every male heart in Whitehall.

"Why so gloomy, Sherlock?" Mycroft said. "I should have thought you'd be pleased to see Beatrice safely home."

"I am delighted," I said through tight lips. "But I do have other demands upon my time."

We sat by the fire—Mycroft seems to have an intolerance to the cold of late—and B told her tale. My brother listened with his eyes closed and his fingers forming a tent. Anyone might think he had fallen asleep.

"You met with some government insiders?" Mycroft asked when B was done.

"Yes." She listed several names and he whistled. "Either you or your friend Zola are well connected. What do they make of this matter?"

"There is no doubt there is a traitor, a real one, and it is not Dreyfus."

"And their reasoning?"

"There is evidence the theft of documents continues even now. A fellow by the name of Esterhazy has drawn attention."

"He was brought to trial in January," I said, "and acquitted in a closed session."

"And another suspect, Lemercier-Picard, was found hanged in suspicious circumstances last month," Mycroft added. "Quite a mess."

"It is," Beatrice said. "There is paranoia and suspicion at every turn. Many of the government know there has been a grievous miscarriage of justice, not that they'd admit it publicly."

"But they told you?" My brother's eyes stared sharply at B. I have seen cabinet ministers quake before that look. B merely nodded.

"France is on the brink of civil war. Those gentlemen I named are anxious to avoid that at all costs. They want to know how England might respond to this crisis. They cannot ask openly, of course, but through an unofficial channel like myself something might be accomplished."

Mycroft sat up straight. "Did they mention my brother or me? No? You are quite certain?"

"My dear Mycroft," she said. "Is it really so difficult to believe that I may have a reputation that goes beyond the name 'Holmes'? They confided in me because I have impeccable credentials in my own right."

"Ah, of course," Mycroft said, sinking back into the bosom of his chair. "Yes, being the Queen's goddaughter must afford you considerable prestige. Forgive me if I was too harsh."

"Were you harsh?" She smiled at him and he chortled.

"I would have you work for the government, Beatrice. You have a knack for learning things mere men cannot discover on their own."

"Of course. Men tell their wives all sorts of things and women will tell other women things they would never tell a man. I do have something for you. I promised I would place it into your hands alone."

She handed him a sealed letter and he whistled when he saw the signature. He handed it to me and I understood his reaction.

"Well, well," Mycroft said. "This is of enormous interest. But you say you never mentioned me?"

"I did not have to. The illustrious gentleman who gave me that letter asked if I might be able to locate you. I said, truthfully, that I had met you at dinner on one or two occasions. The gentleman was kind enough to give me your office address. That is why I asked Sherlock to bring me here. Just in case."

"In case you are being watched? Do you think you might be?" I asked.

"I was certainly followed from Paris by a slight man with a curiously brachycephalic head. Which reminds me, Sherlock, I read an article about the racial geography of Europe in *Popular Science*. I would be curious to hear your opinion. As to my Parisian shadow, I can tell you only that he has been married for at least ten years, has two children, and suffers from arthritis. Beyond that I know nothing about him."

Watson coughed on his fruitcake. When he was able to speak he said, "Surely many people travel from Paris to London? Could it not have been a coincidence?"

"If I had travelled by the usual course I might agree with you, Doctor. However, in the interest of safety my friends took a peculiarly convoluted route. No, I am not mistaken."

An hour later, all our business concluded, B rose to return to Wimpole Street. She would travel alone, she said. I was not happy about this, particularly in light of the news that she had been followed. However, she insisted it would look less suspicious if she did so and Mycroft agreed. "No point in tipping off people about your relationship, Sherlock, if you do not have to. It is bad enough you were together in Paris in January. Go and watch from the window and observe if the lady is followed."

"I don't like it," Watson said. "It seems unnecessarily dangerous."

"If someone wanted to injure me, Doctor," said B, "they have had plenty of opportunity to do so. I was most at risk before I completed my task. I suspect my follower will now return to France with his report."

Watson and I walked her down the stairs and then stood at the window that overlooks Horse Guards Avenue. As B crossed the road, a small man with an unusually short and wide head followed behind her at a distance of some fifty yards or so.

"Watson," I said. "You go follow that fellow. Do not reveal yourself; we cannot let him know we have uncovered him. But make sure you do not lose him."

"I do not understand your alarm, Sherlock," Mycroft said when Watson had left. "The girl is not concerned and her reasoning is sound. Now, read this letter and tell me what you think…"

7.00 pm

Confound it! Must I do everything myself?

Easter Monday 11 April 1898

The church bells have just chimed nine o'clock and the street outside is dark. The family has left and there is nothing now for Watson and me to do but wait.

George Prentiss is working, so it is only his wife, children, and Agnes who have gone to Gillespie's. Bessie has been given permission to return home for the night.

As the family left by the front door, Watson and I arrived by the back. We are now sitting in the kitchen. I suspect it may be some hours before our prey arrives. If he arrives.

I made sure all the doors were locked and the windows secured. Upon reflection, I decided not to slide any of the bolts. If our 'poltergeist' should try to access the house by another route, I do not want him alerted to our presence. No, best maintain the illusion that the place is empty.

Watson and I have made ourselves as comfortable as we can in the kitchen. I expect our intruder will enter via the cellar window, as usual. Once he comes up those stairs, he shall find us waiting for him.

Watson says, "But what if he does not come?"

I am loathe to consider the possibility. Patience will out, I think.

Watson is sucking humbugs.

"Must you?" I said.

"I said I was sorry."

"Yes, but that does not avail us."

"Well, honestly, Holmes, I appreciate your concern but you really might have been more explicit in your instructions. You said to follow the fellow; how was I to know I was to keep on following him after Beatrice reached home? I assumed the whole point was to ensure her safety."

"There's the flaw in your reasoning: you assumed."

More silence. More humbugs.

"Holmes?"

"Yes?"

"I really am very sorry. Did I do so badly?"

"Yes."

11.00 pm

It's getting very cold. I must have shivered because Watson just tossed me my scarf.

Midnight

Still nothing. The streets remain remarkably busy for so late an hour. Possibly some people are dragging the Easter holiday out as long as they can. The sounds of inebriation filter through the house. The clip of footsteps and horses' hooves. We may have some hours left to wait.

I can see my breath but we dare risk a fire. Watson is dozing on the chair but despite his great coat and his hat, he is still shivering. I found a rug in the parlour and tucked it around him. He gave me a sleepy but appreciative grin before settling into sleep. I know the instant he is needed he will shudder into action, prepared to do whatever is necessary to protect me and himself and capture our intruder. This ability to switch from sleep to complete wakefulness is a skill familiar to both the medical and the military professions, so in this instance my friend is doubly blessed.

I am reminded of that night we sat watch in Stoke Moran waiting for the "speckled band" to appear. That was a dreadful watch too. Worse than this, in fact, because the environment was wholly unpleasant. At least here there are some domestic comforts.

I wish he'd come.

Tuesday 12 April 1898

Watson counsels calm but how can I be so when I have been the biggest dunderhead of all time? I had him. I actually had my hands on him. Damnation!

"It's not your fault, you know," my friend says. "You did everything you could."

"I should have anticipated better. I should have realised he'd be armed. I should—"

"My dear Holmes, you really ask far too much of yourself at times. Even if you had known the fellow would have a weapon, how could you have done anything differently? He was a monster. I've never seen such strength, nor such speed."

For several moments, we sat in silence. He finished dressing my wound and said, "I think you should get to bed, old fellow."

"The injury is not as severe as all that," I said. Yes, I will admit to some petulance. I was aware of it but could not keep it from seeping into my voice. I can add another layer of guilt to my sins.

"That the bullet did no irreparable damage is insignificant," Watson said. "You need rest and your body needs time to heal. Come on, old friend, lean on my shoulder."

So like an old pair of codgers he helped me into my bedroom and eased me into my bed. I groaned as I lay down.

I said, "Watson? Am I getting old?"

"Yes, Holmes."

He insisted that I drink a draught of some horrible stuff. In less than a minute, I was sound asleep.

I awoke this morning with a headache, a dry mouth, and a throbbing in my left arm. From the other room, I could hear voices.

I threw on my robe with some difficulty, and shuffled into the sitting room.

Watson said, "Ah, there you are, Holmes. I trust you slept well. Lestrade came to give us an update on the Camden Town incident."

I sank into my usual chair. Watson brought me coffee and I drank the whole cup almost in a single gulp. Then I held out the cup and waited for him to refill it before I nodded to Lestrade that I was ready to converse.

"The doctor has been telling me about your adventures, Mr Holmes. You are lucky that bullet did not kill you. You know, if you'd told me in advance what you were planning we could have had some constables standing by."

"That would not have availed, Inspector. The man has obviously been keeping a close eye on the Prentisses' home. He would not have acted if he'd known it was being watched by the police."

"Perhaps," Lestrade said. "Nonetheless, I am very sorry to hear you've been injured."

"I was too slow," I said. "Much as it galls me to admit it. I misjudged his speed and I underestimated his size. Well, at least now I know what we are up against. I will not misjudge him again.

"But you have news for me, Inspector?"

"Yes, I'm afraid it's not much. The man was spotted a few hours ago in the Holborn district, but then we lost him."

"Holborn again?" I said. "The diamond district, the Hatton Garden area… Something is going on there, Lestrade."

"I recall I referred you to Inspector Glaser. Was he of any use to you?"

"Indeed, he was extremely helpful. I must say, Lestrade, your recent additions of policemen to the service have been exceptional. There was Tavistock Hill who worked on the Hacker and Smiley case, and young Stevens… How is Stevens, by the way?"

"He's doing very well, Mr Holmes. He's a bright lad and a willing one. He's already become a favourite among the other officers." Lestrade grinned and added, "Of course, he can at least say he helped the great Sherlock Holmes. That must set him apart from his peers."

"Soon I shall be obsolete," I said.

A long silence ensued and it continued beyond a comfortable period. After several moments Watson said, "You must forgive Holmes, Lestrade. I'm afraid he's feeling a bit morose at present. It's not uncommon when a man has suffered a bullet wound."

"Well," said Lestrade as he picked up his hat. "You're certainly not obsolete to me. No matter what advances we make, there's only one Sherlock Holmes and the world is not done with him yet." He extended his hand and I shook it gratefully. He's really a very good sort of chap and at least he has the sense to recognise genius though he possesses none himself.

He added, "Don't forget, Mr Holmes, if our young officers excel it's largely because of you. We've made great advances since you first invented the job of Consulting Detective, and those advances came from studying your methods. Now, do look after yourself, won't you, old friend?"

I nodded. I confess I had quite lost the power of speech. Lestrade said his goodbyes and departed, leaving me in a most perplexed state.

"I think you should go back to bed, Holmes," Watson said. "You're looking very pale. A nice long sleep will do you good, I think."

"I need to know more about those documents of Mrs Prentiss. Rickman returned, as I knew he would, because there is something in that house he wants. We have ruled out jewels and other valuables; Kidwell is no longer there so we can eliminate the carnal factor."

"What do you need me to do?" Watson said.

"Go visit Mrs Prentiss and ask her if we can read her documents. Perhaps they will help me deduce what Rickman seeks."

"But she returns her documents to Brahms when she is finished," Watson said. "Would she still have this paper?"

I held my arm and winced. It really hurt like the devil. "I cannot say," I admitted. "The thief seems to think she still has it so we cannot overlook the possibility."

"Very well, I shall speak to Mrs Prentiss and get her permission."

"Bring the papers back here as soon as you can. Then I have one more assignment for you, if you are willing."

"Of course."

"I need you to visit Hatton Garden."

8

I slept all morning thanks to another dose of Watson's disgusting medicine. At some point, I heard him come in but I could not shake myself back to consciousness.

It was late afternoon when I awoke and I felt utterly disoriented. Mrs Hudson brought up some coffee and a tray of food. I surprised myself by emptying the pot and cleaning the plates. Feeling much improved, I then turned my attention to the case of documents Watson had left. I was making slow but steady progress when he return

"Ah, you're up," he said. "Our friend Inspector Glaser was most concerned to hear of your injuries, Holmes," the doctor said. "He insisted on coming to pay his respects himself."

"Very kind of you, Glaser. Won't you join us for supper?"

"Thank you, no; the Solbergs are expecting me. I was sorry to hear you'd been injured, Mr Holmes. Rivkah has sent you her chicken soup. She says it has healing properties."

"Thank you. That was most kind," I said. "Now, tell me all your news: What has been happening in the diamond district?"

"Nothing of any consequence, I'm afraid, Mr Holmes," he said. "I have been keeping careful watch but I've seen and heard nothing of the man you seek. Dr Watson told me the fellow was spotted in the Holborn area. Is it possible his interests lie beyond our small world of precious gems?"

"Possible? Yes. But my instincts tell me there is some link between the diamond district and my case," I said. "What little we know of the man suggests he knows something of jewels; he has been twice spotted in the vicinity of Holborn, and as I discovered to my cost last night, he is willing to shoot anyone who stands in his way. Perhaps I am wrong. It does happen," I added at seeing his bemused expression. "But I would prefer to be cautious."

"I've made sure the merchants and tradesmen in my district have the full description that the doctor gave me. If he makes an appearance someone will let me know."

"I expect so. But is it possible someone might be hiding him?"

"Yes, it is, I'm afraid. There are unscrupulous people everywhere, and though many in our community are religious, we have our share of rogues. Besides, even good people will keep silent if they are afraid enough."

"Ha! In my experience, some of the worst rogues in Christendom have been men of the cloth. No reason to suppose Jews are any different."

"In that respect or in any other," Glaser agreed. "But as to this fellow, I have excellent resources around the diamond district. If Rickman is hiding there, we'll find him eventually. I have instructed my fellow officers to contact me if they hear anything. Of course, Holborn goes far beyond the Hatton Garden area."

There was a ring at the front door and a moment later I could hear light footsteps hurrying up the stairs. A perfunctory knock at my door was followed by B bursting into the room in a state of high dudgeon.

"What in the world," she exclaimed. "You get shot, Sherlock, and don't even bother to send word to me? What were you thinking? Oh, forgive me, I did not realise you had company."

She hesitated, caught between good manners and concern.

I said, "This is Inspector Glaser from the Hatton Garden district. He is helping me with the Camden Town case. Glaser, my, ah, friend, Lady Beatrice."

"Inspector Glaser," B said, shaking his hand. "A pleasure to meet you. Tell me, how fares my old friend Rabbi Steinmetz?"

"You know the rabbi?" Glaser said, looking surprised. "He is very well. He is as old as Methuselah but you'd never know it. I have to run to keep up with him."

"He and my father were acquainted," B said. "My father was a scientist and a man of enormous curiosity. He came upon some Torah scrolls several years ago and donated them to the rabbi's synagogue."

"Beatrice's father was Benjamin Jacoby," I added.

"Professor Jacoby was your father?" Glaser exclaimed. "I met him once. It was a long time ago, five or six years at least. But you said 'was'?"

"He died some time ago."

"I am truly sorry to hear it. He was a good and kind man. The rabbi will be very saddened by the news."

"Thank you. But, forgive me, you were discussing business. I should leave."

"By no means, Beatrice," I said. "We would welcome your insights. The lady has a remarkable mind," I told Glaser.

Briefly, I brought her up to date with the developments of the case.

"And your wound," she said, "it is not serious?" She looked, not at me, but at Watson.

"I have no doubt it is painful, but the bone and the major blood vessels are intact. He was very lucky."

"You both were, Doctor," she said. "All the same, Sherlock, I think you might have told me."

"Forgive me," I said. "I am not used to… such things."

Beatrice and I held each other's gaze until we realised an uncomfortable silence now filled the room.

"And you have borrowed Mrs Prentiss's documents?" she said, recovering. "Surely if there had been anything of value she would have returned them to Brahms already?"

I waited, watching her reason it out. "But Rickman believes she still has it. Whatever 'it' is. He returned last night to get it."

"As you see, Glaser," I said. "Beatrice has a highly logical mind." To my wife I added, "We took only the oldest documents, ones that she has been working on for the past several weeks."

"Perhaps I can help," B said. "My French and German are excellent and even my Italian has improved."

For a moment, I imagined I could hear the orchestra tuning their instruments. I could see B was remembering, too, for her cheeks flushed. Of course, it may simply have been because of the exertion of hurrying to Baker Street to see to my welfare.

"That's not a bad idea, Holmes," Watson said interrupting my reverie. "It took a good deal of persuading for Mrs Prentiss to give up her papers. The sooner we can return them to her the better."

"Your help would be most welcome, Beatrice," I said. "The sooner we catch this Rickman character the better."

"And the Irregulars?" B said, "Can they help?"

"Billy and Tommy are already on the case," I said. "They have the others scouring the city. Glaser, do you have any youths in your district who you would trust to search? What about that fellow, Ari?"

"I have already enlisted the help of my most reliable boys and girls."

"Then I think we can do no more."

Glaser rose to leave. He shook hands with Beatrice and with Watson, then with me. "I wish you a speedy recovery, Mr Holmes. I shall send word as soon as I have something. In the meantime, if you need anything further, send word and I shall be glad to assist."

"A nice young man," Beatrice said after he left. "One of your acolytes, I think."

"Acolyte?" I said. "Why do you say so?"

"It is obvious he has learned much from studying the Master. He was clearly thrilled to be part of the case, to help you with it. I do hope he will be careful. He so wants your approval."

"See, Holmes," Watson said. "Not so old after all."

Friday 22 April 1898

I am sick of contracts. Of letters from whining officials and of endless catalogues of insufferably dull trinkets. We finished late this afternoon with nothing but paper cuts and ink stains for our pains.

The Prentiss family returned to their home last week. It was difficult for the children to travel to school from Gillespie's house in Chelsea. I am not sanguine about it, but Watson tells me people do not live in a vacuum and cannot remain hostage to a dangerous villain forever.

Lestrade's men have been keeping a close eye on Harrington Square and have seen nothing. I was, I confess, somewhat sceptical of their reports but the Inspector assures me his men are highly motivated.

"A man who would dare shoot the great Sherlock Holmes," he said without any apparent mockery. "My constables are incensed. If this blackguard returns, you may be sure we shall catch him."

He has not been apprehended. Does this mean he has not returned? If not, why not? Does he fear that I have set another trap for him, or has he spotted the constables? Too many questions and not enough data.

Though I am not at all sanguine about the Prentisses' return to Harrington Square, at least they have had no disturbances. Thus far. George Prentiss assures me that the house has been secured with double-locks, the windows fixed with bars, and he, himself, has taken a position in British Rail's head office. It is a reduction in salary, but the hours allow him to be home every evening. His wife seems perfectly satisfied with this arrangement. In the meantime, my old friend, Gillespie, has moved in with them for the moment. While he is advanced in years, he has a great deal of experience both as a soldier and as a member of the Queen's own guard. I must be content.

This is what I tell myself: I must be content.

Watson and I went back to Camden Town this afternoon and returned Mrs Prentiss's documents.

"You have done my work for me, Mr Holmes," she said. "I've never been so up to date with my translations."

"My… friend Beatrice did the bulk of it," I said. "She is fluent in several languages."

"Did you find them helpful, Mr Holmes?"

Watson hastily replied, "At least they enabled Holmes to rule out a number of things. Didn't they, Holmes?"

There was no doubting the edge in his voice. I said, as cheerily as I could muster, "Indeed, yes. That is so. Though I must confess I was disappointed we did not find anything more on point."

Watson sighed.

I continued, "Mrs Prentiss, are you sure you gave us everything? Is there nothing more?"

"Nothing, Mr Holmes, I assure you."

I studied the rug on the floor of the study: A deep crimson background with intricately woven black branches and white flowers that I supposed to be cherry blossom. It was far too cheery a thing for my mood. Watson said, "Is it possible there were other documents that you had already translated and returned that struck you as out of the ordinary?"

My head shot up. Sometimes, Watson, sometimes...

Our hostess pondered for several moments then said, "You know, now that you mention it, yes there was. There was the matter of the Egyptian Fathers."

"The what?"

"Yes, I thought it puzzling, too, Mr Holmes. It was at the beginning of the year; January, I think. I had quite forgotten all about it."

"Yes, yes, but what did the document say? Where did it come from? It's been several months, I suppose you cannot remember too much..."

"On the contrary, Mr Holmes," Mrs Prentiss said, rising. She opened a cabinet and, after a few minutes, withdrew a document and handed it to me. It was a long sheet of paper comprising almost entirely of a list of names and years. There were forty-four entries.

"I always keep a carbon copy of the translation for my own records," Mrs Prentiss explained. "Just in case there is some dispute or query later on. I do not have the original, of course. Although, to be clear, I do not believe the copy I received was the original either. It looked like it had been transcribed from another, older, document."

"Thank you, Mrs Prentiss," I exclaimed. "You have done exceedingly well. Why did you think the document was a copy?"

"There were small signs." She sat and pondered, trying to recollect. "The paper was old but not antique. As a linguist, I am a student of philology. Some of the words on the page were archaic."

"So you believe the style of language seemed older than the paper?"

"Yes, precisely. Language evolves, you see. The way we speak and write now is quite different from the Elizabethan era, for instance. This document had something ancient in the language, in the way certain words were used. The syntax and grammar were particularly antiquated, and there were no upper or lower case—something that is exceedingly unusual in a modern Greek document but commonplace in ancient Greece."

"Can you tell us anything about the paper?" I did not hold up much hope, but the woman surprised me.

"Well, it was paper and not parchment. Something else that suggested a copy."

"Anything else?" I asked. "Close your eyes. Imagine it in your hands. Examine it."

She shook her head. "I'm sorry, I've told you everything."

"Be patient," I urged. "Look at the document in your hands. How many pages are there?"

"Three... No, four. Yes... Four."

"Are all the pages filled with text?"

A longer pause this time then, "Yes. Evenly spaced on the first three pages, but more cramped on the last page. The writing was slightly different, too, more rushed."

"Good. You are doing exceedingly well. Now, feel the paper in your hands. How does it feel?"

"Rough. A medium weight type of paper. Not parchment as I said, just paper. It was dry. Brittle."

I took a breath. We had probably reached the limit of her remembrance. One last question came to mind, however, and I said, "What does it smell like?"

Instantly she replied, "Camphor." She opened her eyes and blinked. "Why, isn't that extraordinary? I had quite forgotten. Yes, it smelled strongly of camphor. I remember coughing at the smell when I first took it out of the satchel. Whatever does it mean?"

"It means the paper has probably been stored in a cupboard for a long period of time."

"So it is an old document," Watson said.

"That is by no means certain," I said. "All we can deduce is that the paper seems old, but not ancient, and that it has been stored near camphor."

"Oh, I wish I could remember more," Mrs Prentiss said.

"Not to worry," Watson said. "You have done extremely well. Hasn't she, Holmes?"

"What? Oh, yes, splendidly. Well, it may not matter, in any case. As you say, this was not the original manuscript but only a copy…"

I tried not to sound too disappointed. Even a copy can be of extraordinary interest if one knows what one is looking for.

"You said you took the papers out of a satchel," I said. "Where did the document come from?"

She took the copy back from me and held it, as if the tactile connection could stimulate her memory.

"It was in between two pages of a letter," she said. "I'm afraid I cannot tell you anything about that letter; I did not record the information."

"You did not translate it?"

"No…" Her hand caressed the page and she frowned. "Now, why didn't I? I see I noted receipt of the document on the twentieth-fourth of January and that I returned it on the seventh of February."

Watson and I waited as she continued to ponder. "It was in English… Yes, that's right. It was a bill of sale from the Fleming estate and spoke of the death of old Sir Nicholas Fleming… He had died only two days earlier and I remember I was surprised that his heirs acted so promptly to discharge his affairs. I suppose he had been ill for some time and they were waiting for it. What a horrible thought. But I remember that I thought it was odd to find a document like that in my box of papers."

"Odd?"

"For two reasons: in the first place I don't get documents in English. Sometimes there may be some direction from Mr Brahms, 'I need this urgently'; or 'M Brel sends his regards', sort of thing."

"I understand. And the second reason?"

"Well, Sir Nicholas wasn't someone we would normally do business with. He was an English gentleman and if he had affairs with foreign correspondents, he dealt with them himself. He used to come to the shop from time to time; he and Mr Brahms were acquainted. Yes, I remember that Mr Brahms was very anxious that everything to do with the estate be handled as quickly as possible."

"Sir Nicholas Fleming, the explorer?" Watson said. "He and his partner, Sir Jeremy Jeffrey made their name in North Africa, if memory serves."

"Yes… Tell me, Mrs Prentiss, is there anything else you can tell us about the gentleman?"

"Not really, I'm afraid. I met him once, no, twice. He was very elderly and not in good health. He had three sons but I got the impression he was not on good terms with any of them. He was an antiquarian with a taste for the exotic. He had a particular fondness for documents of the ancient world: Greece, Egypt, and the Middle East. Now and then Mr Brahms received an object associated with one of those places and he always let Sir Nicholas know."

"Did Sir Nicholas ever purchase items from Brahms?" I said.

"From time to time, I think, but only after his health prevented him from going on his travels. I suspect dealing with foreign antiquities helped him remember the places he'd seen. From time to time, Mr Brahms would ask him to appraise rare artefacts. His was a highly specialised knowledge and there really are not many men, not in this country anyway, who shared his expertise. His death is a sad loss."

It seemed Mrs Prentiss had told us all she knew. "Your assistance has been invaluable," I said. "Rest assured we shall get to the bottom of this strange matter as soon as possible."

"Thank you, Mr Holmes," she said. "I hope I have been of some service. It is in my interests and that of my family to assist you any way I can. May I ask how you will proceed?"

"I will take this copy with me, if I may. I should like to study it further. And I think you and I, Watson, should pay Mr Brahms a visit without delay."

Mrs Prentiss glanced at the clock. "I'm afraid you're too late for today, Mr Holmes. The offices closed at five o'clock. It is now five minutes past. Moreover, Mr Brahms does no business on the weekend. You'll have to wait until Monday morning."

"Confound it," I muttered. "Well, we have other business to detain us today. Mr Brahms will keep, I expect. Never mind. Let us see if Connie Kidwell can shed any further light on these peculiar events."

Connie Kidwell was in a sullen mood.

"I was having my dinner," she said. "Little enough they feed us here without you making me miss my meal."

"I'm sure they'll keep it for you, under the circumstances," Watson soothed.

She was not appeased. "You could at least have called when I was doing that bloomin' laundry. Wouldn't mind missing that, I can tell you. Well, get on with it."

"We are still trying to find this Rickman fellow," I said. "If you can you give us some idea of the sort of things that interested him it may narrow the field of search. You mentioned gemstones, I think?"

"Yes, diamonds in particular," she said. "He talked about gems the way most men talk about women, but anything valuable made his beady eyes light up. Greedy bloody bastard."

Watson raised an eyebrow. We were in the matron's office in the home for 'unfortunate' women. The uncompromising white walls held no ornamentation beyond an enormous black cross and a painting of the Madonna and with her fat baby. In this environment, Kidwell's language seemed inappropriate to the extreme. I myself was not offended but I fear it rather put Watson's back up. He bristled like a wet cat.

"Quite," I said. "I don't suppose he showed any interest in artworks or antiquities?"

She shook her head. "We didn't do much talking and to tell the truth, he's not so bright. He did say there were some coins that would be worth a fortune if he could lay his hands on them.

Said the fellow who owned them had no clue what they was worth."

"Really? Can you tell us anything more about these coins?"

"Nah. What would I care about some silly old pennies?" She shook her head and rubbed her back. "They've got us up since five in the morning to start our prayers. Fat lot of good it does." She pointed at her belly. "I just want this thing gone."

Watson snapped, "It's a bit late for that. What happens when the child is born?"

"I'll give it up," she said. "I don't want it. I hope it dies."

We rose to leave. Watson, white-faced, shaking with fury, strode from the room. It seemed we would learn no more. Then, at the door, the girl's mood abruptly changed and she said, "You mustn't mind me. I'm just angry. Not at you. Not even at him. I'm angry with myself for throwing away such a good situation. What a bloody fool... This baby—what's to become of it, eh? Even if you find Avery, he's not going to want me or his kid. Still, I hope you do find him. Make him marry me like he promised."

"You'd still have him?" Watson seemed aghast.

"I know what you think of him, of both of us, but he treated me like a lady."

"Thank you for your time, Miss Kidwell," I said, opening the door.

"They was Egyptian," she said, as she opened the door. "Those coins. I remember that much. The 'fathers', he called them. Isn't that a laugh? A man like him all anxious about fathers. I could laugh."

"Insufferable, foolish girl," Watson seethed as we hurried up Islington High Street. There were plenty of cabs in the area, but

I decided it would be wiser to let my friend walk off some of his spleen for a while. It did not take too long.

About ten minutes later, he stopped abruptly and said.

"Where are we going, Holmes?"

"Back to Baker Street. We can accomplish no more this evening. On Monday we shall visit Brahms and perhaps that will clear up some of our current confusion."

"And what will we do in the meantime?"

"Think!"

9

Sunday 24 April 1898

This morning—it may have been closer to the afternoon—Watson gave me a look a teacher might give a child who has failed to study his times-tables.

"What time did you get to bed, then?" he asked as he poured the coffee.

"Late," I said. I may have groaned. My head, mouth and ears all felt full of cotton wool.

"And did you get anywhere?"

I gulped down the coffee. "No... There are still holes, Watson. There are vast empty spaces where information ought to be and is... not. It's like trying to read a book when the pages are made of Italian lace."

"So it's a dead end, then?" he said.

I downed a second cup of coffee and shook off my lethargy.

"No, not quite. We still have the coins."

"What, those coins of the fathers or whatever they're called? But we don't know anything about them."

"Then it is time we learned."

The rabbi, pleased enough to see me, was positively thrilled to make the acquaintance of his favourite writer, Dr John Watson. My friend, for his part, was equally fascinated by the rabbi. For several minutes, they sat together in a cosy tête-à-tête while the rest of us looked on in amusement. We were in Schwartz's workroom, sitting where the red-haired girl served us tea and cherries. She was not present today.

"I was sorry to hear you had been injured, Mr Holmes," Solberg said as he polished an impressive emerald. "I hope the wound does not trouble you too much."

"It is mending, thanks to Watson's ministrations." So Glaser told them about my little adventure. Well, no harm.

"I am curious about Rickman's continued interest in that house," I said. "I wondered if perhaps he might have thought there was something of value there. An antiquity, perhaps."

"Schwartz is your man for any questions about antiquities, Mr Holmes," Glaser said. "No one can rival his knowledge on the subject."

Schwartz shrugged and presented the palms of his hands in a gesture of humility. Still, there was no denying he was pleased by Glaser's acknowledgement.

Solberg added, "It's true, Mr Holmes. Mordechai is like an encyclopaedia when it comes to all things ancient."

"A poor knowledge," the man said with a scolding look at Solberg for the gentle tease. "But I am happy, very happy to help you in any way I can."

"Well then, have you ever heard of the Egyptian Fathers?" I said.

"Ah, there's a term I have not heard in many years," Schwartz said. "Better known as the Coptic Patriarchs. They are a myth much like the Holy Grail of Christian lore."

"Yes, but what are they?"

"They are coins from fourth-century Egypt. A *nummus,* if memory serves; that is to say, at the time they were in currency they would have been worth about a penny, perhaps less. The 'Patriarchs' were unusual: they are said to be made of copper instead of the usual bronze. It is claimed that they bear the image of a male figure on one side—opinions vary about who it is—and a winged lion on the other."

"A winged lion?" Watson asked. "My Egyptian lore isn't very good, I'm afraid. Is there some significance to that?"

"It's the symbol of Saint Mark the Evangelist," the rabbi said. Watson and I stared at him in some astonishment. The rabbi chuckled. "Does it surprise you that I am versed in things that go beyond my own religion? A man has a curious mind. He reads; he learns many things."

Schwartz added, "The rabbi is quite correct. I am no expert, but I believe St Mark is considered the founder of the Coptic Church in Egypt. The coins are claimed to have some sort of mystical property, not unlike the Grail. They are shrouded in myth and legend. Who knows what the truth really is. Their story is well enough known in certain circles."

"Indeed," said the rabbi. "Even I have heard of them. It is a charming story.

"It is said that one day St Mark came upon a destitute widow who was begging for alms. He gave her two coins and the woman immediately spent them on food. However, upon returning home she found she still had the coins. Being an honest woman, she went back to the shopkeeper but he assured her he had been paid in full. Thereafter, no matter how often she used the coins, they remained in her possession.

"It is a delightful variant on the endless wealth legends, is it not? Some stories tell of people asking genii for a vast store of wealth. Their wish is granted, but always in a way that brings unforeseen negative consequences. There is something charming about having only two coins that always return home."

"How delightful," Watson said. "The spender will never go hungry, but neither can he squander his wealth on extravagant items like..." He fumbled for an example.

"Like carriages or horses," the rabbi said, helpfully.

"What happened to the coins after the widow died?" I asked.

"The story claims they were passed on to her oldest son. After that, they faded into obscurity for several centuries. The next account came from the Holy Roman Empire. It was said that Charlemagne owned them for a period around the eighth century of the Common Era. Then they allegedly showed up again during the siege of Jerusalem in 1187."

"That's very specific for a legend," I said.

"Oh, such stories have a way of recurring over the years."

"I assume if they were found they would be valuable?" I said.

"I doubt they actually exist," Schwartz said. "But, yes. If they were found and could be authenticated they would be priceless. Not only in monetary terms, but in historical interest."

"How would one go about authenticating such a thing as coins?" Watson asked. "I mean, wouldn't it be like trying to distinguish one penny from another?"

Schwartz shook his head. "An enormous difficulty, I agree. There have been fakes, even fakes of the coins. Some appeared in... where was it now? Somewhere in Bavaria, I believe..."

He turned to his friends and a brief, bewildering conversation in Yiddish ensued.

"Rosenheim, we think," Schwartz said, turning back to us. "About twenty or so years ago there was a small outcry because someone claimed he had found the coins. There was a great deal of excitement."

"My wife's brother lived in Bavaria at the time, may he rest in peace," said the rabbi. "And I remember him writing to us about it. Yes, I think it was Rosenheim, near Munich."

"How was the fraud proved?" I asked.

More excited conversation. Schwartz said, "We can none of us really recall. I think it was something to do with the provenance."

"Provenance!" I slapped my knee. "Of course. If you wanted to prove such a thing were authentic you would need to be able to trace it back to its origins. I suppose a list of names of the previous owners and the dates the coins were in their possession would serve, yes?"

"Of course," Watson said. "The list!"

"List?" Schwartz was full of curiosity and excitement. "Certainly that would be of immense use. A record of names and dates, so long as it was sufficiently current, could indeed support the authenticity of these relics, assuming they exist. You have seen such a list?"

I shrugged. "I have heard rumours. Tell me, if such a document did exist I suppose it would be in Egyptian?"

"Or Greek," the rabbi said. "There was a great deal of Greek influence over the Egyptians, I believe. Not that I'm an expert, of course. Do you think the coins are what this crazy man is looking for, Mr Holmes?" the rabbi asked. "Is that why he broke into that poor woman's house?"

"There may be no connection at all," I said. "I suspect Avery Rickman heard the term and for some reason thinks this unfortunate woman knows something about them."

"But she does not?" Schwartz asked. It didn't sound as casual as he intended and I saw Glaser stare hard at him.

"Beyond the fact that she has heard the term," I replied, "She knows nothing at all on the subject. She is just an ordinary English housewife. Perhaps better educated than most."

"I think," Watson said, picking up my cue, "The problem lies with her maid. The girl was trying to ingratiate herself to this Rickman character and probably told him all sorts of nonsense. It's likely she said the house was full of jewels and she herself was a lady's maid, rather than a scullery maid. Even in the serving classes there is a hierarchy."

I forced myself not to smile. Watson is such an expert in reading people and situations, and his explanation sounded perfectly plausible. However, Schwartz was too canny to accept this interpretation of events at face value and he continued to tug at the puzzle.

"But how would a scullery maid have heard about the Patriarchs?" he said.

"From her mistress's reading, perhaps? Possibly from some comment made by Rickman himself." I suddenly felt we were all in a play each portraying a character. What a tableau we formed as we stood there, caught in the sudden unexpected tension like an insect preserved in amber. There was an unease in the air that had not been there before. Schwartz stood before me in a halo of sunlight; his white frothy hair glowed under his black skullcap, and the sharp light turned his head into a skull. Only his dark eyes were alive and these stared into mine. The rabbi, a troubled look on his face, stared at his old friend, and Glaser had been transformed from a genial guest into a policeman. Only Solberg seemed untroubled. He sat at the long bench and sipped his tea.

I continued, "I may be completely wrong of course. This fellow, Rickman, may have been visiting the house in Camden

Town for some other reason entirely. Perhaps he had not heard that his, ah, paramour had been discharged and his interests lay somewhere else entirely…"

"Then why would he have arrived with a pistol?" Glaser said. It is most unsettling when policemen display wit. On the way home, I commented to Watson it was like hearing a dog suddenly start to talk. He said I was being unkind.

At any rate, I was forced to respond to Glaser's reasonable observation. I said, "I suspect you may be right. As Watson said, perhaps the maid had misled him into thinking there were jewels in the house. However, since these coins were mentioned it would be foolish not to learn what we might about them. There seems little doubt Rickman is interested in arcane treasures."

"It's not unusual," Watson said, "for a young woman to pretend an interest in a man's concerns in order to win his affection. The young woman Holmes speaks of was very obviously deeply infatuated with the man. And given how many lies she told her employer over the past few months I think it's evident the glib falsehood comes naturally to her."

Solberg said, "The tea is getting cold. Sit, gentlemen, and let us talk of more civilised things."

"Spoken like a true Talmudic scholar," the rabbi said, easing his creaking bones down onto the bench.

A young man, thin and unpleasantly pale, stood at the door and waved at Schwartz. The old man rose and said, "Excuse me, gentlemen. Business."

We all sat and sipped our tea. The conversation dried up and after some moments the rabbi said, "I understand, Mr Holmes, you are acquainted with the daughter of my old friend Benjamin Jacoby, may he rest in peace."

"Yes." I hesitated. I do not like to be deliberately deceitful with good men unless there is some justification. On the other hand, my relationship with B is known to so few and then only my closest intimates. "She is a very dear friend," I said. "But our friendship is not common knowledge and I would greatly appreciate it if you would keep the matter confidential."

"Of course, of course," the rabbi said.

"You are afraid the lady might become a focus for your enemies if her friendship with you was known," Glaser said. "Yes, there's sense in that."

The rabbi said, "Perhaps one day you might bring the lady here? If it would not cause you too much discomfort you could join us on Friday and share our Sabbath dinner."

"I would be delighted. I will see if Beatrice is free, but I'm sure she would very much like to spend time with old friends of her late father."

"Ah, I was very fond Benjamin Jacoby," the rabbi said. "He was a good man. In fact, you remind me of him a little."

"Do I? How so?"

"You both have the minds of a scholar. It is a rare thing, far more rare than the most precious gem: a man whose only interest is the truth. A man of integrity who is incorruptible."

"You seem to have got Holmes's measure more swiftly than most, Rabbi," Watson said. "I think it's because you have the same values."

The rabbi smiled and sipped his tea. "Perhaps, perhaps," he said as he placed his cup back in its saucer. "Or perhaps it's because I've spent so many years reading your delightful stories, Doctor."

Watson was charmed at this. "I do have to take some poetic license from time to time," he said. "But I try to be honest in the narrative."

"You do exceedingly well."

Glaser said, "I don't suppose you have room at your table for an impoverished policeman this Sabbath, Daniel?"

"It's less me than my daughter you want to see, my friend," Solberg said, laughing. "But we are dining with the rabbi, too."

"Please join us, David," the rabbi said. "The more the merrier. We will drink a toast to old friends and new. What *tsimchas* we shall have!"

"Tsimchas?" I asked.

"Joy."

After a while, we rose to leave. At the door, Glaser hesitated, turned to the rabbi, and asked the question that had been vexing him: "What is *Reb* Mordechai's interest in these coins, rabbi? Come, you saw how he reacted. You know him better than anyone."

Solberg placed a gentle hand on Glaser's arm. "Be calm, David, there's no mystery, it's just *Reb* Mordechai's way. You know how he gets when he hears of rare treasures. They fascinate him much the way Mr Holmes's most unusual cases fascinate you. He's a good man."

Glaser didn't seem convinced and Solberg turned to me and said, "I know how it looked, Mr Holmes. Schwartz has a way of appearing—what's the word?—single-minded when he gets caught up in one of his passions. But he is an honest man and a kind one."

"Mordechai is a very good man," the rabbi agreed. "I would answer for his integrity, Mr Holmes. But he does love his mysteries and his treasures. If I may make a suggestion?"

"Please."

"Include him. Ask him to help you. He knows people, experts that go far beyond our small world. He would not want the coins for himself; he would want to see them housed in a museum where the world could appreciate them. His interest doesn't come from avarice but from a passion of all that is rare. He would dearly love the credit of the discovery, if the coins were to be found."

"Well, I can certainly understand that motivation," I said. "I shall take your advice. And we shall see you on Friday, Beatrice, Watson, and I."

We shook hands and left. Out on the street, Schwartz was showing gems to a couple of prospective buyers. When he saw me, he excused himself from the men and came over.

"I wanted to apologise if I seemed rude, Mr Holmes," he said. "It's just…"

"That it is your business," I said, shaking his outstretched hand. "More, it's your passion. You need not explain to me. I understand obsessions only too well. I would be extremely grateful, Mr Schwartz, if you would make discreet inquiries about the coins. Be careful not to arouse any suspicion, however. This man, Rickman, is very dangerous as I learned to my cost. I share your opinion that the coins are a myth, but whether that is the case or not, the fellow must be found."

"I shall be very careful. Thank you again, Mr Holmes, and good evening."

Glaser walked us to the end of Hatton Garden where we caught a cab. As we prepared to board, I said, "Thank you again, Inspector, for all your assistance. You are really quite invaluable."

He flushed, caught between embarrassment and pleasure. "It is an honour to help a man like you, Mr Holmes. I'll look forward to seeing you and the doctor and Lady Beatrice again."

"Yes... Do please be careful, Glaser. And keep an eye on your friend, Schwartz. No one knows better than I how a man's passions can lead him astray."

"You have my word," he said.

Monday 25 April 1898

Brahms Antiquities is a discreet and elegant building in Knightsbridge. From outside it looks like a private home. One must ring the bell and present one's card to gain admittance. Only then is the visitor escorted through a plush hallway to the back of the building where Ezekiel Brahms keeps his office.

He is a small, bald-headed man who speaks with the exquisitely precise intonation of one who is not a native speaker.

"You are an Austrian, I perceive, Mr Brahms," I said as Watson and I sat on the elegant but uncomfortable divan.

"You have an acute ear, Mr Holmes," he said. "A most acute ear. Yes, you are quite right. I was born in Salzburg, but I have lived in London for almost thirty years. Very few people can tell I am not an Englishman. Yes, yes, you have a very acute ear."

"Holmes is a musician," Watson said.

"Ah, then perhaps you would find this interesting..." He gestured excitedly. "Come, come," he said.

Somewhat bemused, we followed him into a small drawing room. A harpsichord nestled between two long windows. I felt that frisson of excitement that I seldom experience outside the solving of a puzzle, but this piece was special indeed.

"It is very old," I said. I let my fingertips caress the wood.

"It was Bach's. Yes, yes. Johann Sebastian Bach, himself. He composed *The Goldberg Variations* upon it."

"How extraordinary. If true."

He looked hurt. "Mr Holmes, I assure you, I have proof of provenance, unassailable proof. But perhaps you would like to play it?"

"I could not do it justice. I am a violinist."

"Ah. A pity. We do have a number of rather lovely violins, if you are interested?"

"Thank you. I own a Stradivarius."

"Do you indeed? I say, if you are ever looking to sell it, Mr Holmes, I hope you will let me make you an offer."

"Thank you, Mr Brahms, but I have come to you today on rather different business. Tell me, was the thief successful in his attempts to gain access to your premises?"

"How in the world did you know about that, Mr Holmes? You are quite right. We have had three attempts made in the past couple of weeks. Three. And never any bother in as many years previously. How in the world did you know?"

"The bars on the windows outside are less than a week old. There are no fewer than three gouges around the door lock and I see these locks have been changed in the past week."

"Dear me, yes, you are quite right. We have so many valuables here, you see. It's not simply a matter of financial worth, but we are custodians of the world's treasures. We must be good stewards. But to answer your question, no, the premises were not violated. Our security is always excellent and we have, as you observed, added further levels of protection."

"Do you have a security guard on the premises after hours?"

"We didn't until recently, but we do now. He's an upstanding man, above reproach."

"I hope he is armed."

"He is, Mr Holmes. You know, I worried that I might be overreacting but you do not think so?"

"By no means. As you say, these treasures belong to the world. It is only right you should protect them by any means possible.

"Now, I need to ask you about your records of Sir Nicholas's estate…"

We spent the next forty minutes discussing the life and adventures of Sir Nicholas Fleming. The man's time in Egypt, his knowledge of antiquities, his generosity, all these were covered in excruciating detail.

Sir Nicholas died in January after a long illness ("bravely borne"). In June last year he arranged with Brahms to sell off his various art collections immediately after his death. The proceeds were to be divided among his heirs. I forestalled Brahms' discussion about the various nieces and nephews who stood to inherit.

"Were any coins listed among the inventory?" I said.

"Coins? Not that I recall. I would need to check my files."

"May we see your records?" I said.

"Of course."

He rose. A chiming collection of keys hung from his waistcoat and he selected one of these and opened a door behind us. It was a file room some twenty feet long and almost as wide. The walls were lined with shelves that went to the ceiling and these were packed full of files. There were five additional rows of cabinets cutting the length of the chamber. Everything was neat and orderly but exceedingly dull. Watson gave me a glance. I shared his dismay.

"Where are the documents from Fleming's estate?"

Brahms indicated a pair of boxes at the bottom of the back wall. "Here," he said.

Watson whistled. "Good grief. There must be hundreds of papers here."

"Six hundred and twenty-nine," said Brahms. "A separate record for every item and every transaction."

"You have a master list?"

He pulled out a thick folder at the front of the drawer and handed it to me. "Here you are, Mr Holmes."

The document was 35 pages long. I read it twice.

"I do not see any mention of the Coptic Patriarchs," I said.

"The what?" Brahms looked bewildered.

"Egyptian coins. Do you recall if there was a document in Greek? It would have looked like a list of names and numbers. Mrs Prentiss translated it and returned it here."

"And it concerned some patriarchs?" Brahms' confusion seemed to have deepened, rather than lessened.

"Apparently. At present we are concerned only with the document."

"How very odd," he said. "Usually I try to keep a close eye on all the items that pass through here, but given the size of Sir Nicholas's estate, I'm afraid we got a little lax." He took the folder from me and peered at it. "I am very sorry, Mr Holmes. The only possibility is the document was part of a larger number of papers that we had been requested to translate. If that is the case, they would have been sent directly to the interested party."

"And you retain no record?"

"Under the normal way of things we do, of course we do. However, in this instance... I'm afraid not."

"Would Sir Nicholas's partner have any further information?"

"Very possibly, but I'm afraid Sir Jeremy left for Africa immediately after the funeral. I can write to his agents, but the reply may take some time."

"That is unfortunate. Possibly, Sir Jeremy will have little to add. Still, send the letter. It is always best to be punctilious."

10

Friday 29 April 1898

Beatrice, Watson and I, slightly cramped in a cab, made our way to Hatton Garden a little before eight o'clock. The lady was demurely dressed with a high-necked gown and a veil of some silvery, shimmery material on her head. She was in high spirits and I knew I could expect some teasing throughout the evening.

I could feel her warmth through my coat and her hand briefly touched mine. Sitting opposite, Watson continued his dissertation on the traditions of the Jewish Sabbath.

"It is very particular, you know," he said. "I read up on it. There is no work permitted, not so much as a candle may be lit. Still, it is considered a time of great joy and celebration."

"It is indeed," my wife said. Her voice sounded mirthful. "I dined with the rabbi once, many years ago. Possibly he does not remember."

"I cannot imagine anyone ever forgetting you, Beatrice," I said.

She released one of those gurgling laughs that for some reason makes me feel quite giddy.

We arrived promptly at the chimes of eight. The door of the rabbi's house opened before the cab left and our host came to greet us.

"You're very punctual," he said. "I am so happy to see you again, Lady Beatrice."

"Thank you, Rabbi," my wife said. "But I think you should just call me Beatrice. There is no formality between friends."

In the small house, the rabbi introduced us to his wife Miriam and their daughter Esther.

"I wish we'd been here for candle-lighting," Beatrice said. "I do love that prayer."

"You are familiar with the *bracha*?" Solberg said. "That's what we call 'blessing'."

"Oh yes," Beatrice replied. "My father had many Jewish friends and we often joined them for the Sabbath."

"Your father was a good friend to our people, Beatrice," the rabbi said. "He was a benefactor, a man of great generosity and kindness."

"Thank you, Rabbi. I had no idea how altruistic he was until after his death. I received so many letters of thanks and condolence."

"I regret I had not heard of his passing," the rabbi said. "Not until young David told me. Speaking of David, where is that friend of yours, Daniel? I missed him at services."

"He and my daughter had things to discuss, so he said." He grinned. "I am hoping for news of a wedding."

"That would be lovely," the rabbi's wife said. "It's about time that boy settled down."

"Time who settled down?" Glaser said, joining us. The girl at his side gazed up at him with such longing I think we all held our breath.

"You," Solberg said. "That is, you and my daughter."

Glaser gave his friend an affectionate, long-suffering look. "I'm sorry we're late," he said. "It was entirely my fault. We were talking and I forgot the time. We even missed candle-lighting and the services."

"If you were any other man I'd have to chastise you," Solberg said. "But I know I can trust you. Even with my only child." He glinted at his friend and tried to look dangerous. He added, "Right?"

"Right."

"David is a perfect gentleman, Papa," Rivkah said. "How can you doubt it?"

We sat at the table and the rabbi said a blessing over the food. Watson was in his element. He asked an endless litany of questions about the prayers, the food, and the traditions. The rabbi answered with admirable patience.

Beatrice was in a giddy mood and rather than discouraging my friend, she seemed determined to egg him on.

Glaser sat opposite me and did not speak very much. His attention seemed focused entirely on Solberg's daughter. The girl hovered near him ready to fill his cup or his plate at even the slightest gesture. Sitting beside his friend, Solberg could barely control his amusement. Indeed, from time to time, little chuckles of laughter erupted from him. Then he raised a hand as in apology while he forced his glee back into submission. At least for a few minutes until it bubbled up again. Between his mood and my wife's we were in for a giddy evening.

"Sit, Rivkah," Solberg said at last. "You are a guest in the rabbi's house. It is not right that you should attend his guests."

He spoke kindly but the girl's cheeks turned a deep pink.

"Let her be, Daniel," the rabbi said. "What a thing it is to be a young woman and in love. I suppose you know something of that, Beatrice?"

My wife smiled. "I don't think I've ever been one to behave quite the same as other women, Rabbi," she said. "I fear I'd shock you with my modern ideas."

"My husband is not easily shocked," the rabbi's wife said. "Though you may not think it to look at him."

The two exchanged a look of fondness and I wondered what it must be like to have someone be so part of your life for so many years. It is a measure of the old couple's warmth that it suddenly seemed an enviable state.

Again, I became acutely conscious of the woman at my side. My wife. I think I shall never get used to calling her that.

We ate our excellent meal with great enthusiasm. The conversation was lively and entertaining. There were no airs in this house. It seemed a warmer and more delightful environment than many of the great mansions in which I have dined. The rabbi spoke with considerable insight about politics. Inevitably, the subject of the Dreyfus affair arose.

"Beatrice has just recently returned from France," I said.

"A bad time to visit," Solberg said. "What were you doing there?"

She hesitated and I said, "She went to aid M Zola."

"A great man, Émile Zola," Solberg said. There were murmured assents around the room. "A man with a great sense of justice."

"Do you know him, Beatrice?" Glaser said.

"Zola was another friend of my late father's," she said. "If a man was wise or learned, my father knew him or knew of him. When I heard Zola had been arrested I went to see if I could help him or his family in any way. There was little enough I could do for them, I fear."

"You went on your own?" Rivkah asked. She seemed astonished.

"Certainly."

"But no male escort?" Esther seemed equally dumbfounded.

"Beatrice never does the expected," I said. "She is the most independent thinker I have ever encountered."

"Why, thank you," my wife said.

Watson said, "Beatrice is remarkable in many ways. She has a profound sense of justice."

I reflected that my friend has come a long way in accepting my wife's brand of justice since our dreadful time at Rillington Manor last year.

Glaser said, "There's a lot to be said for intelligence, no matter whether the thinker is a man or a woman. Take Rivkah, for instance: she speaks six languages, studies history, and is an accomplished seamstress. Why should her accomplishments be considered any less valuable because she is not a man?"

"You're going to corrupt my daughter, David," Solberg said, chuckling.

The conversation was interrupted by a knock at the door. The maid came in a moment later and said, "There's a boy asking to speak to Inspector Glaser, Rabbi."

"Will you excuse me?" Glaser said, rising.

He left the room but returned almost immediately. "I have to go, I'm afraid."

"A problem, David?"

"I don't know yet, Rabbi..." he seemed about to say more but a glance at the ladies' expectant faces silenced him. "I need to investigate. I'll be back as quickly as I can."

I itched to join him, to see what was going on, but courtesy compelled me to keep my seat. Softly, Beatrice whispered, "Poor Sherlock. Held prisoner by social convention." She squeezed my hand in sympathy.

I did not have to sit for long. About fifteen minutes later, there was another knock at the door. Now the maid returned and, with an anxious look, said, "I beg your pardon, Rabbi, but Inspector Glaser asks if Mr Holmes might join him."

"What has happened, Sarah?"

"I'm not certain, rabbi, but I think someone's been killed."

"*Mein Gott*! Who is it, do you know?"

"I do not know, Rabbi. The boy will take you to the address, Mr Holmes. It's not far away."

"Will you forgive me?" I said as I tossed my napkin on the table. "I hope I shall return shortly but…"

"Go. The cause of justice continues even on the Sabbath, Mr Holmes. I send my blessing for your safety and for David's, too."

"Holmes?" Watson said.

I shook my head. "I'd prefer you stay and look after Beatrice, Watson."

"I'm perfectly capable of looking after myself," she said giving me a scolding look.

"We shall see to the lady's safety, Mr Holmes," Solberg said.

"Indeed, Beatrice can stay here for the night if need be," the rabbi's wife said. "Esther will not mind sharing her room."

"Oh, please say you will," the Rabbi's daughter said.

My wife, none too pleased at being managed, said in a tone that belied her words, "Thank you. I should be delighted." Then she made a face at me.

The body that had been Mordechai Schwartz lay face down in a sea of still-wet blood. Glaser glanced up at me with anguished eyes.

"Stupid old fool," he said. "What in the world had he been up to? Why would anyone want to hurt him?"

Watson, careful to avoid any of the bloody tracks on the floor, knelt down and examined the body.

"Still warm," he said. "Rigor has not set in yet. Dead considerably less than an hour. Possibly no more than twenty or thirty minutes."

We were in the room where I had first met Schwartz. Now he lay not eight feet from the long bench where we had drunk tea sweetened with cherries. The air tasted of blood and death and violence.

"Shot at point blank range," I said. "Through the left temple. You see the stippling around the wound. Death would have been instantaneous."

"Are you all right, Glaser?" Watson said looking up at the inspector. "Do you need to get some air?"

The policeman shook his head but his hand squeezed Watson's shoulder as if to steady himself. "Thank you, no. I'll be all right."

His blue eyes were almost violet in the gaslight, intensified by the redness of his sclera. His cheeks were damp with tears I doubt he even knew he'd shed.

"Who found the body?" I asked.

"Constable de Vine. He's outside; I knew you'd want to talk to him. I sent the other constable, Bing, to start the search."

"Excellent. Ask de Vine to step in, would you, Glaser?"

The policeman hesitated. "Is that really necessary, Mr Holmes? He's never seen a murdered body before. He's pretty shaken."

"He'll have to get used to such things if he wants to be a police officer," Watson said. "Still, maybe it wouldn't be too bad an idea to talk to him outside, Holmes."

Such squeamishness! True, the impact of the bullet had shattered the skull and the wound was dreadful. The arterial spray drenched not only the floor but also the walls and the ceiling. Gobbets of bone and brain tissue spattered the leather tobacco pouches that hung from the big black beam. Dreadful, I admit, but as Watson said, a policeman surely must get used to such things.

He and Glaser were looking at me with such, I don't know, hope, I suppose. In the end, I submitted and went outside.

The young officer, Charlie de Vine, was a sickly greenish colour and he was shaking so hard his truncheon and keys beat a dissonant rhythm against his hip.

"This gentleman is Mr Sherlock Holmes," Glaser said. "He wants to ask you some questions." He spoke matter-of-factly, thank goodness. I can make some concessions to a man in shock but I draw the line at mollycoddling.

"Yes, sir," the fellow stuttered.

I suddenly had a memory of my case last year and another man who died of a gunshot wound to the head. I remember B standing at the doorway looking at him. She was shaken and pale but ten times calmer than this supposed officer of the law.

"Tell me what happened from the moment you arrived, de Vine," I said.

"Yes, sir," the young policeman stammered. "Well, it was a quiet night. I mean, this area on a Friday evening tends to be very dull. Anyway, about..." he glanced at his watch. "About thirty minutes ago I was coming down Hatton Garden and I saw a light in the window of Mr Schwartz's building. It was just a glimpse and I thought at first I'd imagined it."

"It was not the gaslight?" I said.

"No, sir. It was a torch. I saw the beam of light move about."

"Good. Continue."

"I was just crossing the street when I saw a flash through the window and heard a bang, all in the same second like. I blew my whistle and started up the steps. I could smell something, too, something pungent like chemicals or burning.

"I used my torch and made my way down the hall. Then the door at the end burst open and someone came rushing out. He knocked me over. I blew my whistle again and I think I shouted."

I stared hard at the young man and he continued to jangle.

"What happened next?" I said.

"Next?"

"Did you give chase?"

"No." The word came out flat and pallid. "I'm sorry, sir. I know I should have."

"What did you do?"

"I went inside to see where the man had come from. It's that confusing in there. I fell over twice on the flagstones and I bumped my head on one of those beams. Anyway, after a few minutes I found him, that Mr Schwartz gentleman. Gave me a right turn to see all that blood."

I gazed at the man for several moments in silence. Watson knows me too well to interrupt. Glaser remained silent, too.

"Is there anything else you haven't told us?" I said. "Think carefully."

The man looked in my eye and said, "No, Mr Holmes. Nothing."

"What did the man look like? The one who knocked you down."

"He was young, in his early twenties, I'd say. He was tall and clean shaven." The words were calmer now, more fluid. "He had a hat on, pulled down low but I could see he had light-coloured hair, or it could have been silver. He wore a longish coat in some dark colour. Black or dark brown, perhaps."

"What did he have in his hands?"

132

"In his hands, sir?"

"Was he carrying anything?"

The policeman took a moment then said, "No, sir. He had the gun in his right hand, but it was just dangling from his fingers, like he'd forgotten he was carrying it. But he didn't have anything else. He pushed me down with his left hand. Strong as a bull, he was."

"Very well. Stay here, Constable. We need to examine the scene in more detail."

We returned to the body of the late Mordechai Schwartz. At my request, Watson went around turning on all the gaslights. I examined the entire room and traced my way back through the outer chambers, then to the hallway and, finally, the front door of the building. All the windows and locks were intact. There was no evidence the killer had forced his way in.

There was a confusion of tracks in the murder room: Large footprints that slid and skidded in the blood headed in several different directions. It was obvious what had happened: The murder had occurred in the dark. Now, alone, the killer found himself disoriented. I also reasoned that he was agitated. Perhaps the murder had not been premeditated? No. He had brought a weapon so he was prepared to use it.

The smears on the floor suggested the killer had fallen over at least twice. It was definitely he; de Vine is a much smaller man with a correspondingly smaller foot. His own tracks were easy enough even for an amateur to track.

So, the killer was disoriented. He fell. The sound of de Vine's whistle panicked him. How had he found his way to the exit? De Vine's whistle or his torch probably acted as a guide. What a fool that policeman was. Such rank incompetence. If only he'd used his wits, used some stealth, we might have trapped our killer nicely. Or was it mere foolishness?

We went back outside. I said to De Vine, "You'd recognise this man if you saw him again?"

"I think so, sir, though it was dark."

"Had you seen him before?"

"No, Mr Holmes. I'd remember a fellow like that."

"What about Mr Schwartz's neighbours? Who lives in the buildings on either side?"

"I don't know," he said. With a furtive glance at Glaser he added, "I don't know these people."

Before I could reply, a report cracked through the night.

"Stay here," Glaser commanded as he, Watson and I fled down the road in the direction of the shot, for shot it most certainly was.

11

Where Hatton Wall meets Saffron Hill there lay a body.

"It's Bing," Glaser said when we were still forty yards away. The lamplight clearly picked out the stricken policeman's silver uniform buttons and his helmet.

We reached the body and the inspector knelt beside it. "Poor devil," he said.

"A sudden attack," I said. "He didn't have time to blow his whistle."

"The bullet went right through his heart," Watson said. "He was dead before he fell."

"He's just a boy," Glaser said. He raised his anguished eyes to me. "I want this man, this Avery Rickman, Mr Holmes. I will find him. You may depend upon it. I will find him."

"You can count on my help, Inspector," I said.

"And mine," Watson added.

I put my arm around Glaser's shoulders and led him a few feet away from the corpse. "Take a breath. No, no, it's all in hand. There's nothing you can do for the man now."

After a moment, he stopped shaking and took a deep breath.

"It is my experience that work is the best remedy for distress. You'd best call for some assistance, Glaser. You now have two murders to investigate and I wouldn't place much faith in de Vine. Go and telephone the Yard. Watson will stand guard here and I shall begin the search. Speak to Lestrade if he is on duty and send him my compliments. Ask him if a young constable by the name of Maurice Stevens may be available to assist. He is a good man despite his youth and comparative inexperience. I trust him."

Glaser nodded and ran down the road.

I turned to my friend and said, "Watson, will you be all right if I leave you here alone?"

"Go," he said. "I'll be fine, Holmes."

"Be careful. This is a filthy area. There are dangers aplenty even without gun-wielding murderers. If you catch sight of this fellow on no account try to detain him."

"No fear of that, Holmes."

I ran south down Saffron Hill all the way to Charterhouse Street, then west from Holborn Circus to Brook Street, and then back north. I investigated Dorrington Street and Leather Lane, St Cross Street and came back via Hatton Garden, but the killer had vanished.

At last, I returned to where Watson remained with the body. A small crowd had gathered but they kept their distance. In the cramped and crooked buildings people leaned out from their windows, watching everything.

"Any luck?" Watson asked.

"Nothing. Has anything happened here?"

"Not a thing other than the usual busybodies gawking." He nodded towards the macabre spectators.

I approached the crowd. "Did any of you see what happened?" I said. "Come, if this fellow will murder a policeman no one is safe. It is in your interests to help us."

I turned at the sound of running footsteps. It was Glaser. He addressed the gawkers. "Come on," he said. "One of you must have seen something. Lefkowitz? Blum?"

The mob melted, vanished. Only a prostitute and a retired naval officer remained.

The woman said, "I saw him, sir. A tall and slender man he was and hair like snow, though he was young enough."

"It's Maggie Chase, isn't it? Hullo, Maggie. Did you see what happened?" Glaser said.

"Hullo, Davy," she crooned, taking his arm. Then, remembering the horror, suddenly dropped her flirtatious attitude. "It was all so fast. I didn't see the shooting. I heard a loud bang and turned in time to see the fellow run away."

"I saw it," the old sailor said. "The tall man, with very pale hair like this girl says, and he was running down the street. The young policeman asked him to stop for a moment. Very polite he was, called the devil 'sir'. But the man turned and just fired. There was no need for it. No need at all."

"There now, Cap'n, you mustn't upset yourself."

"Which way did they go?" I said.

The pair pointed back in the direction from which I had come.

"He stopped," the sailor said, "in the doorway of one of those houses up there. I saw him stop and bend down."

"What do you think he was doing?" Glaser said.

"Being violently ill, I reckon," the man replied.

I walked slowly back along Saffron Hill examining every inch of the road. All the doors were shut; the windows had their curtains drawn. There would be no help for the police in this place.

Some thirty yards later, I stopped and studied a puddle of vomitus. It reeked of undigested alcohol. There was potato, too. So that was his dinner: a potato and a jug of whisky.

I returned to Watson and Glaser, now standing alone with the dead body. The inspector said,

"Inspector Lestrade sends his compliments, Mr Holmes. He himself is engaged upon another case but he is sending Hill and young Stevens as you requested."

"That is very good news. What else has been happening?"

"I've sent word that there is a dangerous man at large, and have asked that people stay in their homes for now. I've also spoken to the rabbi. He make send a plea for any witnesses to come forward. I doubt there will be any, but we lose nothing by trying."

"That was well thought of," I said. "Have you informed Schwartz's family yet? Good. If you do not object, I should like to accompany you when you do so. Perhaps they might be able to explain what he was doing in that building tonight."

"I'd like to come, too," Watson said. "But we cannot leave the body."

Even as he spoke, I could hear the rattle of the police vehicle approaching. A moment later, Tavistock Hill, Stevens, and four other constables joined us on the pavement.

"Good to see you again, gentlemen," Hill greeted us.

There followed a wholly unnecessary period of handshaking and pleasantries. Stevens, still shiny in his brand new uniform, stood proud yet watchful at the perimeter. His eyes were scanning the ground around the body, the buildings where people sat at their windows peering into the street, and the street itself. I would like to think this acute attention is something he learned from watching me work on the Rillington Manor case, but in truth, I think the man just has an innate capacity for taking pains. He would not have let a killer get away without at least giving chase.

The two inspectors, in the meantime, had caught up on events and made a plan. They would divide the two crime scenes between them with Hill responsible for the murder of the policeman while Glaser handled Schwartz's case, though Glaser, as senior officer, would oversee both crimes. Watson and I would assist the two strands of investigation.

"He has already killed twice, that we know of," I said. "So you must be on your guard and take no unnecessary risks. Use your whistles.

"Stevens, a word with you, if I may."

I took the young man aside and said quietly, "I have a particular task for you, if you would be so kind."

"Whatever you need, Mr Holmes. I'm your man."

I explained and he nodded. "I understand."

"Not a word to any of your colleagues, not even Inspector Glaser. You come directly to me or to Doctor Watson."

"Yes, sir," he said. No quibbles about the chain of command or other such nonsense, thank goodness.

We returned to Watson and Glaser. I said, "I thought since Stevens is a newly minted policeman he might be best served working with Constable de Vine."

"I had thought to send de Vine home," Glaser said. "You saw how shaken he was."

"Which is why I think he could use some company," I said.

"He'd surely see it as a condemnation if you sent him off duty, Glaser," Watson said, following my lead.

"Perhaps," Glaser said. "Very well."

We stopped on our way back long enough for me to indicate the vomitus I had found.

"Whisky and potato. Hardly nutritious," Watson observed.

"Yes," Stevens said. "But what does it tell us?"

"Glaser?" I said.

"Well, the killer dined before meeting with Schwartz. He only ate a potato so he is too poor to afford meat. Of course, he could be Catholic; I believe they do not eat meat on Fridays."

"He may be a Catholic and he may certainly be impoverished. However, I think there is another explanation. Watson?"

"It's the whisky that is significant," my friend replied. "There is no blood or other indication that the fellow is a chronic drinker, though we cannot be certain. There isn't very much food here and what there is is undigested, so I'd venture to say he was nervous and steeling himself for whatever lay ahead."

"Precisely! You see, gentlemen, Doctor Watson frequently builds up my reputation at the expense of his own. Your explanation is the most likely, I agree," I said. "You may be right that the fellow is a Catholic, Glaser. He is tall and fair and not Jewish. A Catholic would not eat meat on a Friday, but he could have dined on fish, could he not? Moreover, while poverty might explain the lack of meat, it does not explain why the fellow consumed so much alcohol. As Watson says, there are no indications the fellow is an alcoholic. So why drink so much so early in the evening? Conclusion: he was steeling his nerves."

Glaser sucked in his cheeks and breathed in deeply, trying to contain his ire. "Then he planned to kill Schwartz all along."

"Almost certainly, I'm afraid. I'm sorry, Glaser. I know you were fond of him." I indicated the stinking puddle at our feet. "He was prepared to kill Schwartz. He fortified himself with alcohol and he brought a weapon. When it came to it, he did the task efficiently enough. But Bing surprised him. That was a killing he was not prepared for and it distressed him."

"Distressed him?" Stevens said.

"He vomited just moments later."

"Yes," Glaser said. "Killing Bing was unplanned. He reacted to that murder by being ill; why did he not react the same way to the first?"

"Perhaps it was cumulative," Watson said. "The shock of not one but two murders overcame his nerves."

"Perhaps…" I straightened my back. "Well, we need to ponder the matter. Let us return to Hatton Garden and I shall resume my examination."

Leaving Hill and three other policemen to handle Bing's case, Glaser, Watson, Stevens, and I returned to the scene of Schwartz's murder.

Saturday 30 April 1898

Around six this morning, weary and discouraged, Watson and I convened with the two inspectors in the rabbi's home. The rabbi's daughter Esther served us coffee and pastries then left us alone to discuss our grisly business.

"You are obviously familiar with this Rickman fellow, Mr Holmes," Hill said. "It might help if you could tell us about him."

"I'm afraid I know very little."

At my nod, Watson told the story of Mrs Prentiss and the Camden Town 'ghost'. He did so discreetly and avoided mentioning Kidwell's name. Other than that, he covered all the pertinent details admirably.

"So you don't even know if Rickman is his real name?" Hill asked when Watson concluded.

"I would be astonished if it was," I replied.

"But at least we know what he looks like," Glaser pointed out. "Mr Holmes caught a good look at him that night he was shot, and so did young De Vine last night."

"De Vine is lucky to be alive," Watson said. "I'm surprised Rickman didn't just shoot him."

"He was taken by surprise," I said. It was a fair point, though. After a moment's contemplation I added, "It's possible that Schwartz was his first murder. He may have been in a state of shock. Still, it did not take him long to recover as the unfortunate Constable Bing discovered."

"Did the wife of the first victim know anything that might help?" Hill asked.

"She was too full of grief to offer much," Glaser said. "But she did say her husband had a meeting last evening with someone about the Fathers, and that is very curious."

"Why so?" Watson asked.

"We do no work on the Sabbath. That includes even discussing any sort of business matter. That Schwartz should be willing to take such a meeting after sunset on Friday suggests he did not consider it business. That's not to say there wasn't a work-related aspect to it. Schwartz was religious but he was also pretty single-minded. He may have persuaded himself that the meeting was simply to gather information. Yet..."

"Yes?" I urged.

"I don't understand why he'd want to meet someone in his business premises. Why not bring the man to his home where it was warm and comfortable?"

"When I examined the body, I found Schwartz had a bruise on his right hip," Watson said. "From its position and shape, I think he went into the building in the dark and bumped into something. He would not have put the light on and was trying to feel his way around. I don't know if that's significant."

"Everything is significant until we can prove otherwise," I said. "I think you and Glaser make some excellent points, Watson. Schwartz entered the building in the dark. He did not put on the gaslight because it was in violation of the Sabbath. Hill, your thoughts?"

"Well, I don't understand the religious aspect of things like Glaser here, but everything you've said makes sense. But why would Rickman want Schwartz dead?"

"That is, indeed, the question."

The door opened and my wife entered. Though her features were perfectly composed I sensed she was vexed. I cannot say I blame her: I should be exceedingly annoyed to be kept away from such a deliciously interesting case merely because of my sex.

"Good morning, Beatrice," I said. "I do not believe you've met Inspector Tavistock Hill?"

She shook his hand. "Mr Holmes has spoken of you, Inspector," she said. "He holds you in high esteem."

Hill beamed. "Most kind," he muttered.

"Did you have a successful night?" she asked as she poured herself a cup of coffee.

"Not very. Two murders and the elusive Avery Rickman seems to be responsible for both."

"Two?" she said. "Who?"

"A jeweller by the name of Schwartz, and a young policeman by the name of Bing."

"How dreadful," she said, but I could see the same excitement in her eyes that burned in my own heart. She sat at the table beside me and asked, "What have you learned so far?"

To Tavistock Hill's astonishment, I related the details of the murders. Beatrice listened intently then said, "So the killer apparently met with Schwartz, killed him, and then fled. Why kill the second policeman? Surely he could have hid. Would that not have been easier than murdering a policeman? And why kill Schwartz… Inspector Glaser, you said your friend was fascinated by the Patriarchs. Is it possible his inquiries attracted the attention of the killer?"

"I think that's probably what happened, yes."

"But if Rickman is looking for the coins, wouldn't Schwartz be more valuable to him alive? How many people would be able to authenticate them? Why kill one of the few people who seemed able to help him?"

I slapped the table and chuckled. "As always, Beatrice, you get to the crux of the matter. All excellent questions."

"They could have argued over money," Hill said. "Perhaps Schwartz wanted a larger share of the profits than Rickman was willing to give him."

"No," Beatrice said, firmly. "No observant Jew would haggle on the Sabbath. You'll correct me if I'm wrong, Inspector Glaser."

"No, you are quite correct," Glaser said. "*Reb* Mordechai was very observant. He would not have discussed money on the Sabbath."

"Which brings up a point Watson made earlier," I said. "Why choose Friday night for a meeting? Unless..."

"Unless?" Hill urged.

"Rickman knew enough about the area to expect most of the community would be indoors. Once people got home from Friday evening services they would be inside having dinner..."

"Which means there would be no one around to identify him," Beatrice said. "Still, even in a community like this there must be people who are not observant?"

"True," Glaser said. "We have our share of the irreligious just like any other community, not to mention it's not only Jews who live in the area. Still, it would lower the risk considerably."

144

I was tired and I suddenly wanted to be gone, to be back home in my familiar seat and able to just think my thoughts without interruption.

Watson, glancing at me, said with eerie prescience, "Well, I think we should head back to Baker Street, Holmes. We all need some rest."

"If you do not mind, Sherlock, and if the rabbi has no objection, I think I will stay here." Beatrice said the words so innocently. I have learned over the past several months that it is when my wife sounds innocent that she is most dangerous. I had a sudden ghastly surge of unease. I said, "For what reason?"

Watson and the two policemen made some excuse and left the room. B and I faced each other.

She said, "I thought I should call upon the wife of the dead man. I'll go with the other women so you need not worry about me."

"Beatrice—"

"Sometimes a woman will tell things to other women that she will not tell a man. Especially if the man is a police official."

"Beatrice—"

"No reflection on Inspector Glaser, of course. He's perfectly charming. Handsome, too. But he is still a policeman."

"Beatrice!"

She seemed not at all dismayed by my sudden shout. "Please, Sherlock," she said calmly. "You'll wake the household."

From the sounds above it was evident we had already done so.

She rested her hand on mine and said, "Please do not worry. I promise I will do nothing dangerous. I shall merely be one of several women who makes a condolence call upon a widow."

I took a deep breath then slowly nodded. "I have no right to tell you what to do," I said. "But I must confess I am not easy about you staying here when there is a murderer at large."

"You've never told me what to do," she said. "You have followed the terms of our contract to the letter. And you are not telling me now; you are expressing concern, which you are perfectly entitled to do as my friend if nothing more. But, my dear Sherlock, you must see there is no cause for worry. It is broad daylight, I shall not be alone, and I give you my word I shall be careful."

I swallowed back my irrational fears. "That is all I ask," I said.

We both took a breath as if we had just overcome some great challenge. After a moment I said, "Something about this case does not ring true. There are too many oddities, too many things that do not seem to belong to the same puzzle."

"Like someone mixed up a box of chess pieces with draughts?" she said. "Yes, I see what you mean. And it's even worse than that, isn't it, because there are still pieces missing?"

"True. I have a knight, a couple of bishops and some draught men…"

"But you're missing a pawn and a queen."

"Exactly." I couldn't help but laugh at her description.

"Never mind," she said. "You'll sort it out."

"You will not forget this man has killed twice? He seems to have adjusted to the terrible deed with unsettling ease."

"I forget nothing, my dear," she said. She kissed my cheek.

12

Saturday 30 April 1898

About an hour after we returned to Baker Street there was a knock on the door. Stevens arrived, still resplendent in his uniform, and as cheery as he was last night.

"Well," I said. "How did you get on?"

"Not as well as I would have liked to be honest, Mr Holmes, but it wasn't a total loss.

"I spent the night keeping watch with de Vine, just as you said. He was a bit bossy at first, saying he knew what was what, but after a while he started to relax. He told me about the borough—he hates it, by the way, and thinks it's beneath him.

"I asked him about the dead man and he said he didn't know him. 'All those black-hatted fellows look the same. They wouldn't give you a cup of water if you were parched, not unless you could pay for it.'

"I swallowed all this nonsense down and acted like I just wanted to learn from his experience."

"You sound sceptical about what this fellow had to teach you, Stevens," Watson said with pretended surprise. "Not an ideal mentor then?"

"Hardly! Lazy as sin if you want my opinion. He can't stand Inspector Glaser because he keeps after him and makes him do his work. De Vine has a secret place down on Saffron Hill where he skips off for a 'rest', as he put it. In the middle of his shift!"

The young man's outrage was delicious. Watson and I suffocated our laughter with the greatest difficulty.

"But you were spot on about this fellow, Mr Holmes," he continued. "He knows something about Schwartz's murder that he's not saying, and no mistake."

"Has he given you any hints what it might be?"

"Only that he feels guilty about something. He started to say he was to blame but then the inspector came back to check on us and he clammed up. I wasn't able to get him back on the subject, I'm afraid. Oh, he did say the deceased was an old fool to think it would work."

"To think what would work?"

Stevens shook his head. "I'm sorry, Mr Holmes. That's as much as I got."

"You did very well, Stevens. There were too many holes in his initial statement to be credible. He feels guilty, then. That is very interesting."

"Begging your pardon, Mr Holmes, but what sort of holes?"

"Hmm? Oh, well he said, for instance, his attention was drawn by the light of a torch in the window. He was in the process of crossing the street when he heard the gunshot. But if that is true it means Schwartz and the killer were already in that inner room, and it doesn't have a window that looks out on the street."

"So how could he have spotted the torch?" Watson said. "Ah, I missed that. Very well reasoned, Holmes."

"De Vine also claimed to know none of Schwartz's neighbours, and yet he seemed to know the dead man by sight."

"He didn't know him, not by name, before last night," Stevens said. "He told me he'd never so much as exchanged a word with the man before yesterday."

I sat upright in my chair. "Were they his exact words? Be specific, Stevens."

"He said, 'They all look alike, those Jews, and they'd never give you the time of day. That fellow, Schwartz, I never even got so much as a hullo out of him before yesterday.'"

"Sounds like he and Schwartz had a conversation some time yesterday, then," I said. "You have no idea what it was about?"

"I said wasn't that an odd thing. I got the feeling de Vine was about to say something but shut right up and I got no more out of him."

"You've done very well, Stevens. My trust in you was not misplaced. Can you shadow de Vine again this evening?"

"If you wish it, Mr Holmes."

"But you'd rather be in the thick of things, eh?" I said. "I sympathise. Never fear, Stevens, we shall find better use for your talents. Just stick with de Vine for now. I would dearly like to know what he's been up to."

Stevens rose to leave. "I'm glad to be of help and I shall do as you ask. There's just one thing…"

"You're wondering why I have kept Inspector Glaser in the dark? Yes, I understand. The inspector is a good man and I have great faith in him. But he is an inspector and has protocols that he must follow. Besides which, Schwartz was his friend. If he had a suspicion that de Vine had been even tangentially involved, he would react with great passion and I am not sure that is wise. Best stay with this lazy policeman for a while. Become his friend, Stevens. I shall deal with Glaser."

After Stevens left, I spent several hours sitting in my chair by the fire. The morning turned into afternoon and then into a russet-coloured evening. Watson dozed and finally decided to surrender to his bed.

At the door, he turned and said, "She'll be all right, Holmes. She's a clever girl and won't take any unnecessary risks." That word, unnecessary, stuck in my brain and it was some time until I was able to ignore it and move on to the case in hand.

I went back to the beginning and pondered the questions that were in the forefront of my mind:

Assuming Rickman, or whatever his name was, had courted Connie Kidwell simply to gain access to the Prentisses' house, why had he not discovered the document he was looking for? True, Mrs Prentiss had already returned the original document to her employer, but she had kept a copy. Did Rickman simply not know about that? Perhaps. It is doubtful Kidwell knows much about her former mistress's business. In any case, it certainly seems likely that Rickman was looking for information on the Patriarchs. Nothing else appears to fit. But how did he know that Mrs Prentiss had that document in the first place? Well, I obviously need to learn more about that peculiar paper. Does it serve as provenance of the coins? I shall proceed with that as my hypotheses until evidence proves otherwise.

Why did Rickman fail to kill me in the Prentisses' house? He had a weapon and, for the briefest of moments, had the opportunity. Yet he failed. Was he merely squeamish? Surely I prove a far more dangerous threat to him than Schwartz or the unfortunate Bing. These were my thoughts. I closed my eyes, puffed on my pipe, and replayed that unpleasant night in my mind.

It was cold and dark, I remember. Around one o'clock I was alerted by the sound of the front door opening and by a sudden draft. Watson woke the instant my hand touched his shoulder. He frowned at me, as surprised as I that the sound came, not from the cellar, but from the front hallway.

So Rickman had a key to the front door. I was taken aback by that at the time; though in hindsight I should probably have anticipated it. I assume he stole Kidwell's and made a copy. I doubt she knew; why else would he continue the charade of entering through the cellar? Was it that it seemed mysterious and therefore romantic? That sort of thing might appeal to a gullible young woman.

Then he flung open the kitchen door... He was expecting us, surely? That grimace on his face, the way the pistol was ready to be fired... No, he knew we were there. So was he really looking for a document or did he intend to frighten us off and return later? Or was it his plan to kill me, only to fail at that instant? Something does not fit.

As to the murders in the diamond district, I am even less certain. Why kill Schwartz? Was he a serious threat or had there been a quarrel of some sort? It is unfortunate Mrs Schwartz claims to know so little of her husband's dealings. Perhaps Beatrice will fare better.

I hope she will be careful.

At around half-five Watson came back into the living room.

"I can't get to sleep," he grumbled. He went downstairs and brought back a carafe of coffee. I did not move. I sat in my same spot following all my thoughts. Around and around I go. Perhaps I am ascribing too much intelligence to the man. Or too little. There may be a dozen explanations for his actions. Something gnaws at me. Something I have overlooked.

Around six o'clock my wife arrived. Mrs Hudson fussed about her as if she was a royal instead of merely the Queen's goddaughter. Beatrice accepted my housekeeper's plea that she stay for dinner with good nature, and then she joined me in the sitting room.

"You have news," I said.

She grinned at me and I could feel her excitement. Watson rose and said, "I think I'll go for a walk."

"It's not a very pleasant day, Doctor," Beatrice said. "Please stay. I've no doubt Sherlock will find your observations helpful as always."

"That weather will play the devil with your war wounds, Watson. I beg you sit. Well, then, Beatrice, tell us your news."

"After this morning's services, I went to see Mrs Schwartz in the company of the other ladies. There was much conversation about what a good man her late husband was. For the most part, I believe it was true. A man easily carried away by his passions, but with a good heart. That was my impression.

"At length, the rabbi's wife Miriam asked what I as a stranger could not: What Schwartz was doing in his business building at that hour."

"Ah," I said, rubbing my hands together. This was what I had been waiting for.

"The widow said Schwartz had been making inquiries about some Egyptian coins. On Friday afternoon he received a telephone call and was very excited afterwards."

"Did he tell her the nature of this call?" I asked.

"He told her the man had a Germanic accent. Schwartz seemed to think that was significant, according to his wife. He was very excited and said, 'We have him.'"

"She was sure those were his words?"

"Yes. She added that he arranged to meet the man at his work premises after evening services."

"Schwartz had no reservations about that?"

"None at all, apparently. He evidently did not expect the meeting to take long because he told his wife he would be home in time for dinner."

I said with as much cheer as I could muster, "Thank you, Beatrice. That is something at least."

"Oh, don't fob me off with that, Sherlock, it doesn't become you. That is not all the news."

The glimmer in her eyes should have told me so. I smiled, genuinely this time, and said, "So what other treasures do you bring?"

She stared at the ceiling and said, "Do you know, it is a long time since you played the violin for me. I think you owe me a tune after we have dined."

"Beatrice—" I stopped and made an exaggerated sigh. "You may have anything you wish, but please tell me what else you have learned."

"Anything?" she said in a dangerous tone. Then, laughing, "It is not fair to tease you when you are so vulnerable. Yes, vulnerable, Sherlock. You would offer anything in order to get the information. Very well. Schwartz kept a diary. Mostly it was to record his transactions, sales and acquisitions, that sort of thing. But from time to time he also made notes about other things."

"Ah! Do you have it?"

"No," she said. "I could not read it and neither could you. It is in Yiddish. At my request, Miriam got it from Widow Schwartz and gave it to David. He will translate it and come here this evening with his report."

David?

"Well, that will do," I said. "Did he tell you what time?"

"He said after he had slept for a few hours he would read it and bring it to you. I imagine he will be here by the time we finish dining."

153

For the next hour, I forced myself to be genial company. As promised, I played a few pieces on the violin to the lady's great pleasure (or so I tell myself), and managed to eat enough of my meal to satisfy both my friend and my wife.

Around eight o'clock there was a knock at the door and a few moments later Glaser came into the room.

"Come and sit here, Inspector," I said. "It is a filthy evening. Can I pour you some coffee? Or perhaps a brandy might be preferable?"

"A brandy would be just the thing. Thank you, Mr Holmes."

His eyes were shadowed with fatigue and even his curly hair seemed to lack its natural buoyancy.

"You did not sleep?" Watson said. "You look done in, poor fellow."

"I should not have asked you to come here, Glaser," I said. "I should have come to you."

"You did not ask; I did," Beatrice said. "And I agree it was a very thoughtless thing to do. I apologise."

Glaser smiled and took the snifter from me. "Thank you," he said, and downed a mouthful. "Ah, that's the ticket. But there's no call to apologise, Beatrice. I made the choice to come here. To be honest, I felt like I needed to get away from the diamond district for a while. There is so much alarm and distress. I can hardly walk five paces without someone stopping me and needing reassurance."

"And in the meantime, you're still dealing with the loss of one of your friends and a fellow police officer," Watson said. "You need some time on your own to grieve."

Glaser's smile was unconvincing but I gave him credit for the attempt. "I shall grieve when we catch Mordechai's killer," he said. "I think my friend's own words might help." He pulled a small journal from his pocket and showed it to me. As Beatrice said, I could not read it. Such a deficit in my education.

"I have not had a chance to study it properly, but I skimmed some parts on my way here. Up until last Sunday when you spoke to him about the coins, Mr Holmes, the journal is fairly straightforward," Glaser said. "Mordechai registers the receipt of various gemstones, as well as their quality and appearance. He writes about sales, customers and amounts received. This isn't his official business ledger. It is a personal log of the precious things that he handled or hoped to acquire. Almost a love letter. Schwartz once told me that he remembered every stone he had ever held. He could describe the cut, the colour, and the flaws the way a proud father might describe a child."

"And since Sunday?" I asked.

"He notes your conversation, writes the word אבבא, 'Abba', father, and a question mark. See, here? Now," the inspector continued, "He lists the names of—I am not sure if it is two or three people who might be able to tell him more about the coins. There's a Dr Bazalgette."

"He is at the British Museum," I said. I made a note. "His expertise lies in ancient Egypt. It is possible he might know something about the coins but I would have thought it unlikely. Who is next?"

"A Greek, I assume, by the name of Demosthenes, no last name and no address or indication of where the man may be found."

"He is not Greek, he is an Englishman. Demosthenes Jones. He has a shop in Soho. I would not have put him down as a reliable source. And the third?"

"There's a reference to Bashir."

"Bashir? Is that a Jewish name?" Watson asked.

155

"Arabian," B said. "It means one who brings good news."

"How in the world did you know that?" Glaser said.

B said, "I knew a man named Bashir at one time. It can be either a first or a last name."

"There is also a town by that name in Iran, I think," Watson said.

"Yes, yes," I said. "But this does not advance our investigation. Did Schwartz speak to any of these gentlemen?"

Glaser peered at the script and said, "He telephoned Bazalgette and was told quite firmly the coins are a myth. Then he left a telephone message for Bashir. I cannot see any sign that Bashir called him back. Ah, but then he spoke to Demosthenes. This is interesting. It appears Schwartz implied that he had the coins or knew where they were. He asked Demosthenes to help him find a buyer. That was on Friday afternoon."

"Tell me, Glaser, does Schwartz make any notes regarding his Friday night meeting?"

"He says something about the 'Emissary from Ngozi' and the hour. You'll see the time is when he was killed."

"So we need to find a person called Ngozi?" Watson said.

"No, we need to find Rickman. There is no Ngozi."

Glaser hesitated. "That is true, Mr Holmes," he said. "From the way Schwartz has written this, I believe he knew the fellow was a liar. He writes 'German' and 'South African' with a question mark. I think he knew this fellow was Rickman. What I do not understand, though, is if he believed that why would he agree to meet the fellow alone and in the dark?"

"That is curious," I agreed. "Another puzzle for us to investigate."

"But not tonight," Beatrice said. "We are all tired and we shall think more clearly after a quiet evening and a good night's sleep."

Glaser rubbed his eyes and stretched. "Yes, I ought to get back."

"Must you?" Watson said. "I really think you could use a night off. Surely this 'Rickman' fellow will not return to the diamond district so soon."

"I agree," Beatrice said. "You need a break. You will function much better for it."

"It is a kindly thought," the inspector said. "But my people need me there. My presence—perhaps I flatter myself—but I believe my presence is a comfort to them."

"You cannot look after your community if you do not first look after yourself, David," Beatrice said.

David again. She pronounced it in the Jewish way. *Da'veed*.

She added, "I know there is no room here to accommodate you, but you could stay at Wimpole Street with Sherlock and me."

"With you and...?" Glaser looked at her with some embarrassment.

"I think we should let the inspector in on our secret," I said. "Or he shall think we are characters of ill repute. Beatrice and I are married, Glaser."

"What?" Embarrassment ebbed as astonishment flowed.

"It is not common knowledge. Indeed, no one outside our very small circle knows."

"They married for convenience," Watson said in a curiously amused tone. "They even drew up a contract outlining the particulars of their arrangement, right down to the number of concerts they will attend together each month."

157

"It is a perfectly rational arrangement," I said with some pride, justifiable, in my opinion. "We both know what is expected of us. We live in our own homes and do not infringe upon one another's freedoms. We do share accommodation from time to time, when it is warranted."

"I see," Glaser said. He plainly didn't. "But why the need for secrecy?"

"Last year my godmother would brook no further delay and insisted I marry," Beatrice said. "Unfortunately, the suitor she had in mind was not to my liking."

"He was a loathsome cad," I said. "A bounder of the worst sort. Beatrice would have been dead within a month if she'd had to marry him."

"But surely your godmother couldn't wield such influence," Glaser said.

"She can when she is the queen," Watson added.

"I was at my wit's end," Beatrice said. "Then Holmes suggested I marry him instead." She smiled at me and added, "Quite the knight in armour, right out of a story book. All you needed was the white charger."

I have never seen myself in such light but I cannot pretend to be dismayed that Beatrice does.

Glaser said, "I still don't understand the need for secrecy."

"At the time we married," B said, "Sherlock was being harried by a cutthroat gang. He felt it was safer to keep our arrangement as quiet as possible."

"Yes," I said. "Even now there are those who would attack me through the people I—that is to say, through my closest friends."

"You see the way of it, Glaser?" Watson said, still with that peculiar mirth.

"To return to the subject," Beatrice said, "What do you say to spending the night in Wimpole Street, David? It will give you a much needed break and you'll feel the better for it."

I added, "I'm sure Tavistock Hill will keep an eye on things in Hatton Garden for the night. You can send word to the rabbi and tell him what you're doing; he can contact you if there is an emergency, though I doubt there will be."

"Well... Yes, why not?" he said. "Thank you, Beatrice. It is very good of you."

"I'll ask Mrs Hudson to call a cab," Watson said. "You should be able to head off right away."

Beatrice said, "Aren't you coming with us, Doctor?"

"Oh," Watson said. "I did not realise you meant me, too."

"But of course, silly goose. Go get whatever you need for the night. There's no rush."

"Do you have room for all of us?" Glaser said.

"Oh, yes. It's a big house and far too empty. I shall be very happy to share it with my friends."

I have not had occasion to enjoy Beatrice's music since her return from France. This evening we all sat as she played some favourites for our young friend. She delighted us with some of Mendelssohn's *Songs without Words*, as well as selections from Offenbach and Saint-Saens upon the piano. Then she rose and said, "Someone gave me a special gift." She ran her fingers over the harpsichord. "Is it not it splendid? It belonged to Bach."

She sat and played a selection of preludes to the *English Suite* by way of a thank you.

The maestro would have approved.

After a while, the lady took a break and joined us for brandy. The conversation wound back to the case in Hatton Garden as though it had some sort of gravitational pull upon us all.

"It must be very hard for the community," Watson said. "Two murders on the one night and the killer still at large."

"It is," Glaser said. "Schwartz was well liked by most. He was an honest businessman and I do not have to tell you how rare a thing that is. He was also very generous; he gave money to people in need and to the synagogue, too. And young Bing… he might have become a decent policeman, in time. I shall miss him." He rubbed his eyes and said, "But I must thank you, Mr Holmes, for recommending young Stevens. He's intelligent and motivated. Not like…" He bit his lip as if he felt he had betrayed a confidence.

"You mean not like de Vine?" I said. "I do not think it is disloyal to speak the truth, Glaser."

He admitted, "Some men become police officers because they have a thirst for justice. Others see it as an excuse to bully others. De Vine is not interested in justice."

For a moment he hesitated, then blurted, "His story last night rang false. When you questioned him about how he came to be outside Schwartz's building, he shook as if he had the ague. But he answered all your questions about the gunman's attire perfectly calmly."

"Ah," I said, rubbing my hands together. I knew Glaser had a spark. "You spotted that, did you? What conclusions did you draw?"

"That he was lying about everything but the man's appearance." He shook his head and I saw he was trying to fight off fatigue. "His statement bothered me… Why was he there?

His beat should have taken him up Clerkenwell Road at that time of day. He was lying about seeing a light in the window. Why?"

He opened his eyes and stared at me. "You knew all this already. Why did you not say anything?"

"I am still gathering data. I did not want to accuse one of your policemen without further proof."

"And that is why you asked Stevens to stay with de Vine," he said. "Ah, now I understand. I really ought to talk to de Vine, though, Mr Holmes. Give him a chance to explain himself."

"All in good time," I said. "Give Stevens a chance to win the fellow's confidence. It is always best to have proof before confronting a liar."

Sunday 1 May 1898

We had just sat down to breakfast when the telephone rang. Mrs Hudson: a body pulled from the Thames. Inspector Lestrade asks if I could meet him at the site.

Glaser, much brighter this morning, asked if he might accompany Watson and me.

"It is a grisly thing," Watson said, "to see a body that's been in the water. Are you sure you want to come?"

"Oh yes," he said with such relish that Watson was dumbfounded.

Glaser laughed and said, "I never get a chance to see such things, and I dearly like to observe you work, Mr Holmes. It does seem odd, though: why would Lestrade want you to see a drowned body?"

"There are several possible explanations, but we cannot know until we go and see."

Beatrice said, "I suppose there is no possibility of my coming? No, I did not think so. Very well, off you go and be men together. I'll..." she sighed elaborately, "embroider something."

She sounded so tragic I chuckled. "I am sorry, Beatrice," I said. "But I think it would be unwise to have you join us. It would cause too much comment."

Lestrade, well wrapped up against the wind with his felt derby pulled down low on his head, waved at us from the pier.

"Ah, here you are, gentlemen. Glaser, too; a nice chance for you to get away from the Chosen People, eh?"

Glaser winced.

"What did you want to show us, Lestrade?" I asked.

"Over here, Mr Holmes. I thought you'd want to see for yourself."

The woman had not been in the river for long. Her body was still intact and the bloating was minimal. Her features were still recognisable.

"Connie Kidwell," I said.

Watson knelt beside the mottled corpse and examined it. "Strangulation," he said. "I thought she'd done the deed herself, driven to despair... but no. She's been murdered, Holmes."

13

We left Glaser in Holborn then Watson and I continued on to the Home for Unfortunate Women in Holloway.

Mother Angelica met us in her office. She is as stark as her surroundings. Nothing is allowed any colour. No doubt she thinks it frivolous. Dressed entirely in black she sits behind a black desk. Her gaunt, hawkish face is pale and there is something cruel in the tightness of her mouth. From her black leather belt there hangs a long piece of cord jutting at even intervals with a series of knots. I can deem no purpose for such an object except as an instrument of abuse. I suppose she would use the word 'correction'.

"Doctor," she said, shaking my friend's hand. "It is always good to see you. How do you do, Mr Holmes? It is an honour to meet you. I apologise I was not here the last time you called. Please take a seat, gentlemen. How may I help you?"

"I sent a young woman to you a few weeks ago," Watson said. "Her name was Constance Kidwell."

The thin mouth pursed. "Yes, she came here…" She checked her diary. "On the twenty-ninth of March."

"And how did she get along?"

"It is always a difficult transition for these girls," she replied. "The ones who acknowledge their sin and who show genuine repentance make the adjustment more readily."

"And Connie?" Watson said.

The mouth pursed even tighter. A white mouth with thin wrinkled lines through the lips. A mouth that had never smiled nor found pleasure in any part of the world.

"Miss Kidwell was of the other sort, I'm afraid. She was a very headstrong girl. She had no sense of decency and even less of discipline."

"What sort of discipline do you mean?" I asked.

"The girls are required to rise at five o'clock every morning. They attend chapel and then prepare breakfast for themselves and the sisters. The rest of the day is a fixed routine of prayer, contemplation, and manual labour."

"And Connie?" Watson pressed. "You suggest she had difficulties. Can you elaborate?"

"Well, she was not religious," Mother Angelica said, "Far from it, indeed. She was found sleeping during morning prayers on three occasions. She said she was too cold to sleep. She resented having to work in the laundry. In short, she needed daily correction. I must say I was surprised."

"Why so?"

"Well, generally serving girls are much more robust than those from a better class. They are used to rising early and to hard work."

"And to the cold?"

"Exactly." Mother Angelica was either oblivious to my sarcasm or chose not to acknowledge it. "She needed frequent reminders that she was exceedingly fortunate to have been given a bed here. We are not a wealthy organisation by any means. We have to be careful whom we take. I may say, Doctor, if it had not been for your recommendation, we would not have accepted her. All these things I reminded her."

"No doubt," I said. "And when did she go missing?"

"Two days ago. Sister Michael had the foolish notion to take two girls with her to the market. A way of raising their spirits, she said. Such nonsense. In any event, Miss Kidwell vanished in the middle of the outing."

"You did not report her disappearance to the authorities?"

"Whatever for? She's an adult; more addled than most, perhaps, but if she chose to leave we could not detain her. I'm afraid we cannot accept her back."

"She is dead," Watson said.

The news seemed inconsequential.

"It is unfortunate that she took her own life, but hardly surprising," the matron said.

"Why do you say she took her own life?"

"I just assumed."

"I take it others of your girls have ended their lives?" Watson said.

"On occasion. It is most unfortunate." At our silence, she added, coldly, "They compound the sin of their lust with self-immolation. No one can help girls with such a wicked nature."

I felt sickened and kept my temper with the greatest of difficulty.

"Connie Kidwell was murdered," I said. Again, there was no reaction. "We need to speak to Sister Michael."

The woman glanced at her watch. "Well, she is leading a discussion on the nature of sin at present."

"This is a murder investigation, Mother Angelica," Watson said. "I'm afraid we must insist."

She sighed. "Oh, very well; I shall send for her."

She rose and pulled on the bell. We sat in silence as she gave instruction to a terrified maid to fetch Sister Michael. Moments later, an equally terrified young nun joined us.

"We need not detain you, Mother," I said. "We have already taken up enough of your time."

She would have argued. However, she knew she had no hope of prevailing and did not wish to look weak in the eyes of her subordinate, so she rose and gave us a stiff bow then left the room. All three of us sighed with relief.

"Please be seated, Sister Michael," Watson said. "I am afraid we have some bad news concerning Connie Kidwell."

"Oh, I pray she did not harm herself," the nun exclaimed.

"I'm afraid she was murdered," Watson said. "We need to ask you a few questions. It is the last service you can do for her."

"Oh, what a terrible thing," she sobbed. "It is all my fault."

"It is nothing of the sort," Watson said. "Come now, dry your eyes, and answer our questions. You may be able to help us find the person who took her life. Now, you will help us, won't you?"

"Of course, sir," she said. "Anything I can do."

"Good girl," Watson said.

I sat back and let my friend go on with the questioning. He's very good with distressed young women. Well, all women really. He could be quite a jack-the-lad if he were not such a gentleman.

"Tell us what happened the day she disappeared," Watson continued. I hooded my eyes and listened to the woman's tale.

"We left the Home at about ten o'clock. We walked to the Islington High Street to do our shopping. There was me, Mary Dobbs and Connie."

"How did Mary and Connie get on?"

"Well enough. Neither of them was very happy at their lot and felt... well, a bit hard done by, I suppose. They are—were—good girls at heart. I am sure of it. I thought the fresh air would do them some good." She dabbed at her eyes with a handkerchief.

"I had to keep a close watch on them because they were so easily distracted. Every time we passed a shop or a puppy or...

well, really anything at all, they wanted to stop and stare. They weren't being difficult, you know. Just giddy."

"I understand," Watson said. He frowned at my sigh and said, "Perhaps you could skip ahead to the point where you noticed Connie had gone missing?"

"Yes, sir. I had gone into the bank to make a deposit for Mother. The two girls said they were tired and it is true the bags they were carrying were very heavy. I told them to wait for me outside. I really should have made them come into the bank with me, but... Oh, if only I'd known..."

"It was not your fault," Watson soothed. "Please go on."

"When I came out, Mary was there on her own and Connie was gone. She said the girl suddenly ran off for no good reason. I thought she was just being silly, Connie, I mean, and she'd come back when she got tired of her game. After all, where could she go? But..."

Her voice sank beneath a hiccough of sobs.

There was no more to be wrung from her. We sent her away and spoke with the remorseful Mary though Mother Angelica insisted on standing watch as we did so. Presumably a young woman of such ill-repute could hardly be trusted in a room alone with two gentlemen. What that says of Watson and me does not bear contemplation.

Whether because of Mother's presence or a mere lack of wits, the girl had little to add. She liked Connie well enough but did not really know her. She was secretive, you see. Connie. Always looking for some sort of angle.

Outside the bank, they set down their heavy bags and Connie had said she needed to go to the lavatory. She set off towards the nearest public convenience before Mary had a chance to remonstrate. She never returned.

"Thinking over it now," Watson said. "Do you think she had planned to leave you like that?"

"Oh yes," the young woman said. "Indeed I do. She had been skittish all morning and kept checking the time. I even asked her if she had a secret rendezvous—it was only a jest. I didn't know… Connie laughed and said oh, yes, she had arranged to meet a very elegant young man, and they were headed off to Capetown that very evening. Where is Capetown?"

"You never saw her speaking to a man?"

The girl glanced at Mother Angelica and said, "No, indeed, sir." Then, softly, "But she had a note. She had it hidden in her glove but I caught her looking at it a few times."

"And you did not get to see what the note said?" Watson said.

"No indeed, sir."

I said, "Do you have any idea how Connie received the note?" To the nun I added, "I imagine the ladies are not permitted to receive private communication?"

"The women," Mother Angelica corrected. No ladies these. "Certainly not. All post is read first by me and then, if it is harmless, it is passed on to the women."

"What would you deem harmful, Mother?" Watson asked. His voice was even. She'd wither if she knew the fury it masked.

"Some of the girls are asked to meet gentlemen for a rendezvous," she said. "Now and then the letters are very upsetting, parents disowning their daughters or informing them that a member of the family has been taken ill as a direct result of the girl's condition. It may seem harsh, but all my actions serve to protect these women to the best of my ability."

"So we have no way of knowing how Connie received that note."

"If you please, sir," said Mary, "but there were a lot of people about in some of the shops. The butcher's was a right bast—that is, it was particularly bad. Connie had been in a bit of a mood before we went in, but she perked right up afterwards."

"And you think someone in the crowd slipped her the note then? I do not suppose you can remember if there was anyone in particular in the butcher shop?"

"No, sir, it was just maids and housewives, I think. But, there, it was that busy the Pope himself might have been present and I'd not have seen him. Begging your pardon, Mother."

So that was that. We rose and thanked Mother Angelica. Although the matter had nothing to do with our case, I was curious and said, "Tell me, Mother. What happens to the children of these young women when they are born?"

"Adoption," she said. "These girls are in no position to keep a child." At my expression she added, "We find them very good, Christian homes."

Watson and I returned to Baker Street. I sat in my chair by the fire and stared into the flames. Someone put a cup in my hands. At some point, I tasted the contents.

"This is cold," I said.

"It wasn't when I handed it to you," Watson said.

"Oh."

I put the cup down on the mantle and sank back into my reverie. Tried to. Watson said, "Is it the case that preoccupies you, Holmes, or that Home for Unfortunate Women?"

"Both. What a stupid, stupid girl she was. A born victim."

"She didn't know when she was well off," Watson said.

"Quite so," I said glancing at him. "Anyone who knows us must assume you would be the one who was outraged and I unmoved."

169

"Anyone who knows us slightly, perhaps," Watson said. "You and I know better. So do the people who know us best: Mycroft, Mrs Hudson, Beatrice. None of them would be surprised by your disgust. And you're right to be disgusted; it's a disgusting place."

"But you sent her there. Connie."

"So it is my fault?"

I said nothing. I was in a quarrelsome mood and could not find my way out of it.

"Where else was she to go, Holmes? Believe it or not, the Holloway Home is one of the better institutions of its kind. Yes, really. The women who must go there are not treated savagely. They get enough to eat and they have shelter from the elements. True, they are forced to endure a ghastly amount of religion but who is to say that's a bad thing?"

"It is deplorable," I said.

"It is not the place so much as that ghastly Mother Angelica. Was ever a woman more inappropriately named? The whole place reeks of terror and guilt and it is entirely because of her."

"What do you think she meant by correction? Mother Angelica said Connie needed 'correction'."

"It may have been no more than a bad scolding."

"But you do not think so."

He said nothing for several minutes then he poured a generous thimble of scotch and handed it to me. He poked at the fire and said, "You never used to be so interested in the way women are treated by our society."

I swallowed a mouthful of the whisky and coughed. I felt its fire work through my body. Warmed at last, I said, "You are saying I have become a sentimentalist?"

"You?" He dissolved in giggles and I could not help but smile. "Not sentimental; never that. But perhaps that great heart of yours has become a little less hidden. You have, if you will forgive me saying so, been a new man since you returned from Italy."

"Marriage," I said. "I thought myself so clever, Watson. I was going to marry and it would not change my life one iota. What a fool I was."

"Not a fool. Just a man. Then again, perhaps they are the same thing. In any case, it is not marriage that changes a man, it's love."

I shook my head. "Beatrice and I do not—"

"Have that sort of relationship?" he finished.

"Well, we don't."

"Whatever helps you sleep at night," he said.

"I have been wondering why she left."

"Beatrice?"

"Connie."

"Ah. A rendezvous, Mary Dobbs said."

"But how was it arranged? How did he know where to find her? And how did he get the message to her?"

"The butcher shop?"

"Filled with maids and housewives it may have been, but a man, a tall man would have attracted even Mary Dobbs' attention."

"So he has an ally?" He thought about it for a moment while I sipped the scotch. "But, no, not necessarily. He could have seen her in the street and just asked some woman to do him a favour. Perhaps he paid her to do so."

"Yes," I said slowly. "I cannot find fault in that theory."

"Then again," Watson added, now warming to the theme, "Perhaps there was no note. After all, we did not find one in her belongings or on her body."

"Neither signifies," I replied. "He may have told her to destroy anything in writing, or he could simply have taken it off the body after he killed her."

"You don't suppose…" Watson began.

"What?"

"Well, we are assuming Rickman is the killer and I'll grant you he seems the most likely culprit. All the same—"

"All the same, we cannot rule out the possibility that she was murdered by someone else. I agree. But there was a rendezvous. Coincidence may work in novels, but real life is seldom so lazy. No, much more likely there was an assignation. It seems unlikely Connie Kidwell should have found another paramour so swiftly, particularly not in her situation."

"Pregnant, you mean?"

"Quite so."

I downed the rest of the whisky and said, "I'm sick of the whole thing. What do you say to us going out to dinner and then perhaps a concert?"

14

Monday 2 May 1898

I slept late but felt much more refreshed when I awoke. Last night's music, though of far inferior quality to my wife's playing, was stirring and enabled me to set this troublesome case aside for a few hours. After breakfast, Watson and I set out for the British Museum to meet with Doctor Basil Bazalgette.

At least one advantage of being the "famous Sherlock Holmes" is you can command attention even from busy experts.

"I appreciate you taking the time to speak to me, Dr Bazalgette," I said. "I wanted to ask you about a telephonic conversation you had last week with Mr Mordechai Schwartz."

"Schwartz, yes, yes. But he did not telephone; he came to see me. We are old friends. He is very learned you know. A broad knowledge rather than a deep, but one always appreciates an enthusiast."

"He asked you about the Coptic Patriarchs?"

"That is so."

"May I ask what you told him?"

"Just the obvious. They do not exist. They are a myth."

"You are sure?"

"Positive. I am an expert in my field, Mr Holmes, just as you are in yours. Certainly they are a myth."

"Miraculous objects do exist," Watson said.

"Nonsense." Bazalgette leaned forward and placed his hands on the table. "Truly miraculous objects do not exist except in story books."

"And yet a man has murdered three people apparently because he believes he has found these coins. One of the victims was your friend, Mr Schwartz."

"Schwartz? Dead?"

Bazalgette's face drained of all blood. Watson poured him a glass of water and helped him drink it. "Slowly, slowly," he said. "You have had a shock."

"But, but he was here. Just here last week. He sat in that chair where you are sitting now, Mr Holmes. Oh dear, oh dear, what a terrible thing. I am sorry to hear it. Yes, very sorry. He was a decent fellow, you know. Very knowledgeable and interested in so many things. In his own field, that is to say as a jeweller, he was quite exceptional. A master craftsman and creative, too. He once showed me a pin that he made of a bunch of daffodils all in gold. Quite exquisite. Oh dear. I shall miss him."

"Can you relate your last conversation with him in as exact detail as you can recall?"

He loosened his tie and sipped more water before replying.

"I had a telephone call from Schwartz on Tuesday night and I agreed to meet him the next day. He arrived promptly at four o'clock and sat, as I said, in that chair. He said he was trying to learn as much as he could about the coins of the Coptic Patriarchs.

"I told him bluntly the coins were a myth and not worth his time. He said, as you did, Mr Holmes, 'I suppose there is no doubt about that?'

"'None at all,' I said. I reminded him of the particulars of the tale: Saint Mark had given a gift of the coins to a poor widow who lived in the city of Akhetaten and no matter how many times she spent them she always found them in her purse. These details never vary. However, the Royal City of Akhetaten was abandoned during the reign of King Tutankhamun. That king died in 1325 BC, while St Mark was martyred in the 64th year of Our Lord."

"Akhetaten?" I said.

"Or Tell el-Amarna as the archaeologists call it. It was excavated some eight or nine years ago."

"And you told all this to Mr Schwartz."

"I did. I also pointed out the impossibility of proving that one coin is more special than any other of its type. Could you say with any certainty, Mr Holmes, that one of the pennies in your pocket is more valuable than any other penny?"

"And when you made this point to Schwartz he asked you about provenance?"

"Yes, that is correct. He said what if there was a document that outlined the tale of the coins and listed the names of all of its owners since the widow. I told him such a document would have to be a forgery. There was just such a case in Bavaria about twenty years ago. Someone had a couple of coins allegedly dating to the early Christian Church in Egypt. They produced the coins and a document much like the one Schwartz described. Of course, tests proved conclusively the thing was a forgery. The blackguard vanished before he could be arrested."

"What was Schwartz's response?"

"That everything I said fit in with his own thoughts and recollections. That was all. We shook hands and he left."

"Did he mention the name Demosthenes Jones?"

"Jones? No. Mr Schwartz would never have dealings with a villain like that, Mr Holmes. The man is a thief and a liar."

"What of someone called Bashir?"

"There are several people of that name, but off hand I cannot think of anyone who has any particular expertise in this subject.

Certainly, my old friend did not mention the name. Dear me, I am really very sorry he is dead. I wish I could be of more help."

"On the contrary, your help has been inestimable," I said.

Despite his elegant name, Demosthenes Jones is no more than a conduit through which stolen works of art are processed. He is a big man, only an inch shorter than I, but his girth... I vow it would take a full twenty seconds to make a circumference around him. He has a small shop in Soho and spends each day sitting in the back smoking some noxious weed that certainly is not *Nicotiana tabacum.*

Today his hooded eyes glinted as he looked up at Watson and me when we drew back the heavy velvet curtain and violated his inner sanctum.

"Mr Holmes," he said, wheezing as always. The gap in his two front teeth gave a whistle to his 'S's and the words sounded like Misster Holmess.

He was sitting cross-legged on a huge red cushion puffing on a hookah.

"I need to speak to you on a matter of business," I said, sitting on a decidedly ill-advised statue of an Indian elephant. Watson stood at the doorway, his arms folded. Now and then, he turned his face away in order to inhale some of the slightly less noxious air of Soho.

"Always a pleasure to speak with you, Misster Holmess," Jones replied. He offered me his pipe; I waved it away with a lazy hand.

"What can you tell me about a man called Schwartz?"

"Schwartz?" He puffed and avoided my eye.

I jangled the coins in my pocket. The puffing stopped.

"I met a Jew by that name a few days ago," he said.

"What did you discuss?"

More puffing. I shifted my position and a china statue of Vishnu crashed to the floor and shattered into a hundred shards.

"Oh dear," I said.

"Oy! Be careful!" Jones hissed.

"Schwartz," I said.

"All right, all right, he wass here. Last week it wass, Tuessday or Wednessday. He were assking about ssome tale. Egyptian coinss."

"And what did you tell him?"

I rested my finger against the base of another statue, a plaster bust of Napoleon.

"Sstop!" cried Jones. "All right. I told him that ssome do ssay the coinss are a myth, though I have heard different."

"What have you heard?"

"Iss it worth ssomething?"

"Goodwill, Mr Jones," I replied.

"Your goodwill iss like money in the bank," he said and bowed slightly. "All the ssame, it don't pay the rent now, do it?"

I took a guinea out of my pocket and showed it to him. "For the broken statue," I said. "How much hashish can you buy for a guinea?"

He laughed and his laughter turned into a cough. "Not ass much ass you might think. Sstill, in the interesst of cooperation...

"I have heard from very good authority that the coinss are quite real and are in right here in London." He reached out his pudgy fingers to take the coin but I covered it with my hand.

"What authority?"

He sighed, puffed on the pipe, and then said, "This must remain between uss, Mr Holmess. It could be difficult for me if it were known I talked to you."

"You may rely on my discretion."

"Well, then... There iss a man by the name of Bashir. An Egyptian by birth, it iss ssaid. He had some dealings with the estate of Ssir Nicholass Fleming."

Fleming! Ah!

"And now?" I said, careful that neither my mien nor my voice betrayed my excitement. "I believe Fleming died some months ago. What happened to Bashir after that?"

"You'll find the gentleman in Chapel Market."

"You told all this to Schwartz?"

He nodded.

"Thank you, Jones, you've been very helpful."

"You, ah, won't mention my name?"

I slid the coin across the counter and his greedy hand grabbed it. "Not a word," I said.

"Well, well," I said as I climbed into a hansom with Watson. "Now the threads start to come together."

"Do you think Bazalgette was wrong and the coins do actually exist?" my friend said.

"Not necessarily. It is entirely possible this Bashir gentleman was misled or duped by someone, or perhaps he's the one doing the duping. A clever fake could be worth a fortune. We still have a great many questions. What is the link between Bashir and Rickman, for instance."

"You do not think they can be one and the same?"

"Unless a tall, fair man can pass himself off as an Egyptian..." I paused.

"Something has struck you," Watson said. He lapsed into silence, understanding, as he always does, when I have a need for quiet contemplation.

As we neared Baker Street he said, "I say, Holmes, I think we should go to Camden Town."

"Why so?"

"Someone ought to break the news to Mrs Prentiss about Connie's death. She ought to know."

"Really? Oh, if you insist. Would you mind taking care of it, Watson? And since you will be in Camden Town anyway, see if you can find out anything about the newcomers to the area. There was an African man, I believe."

"And a widow," he said.

"Trust you to remember the woman."

"And trust you to forget."

"I forget nothing. It is unfortunate that Chapel Market is closed on Mondays. We shall have to delay our investigations into Bashir until tomorrow. I am anxious to see if there have been any further developments in Hatton Garden. We shall rendezvous in Baker Street later."

I found Stevens on Saffron Hill. He was helping an old woman with her bags. He nodded towards me and then, with a jerk of his chin indicated I should meet him down the street.

He joined me a few minutes later. "Good afternoon, Mr Holmes," he said, greeting me with a smile and a handshake.

Saffron Hill is a little too narrow, a little too overlooked for quiet conversation, and we headed for the wider thoroughfare of Hatton Garden.

"Well," I said as walked down the street. "What news?"

"That fellow de Vine is a slippery customer and no mistake," Stevens said. "I am glad to have a chance to talk to you, Mr Holmes, because I think I must report the fellow to Inspector Glaser, but I wanted to talk to you before I do."

"Well?"

"I said he was lazy but, my word, that's not the half of it. He takes bribes; he uses his position to bully people. In all, he is a thorough disgrace to his uniform."

"Does he know he has been so unfortunate as to lose your regard?" I asked.

The man was too distressed to catch my humour. "No," he said, earnestly. "I have been very careful to play the part, wretched though it makes me."

"If it is any comfort to you, Stevens, Glaser already knows de Vine was lying."

"Oh, that is a relief. He's a fine gentleman is the inspector. As to de Vine: He tries to avoid discussing the murder but of course, he thinks I'm just some dolt who knows nothing, and I play that up.

"I told him I thought he was very brave to go into that house after hearing a gunshot. He admitted he didn't realise it was gunfire at the time. I do believe he was horrified by what happened. He says remembering makes him ill and from the way he looks when he remembers I'd say that much is true. He did say one very odd thing though. He said, 'Old fool should have waited.'"

"'Old fool should have waited?'" I repeated. "Ha! Excellent! Well done, Stevens, well done indeed."

"What does it mean?" Stevens said.

"It means we need to find Inspector Glaser."

These things never go as smoothly as one expects. Firstly, Glaser had to be found and informed; then Hill had to take over in Glaser's absence; Lestrade had to redistribute his own work; and then we had to rendezvous at Scotland Yard. An hour and a half passed before we could confront de Vine.

The fellow marched into the room the very model of a good policeman. On the outside, anyway.

I sat in the corner and let Glaser and Lestrade get on with it.

Seeing us shook the fellow and the good policeman façade began to crack.

"Have a seat, de Vine," Glaser said.

"What's this about, Inspector?" he asked. His chair chattered on the floor in answer to his trembling.

"I think you know full well," Glaser said. "Your only hope is to make a clean breast of it."

"I should caution you," Lestrade said, "If you attempt to lie you may face prison for obstruction of justice. Let's have it. The whole story. The truth, mind, or I shall march you down to the cells myself."

The fellow's teeth chattered. "I didn't mean no harm," he stammered. "It was just… I didn't know what was going to happen, did I?"

"Start at the beginning, de Vine," Glaser said. "When Mordechai Schwartz asked for your help."

The fellow was sweating profusely. His body emitted a terrible odour, the stench of fear. I had a flicker of sympathy and then I remembered Schwartz and my heart hardened.

"I didn't know him," de Vine said. "I mean, I'm sure I'd seen him but I don't know those people. Those beards and the hats, they all look the same to me. Anyway, it was Friday afternoon and he was hurrying up the street. He stopped me and asked if

I'd seen the inspector. I said I hadn't and he was probably on his patrol.

"'Well,' says the fellow, 'it's very important that the inspector and his officers meet me in my workshop this evening after services. Ask Glaser to tell Mr Holmes that we have him.'"

"But you did not tell me, did you?" Glaser said. "And you were not there at the workshop. You let Schwartz face that villain alone."

"I did go," de Vine protested. "Only I was a bit late."

"Because you were sleeping," Glaser said.

Lestrade leaned forward. "Is this true? Were you sleeping? Is that why you didn't let the Inspector or Mr Holmes know of Schwartz's plan?"

"It was just... I mean... I was sick," de Vine said with a wail. "I had to take some medicine for my back and it put me to sleep. I did head over there as soon as I remembered. I looked for the inspector and for Bing but I couldn't find them.

"Look, I've been a copper for eight years now. That's four years longer than most other fellows and what have I got to show for it? Bad hours, bad pay, and no respect."

"Well, you need not worry about the unfairness of your lot any longer," Lestrade said. "I am discharging you. You may face charges—"

"You? Discharging me?" de Vine, shouted, interrupting the inspector. "Fine. Stuff it, I say." He tore off his uniform jacket and his hat and flung them across the table. Both hit Lestrade in the face. Then came his truncheon and other items of his profession.

A moment later, he was gone and we all sat in silence.

"I am sorry, Glaser," Lestrade said. "I should have listened to you all those times you complained to me about that fellow.

If I had, Schwartz would not be dead and Rickman would be in custody."

He rose to his feet at least ten years older than when he had sat down.

"Are you all right, Lestrade?" I said.

He shook his head and left.

For some moments, Glaser and I sat in silence. I was seething at the rank stupidity of it all. Schwartz had him, had arranged for us to catch him, and because of one lazy, worthless policeman it had all come to nothing. No, worse than nothing for Schwartz had paid for his good intentions with his life.

"How are things in Hatton Garden, Glaser?" I asked after I subdued my fury.

"What?" It took a moment for Glaser to shake out of his reverie. "Oh, there was a report of a sighting," he said. "Someone claimed they had seen Rickman up by Montague Street again. Strange that he is still in the area.

"I've been thinking: What if he's part of a gang? Maybe there's a few of them holed up together somewhere, keeping an eye on the diamond district while they plan a robbery."

"He is almost certainly being directed by someone," I agreed. Glaser looked crestfallen.

"Oh," he said. "You already worked that out. Well, of course you did. I'm a fool."

"Do not berate yourself, Inspector. Most of your colleagues would have missed all the clues that you spotted."

"Well, I reckon if he was left to his own devices he'd have scarpered by now. That he is still staying around says he probably has people, or at least one person, telling him what to do. Though I suppose if the job was big enough he might think it worth the risk. But why him? A man like that will stand out anywhere, even more so in a district such as this."

"Precisely," I said. "You have put your finger on it, Inspector. Why Rickman? If you wanted to hire someone to commit murder, why would you choose a man who must attract attention, unless attention was the point for some reason? And why kill Schwartz? All the evidence suggests a premeditated murder, and yet the killer was so distressed when he killed Bing that he was violently sick. No, someone else is pulling the strings, but who? Why?"

We both sank again into silence. I broke it by saying, "Other than the reported sighting of Rickman, have there been any other developments?"

"Only the usual petty thefts and arguments that you'd find anywhere. If anything, things have been quieter than usual. People are afraid."

"That fear will not last long."

We returned to Hatton Garden and I watched how his keen eyes scanned his district with a fierce protectiveness that seems to define him.

I said, "You will be careful? Beatrice is very fond of you, you know."

"And I of her," he said. "I shall be careful. At least I have Stevens now; he is worth ten of de Vine. Good evening, Mr Holmes."

Watson arrived in Baker Street not long after I. "Ah, you're back, Holmes," he said. He took off his coat and rubbed his hands together before the fire. He was trying to act coolly but his excitement enveloped him like a cloud.

"You have news," I said. "Tell me everything."

He smirked and sat in his customary seat. "You know me too well," he said. "I visited Mrs Prentiss's house first. I told her about Connie's death. Not any of the details, but just the fact that the girl was dead.

"She was upset, of course, and I think she blames herself for being too liberal a mistress. I tried to reassure her, but the wound is still too fresh. At least Bessie is working out a treat. Mrs Prentiss tells me things have returned to normal. There have been no more disturbances."

"Good, good," I said impatiently. "But the people—"

"I was coming to that," he said, giving me one of those frowns that medical professionals do so well. I half-expected a scolding about my diet. He continued:

"I remembered your advice of old and took myself off to the local pub. There I engaged in conversation with some of the gentlemen from the area. In the space of an hour, I learned that the African gentleman who moved in at the beginning of the year is, in fact, Egyptian. His name is Amun, he is married to an Englishwoman, and he works at University College London.

"Ah! He is an Egyptologist?"

"Well, I assume so. I should have asked. Sorry, Holmes."

"I doubt the locals could have told you in any case. No matter. We can make inquiries of the university. What do we know of Amun's wife?"

"Not much. She is a housewife. No one seems to know much about her. She is quiet and keeps to herself. Other than the fact that she married an African, they don't seem to have anything against her."

"And what of the other woman?"

"What other woman?"

"The widow who moved into the district. Mrs Prentiss mentioned her."

"Oh."

"Watson, really..."

"Ha!" he said. "I had you going there, didn't I? Her name is Mrs Portnoy and she has two children. It is rather a tragic tale: Her husband died just a few months ago and left them in rather reduced circumstances. Around the same time, her mother passed away from a long illness. I am told she is quite a gentlewoman for all her current social standing. The locals describe her as 'a shapely blonde.'"

"When did she move in?"

"Some time in January. She doesn't actually live in Harrington Square proper. It's probably a bit rich for her. She has the top floor flat at the end of Mornington Crescent where it meets the Square. I've been all down the Crescent, Holmes, and as far as I can tell, she and Amun are the only newcomers who have a view of the Prentiss house."

He put his notebook back in his pocket and said, "I, uh, did all right, didn't I, Holmes?"

"Oh, you did very well, my dear Watson. I suppose you had no opportunity to see or speak to these newcomers on your own, did you?"

"I didn't get to speak to Mr Amun. I knocked but there was no answer. However, I did see Mrs Portnoy. I said I was a doctor who had been called to see a patient but couldn't find the address. She was kind enough to give me a glass of water. I did not stay long. The woman is still in deep mourning and I felt my presence was intrusive."

"Did anything about her strike you as unusual or odd?"

"No, indeed. I could see that she used to be wealthy. Her clothes were a fine quality and she wore an exquisite sapphire ring. Her husband gave it to her, she said, and she would sooner starve than give it up. I think starvation may be a real possibility. She has lost at least two stone since she first purchased her gown and her attempts to take it in were, well, not very skilled. The flat was shabby and attempts to make it look elegant somehow made it seem even poorer. It was a very sad thing to see."

"Excellent, Watson. You never give yourself half enough credit for your observations."

"After all these years of our friendship I hope I've learned something from watching you, Holmes. I'll never be your equal, of course."

"True. Still, you did better than most men. You have really come a long way since you tried to get information about the man who followed Miss Violet Smith on bicycle."

"Ah, 'The Solitary Cyclist'. I was very fond of that story, Holmes."

"Really? You astonish me. At any rate, we need to get some rest tonight. Tomorrow we have a rendezvous at Chapel Market."

15

Tuesday 3 May 1898

This morning after breakfast, Watson and I went to the Angel and its market on Chapel Street. Like all street markets, this one is noisy, chaotic and smells of rotting fish. Women bargain with butchers over the right cuts of meat; men haggle over items of clothing and jewellery; and children run amuck through all of it. Every nationality and every language can be encountered if one stays there long enough.

Watson and I picked our way through the cabbage leaves and the pools of spilled porter pretending an interest in all the market had to offer. We had already planned that Watson would pose as Mr McAdams, a writer from Scotland, and I as his guide around the wicked city of London. People will tell a writer things that they would never tell a detective.

As we trailed along speaking to the merchants, a waif wandered a short distance from us, always keeping our pace and never letting us get more than thirty feet away from him.

Now and then, we stopped at a stall and engaged a merchant in conversation. After my brief introduction in which I said Mr McAdams was writing a book about the rare treasures that may sometimes be found in a street market, Watson took over and asked a variety of questions that he had prepared. He nodded his head and wrote in his notebook. I cannot remember when I've seen him so entertained.

In this manner, we proceeded through the market and so by the time we reached the stall of Habib Bashir we had established ourselves as harmless curiosities, people any vendor in any market would accept without question. If they had any complaint at all, it was that we were not there to buy. Still, there was the hope that Mr McAdams' book might lead to more business for them in the future and so they were, for the most part, happy to indulge us.

Bashir is a small man with delicate features and large brown eyes. His complexion is more golden than brown and he could pass for almost any ethnicity. When we first spied him, he was talking very quickly and his gesticulating arms kept time with his speech. He seemed like a parody of a musical conductor but his business was altogether more prosaic: he was trying to interest a customer in a brass figure of the Buddha. The shopper, a middle-aged gentleman with a spoiled wife and two spaniels, shook his head and left. Bashir sighed then turned to the illustrious Mr McAdams and me.

"What can I do you for, gentlemen?" said he in the most genial tones. His accent was a curious combination of the Far East and the East End.

"Good morning," I said with equal warmth. "My name is Cuthbert Culpepper and this is my friend the esteemed writer, Mr John McAdams."

"How'd'do?" said Bashir shaking our hands.

"Mr McAdams is writing a book about the wonders to be found in markets such as this one."

"That is true," said the merchant. "Very true. I've seen it myself I don't know how many times. We're not antiquarians you see. We just sell whatever crosses our path. Might be gilt or it might be gold. You never can tell."

Watson studied the man's collection of bric-a-brac. He said, "I'm curious about where things come from and how they end up in the market. Where does a man like you find his treasures?"

"Treasures," Bashir said, savouring the word. "That's it exactly, sir. That's it. You've said it. Yes, we all pick up things from a number of places. I tend to go door to door. You'd be astonished to know how often ladies in fine homes have things they went to sell for a few pennies. Well, it's money they don't have to tell their husbands about, ain't it?" He nudged Watson with his elbow in a 'we're all men of the world' conspiratorial manner.

"Yes, quite," Watson said, rubbing his ribs. "And is that where all your wares come from, sir?"

"Oh no, not all. Now and then, I get word about an estate sale. Sometimes someone dies and leaves no family so their things are auctioned off. All the big houses go after the expensive items: the jewels and the furs and the artwork, but they don't care much about the little trinkets and I can sometimes pick things up for a song."

"Is there a regular dealer you work with?" Watson said. He delivered the line innocently enough but Bashir looked at him suspiciously.

"'ere, what you want to know that for?"

Watson blinked and looked at Bashir in some surprise as if he could not understand why the man even asked the question.

"I mean," he said, "Do you have a relationship with certain people in your trade who might tell you when they have something of particular interest?" He said it exactly the right way. That is, he implied that Bashir himself could not tell a genuine objet d'art if it flew up in his face and bit him on his rather large nose.

"I work with several auction houses and people in the business, but I don't need to be told when something is valuable. I have expertise of my own."

"Ah," said Watson as if Bashir had just said something of enormous importance. He made a note in his book. "Now, that's what I'm looking for." To me he said, "I told you these men were experts." And to Bashir, "I told my friend he could depend that the gentlemen here in the market would have to have an eye to a real find. No, says he. They're all just petty merchants." He gave me a disdainful look.

Bashir clapped his hands with delight, all suspicion forgotten. "And you were right, sir. You were indeed right."

"Well," I said, defensively, "I do not think it is fair to say all the vendors here in the market have skill. Mr Semple back there..."

"Oh, Semple," said Bashir. "Yes, there are hucksters and fools in any business. You will allow for that?"

"Yes," I said, with a show of reluctance. "Still, I cannot see—I mean no disrespect—but I cannot see that many of the merchants here would recognise something unusual. I mean, anyone can tell a piece of Delft or an ivory carving, but if something outré crossed your path you'd never spot it."

"Depends on what it is, don't it?" he said. "I have a good eye and I can tell a genuine gemstone from paste. I'm well known here. Ask any of the merchants around the Angel and they'll tell you Habib Bashir can spot a treasure a mile off."

Again, Watson made a note. He said, casually, "Mr Ferguson back there told us he specialises in Napoleonic treasures, and Mr Sykes says he knows everything there is to know about religious icons. Do you have an area of specialty, Mr Bashir?"

"Egyptian art," Bashir said. "Anything to do with ancient Egypt and I'm your man."

"Indeed? What, you mean like papyruses... papyri? What's the plural?"

Bashir gave a loud chuckle and revealed a set of perfectly even and white teeth. "Oh, I can tell a piece of papyrus from a

191

fake. Not that you'd find a legitimate papyrus in these parts, they're almost all fakes."

"Well, that's disappointing," Watson said, laughing. "I'm afraid I don't know much about Egyptian treasures."

"We have them though," said Bashir. "Mind you, you'll find more in the British Museum than you will in Cairo these days."

"Is that a fact?"

"Oh yes. Still, history keeps her secrets and who knows what the sand is still covering."

Watson turned to me and said, "What was that story we heard about Egypt?"

"What story?"

"I cannot remember. Something about a coin. A magical coin. I really cannot remember."

"Something from the Arabian Nights?" I said.

"No, no. It had something to do with a coin—or it might have been a few coins—that you couldn't spend, or they could never get lost or something." He scratched his head with his pen. "I think they had something to do with the Coptic Church."

"Oh, it's the Coins of the Fathers you're meaning," said Bashir.

"That's it! That's it exactly. What is the story, do you know?"

He recited the story of the Coptic Patriarchs as if he'd committed it to memory. It was identical to the other versions we'd heard.

"That's it," Watson exclaimed. "Why you are a font of information, Mr Bashir." He lowered his voice and in a conspiratorial tone said, "I may say your exotic anecdotes are far more interesting than some of the other tales we've heard here today."

"Fairy tales," I said, playing the part of the sceptic. "No more exciting than Mother Goose." I made a show of trying to stifle a yawn.

Watson gave me an irritated look. "Not so," he said. "All myths and legends have some foundation in truth. Do you not agree, Mr Bashir?"

"I do, sir. I do indeed. I know for a fact that the story about the Egyptian coins is true. I've seen them with my own eyes."

"You never have!"

Careful, Watson, I thought, but the merchant was far too engrossed to see anything amiss in my friend's excessive wonder.

"One of those estate sales I told you about," said Bashir. He looked around to make sure no one was listening. I was amused at his caution, given that he was revealing his secrets to a man who was supposedly a writer and planning to share all with the world. I suppose by now he'd forgotten Watson's alleged task.

"Go on," my friend urged.

"Well, I was told of the estate of a man by the name of Nicholas Fleming. Don't know much about the gentleman except he had a big house in Holloway. Off I trot, and because of my connections, I was able to get a look at his merchandise. The man died, you see, and his heirs didn't care two hoots for art so everything was to be sold.

"The big merchants, they were putting in their bids for the Wedgewood and the paintings. Nice stuff, most of it, though not to my taste. Anyway, I spotted a box of Egyptian treasures, all of it legitimate, on my word it was, sir. There was a small wooden box, hand carved and very old. I opened it and saw the coins. Ancient they were but still in mint condition. Made of pure copper I'd guess. They were in pristine condition. You could still see the symbol of St Mark on them. St Mark being the patron of that Church, you see."

This certainly matched the description we had heard. Watson said, "What happened? Did you manage to get them?"

"Me, sir? No, sir." He hooted. "They're priceless! The sort of thing that would likely end up in a museum. What they were doing in England is anyone's guess, but there they were."

"So what happened to them?"

He scratched his remarkable nose. "Most of the stuff went to Brahms in Kensington, but some of the smaller pieces were to be auctioned off. I reckon that included all the Egyptian stuff and the papers, too."

"Papers?"

"Well, the coins on their own are valuable, but there will be doubt as to whether they're the real article what with them bouncing around the world for the last two thousand years. So the first owner, a widow woman, wrote how the Saint had given her the coins. Then, when she died, her son wrote his piece about how the coins were his inheritance... And so on. Everyone who has owned the coins has added to the document. I believe it later became no more than a list of names and the dates the coins were in their possession. It was to prove provenance... That is to say, proving how something ended up where it did and tracing back its lineage. A bit like a nobleman showing his line of ancestry."

"Except many nobles have extremely ignoble origins," I said.

The man hooted again. "You've never said a truer word, sir, and no mistake."

We prepared to leave and I said, casually, "I do not suppose you know who the auctioneer was? It might make an interesting side-piece to your book, Mr McAdams."

"It would indeed. An unusual angle, too, to see how the auction houses feel about these markets. Can you help us, Mr Bashir?"

The Arab frowned then reluctantly said, "Well, I suppose it won't do no harm. Bramley and Sons it were. Up the Caledonian Road."

To indulge the man we purchased a pair of silver (nickel) candlesticks then we said goodbye and merged into the crowd. As soon as we left, the street urchin who had been following us slipped in behind Bashir's table and waited.

Addendum:

I spent the afternoon investigating Mr Amun. He is a refined, gentle sort of man who teaches Egyptian studies at the university. My preliminary findings reveal nothing of any import but I should like to meet the man for myself before I make up my mind.

Midnight:

This evening a little after ten o'clock, a knock came to the door followed hard on by a pair of thundering feet. A moment later, the door opened and young Billy bounced into the room.

"Watcha, Mr 'olmes. Doctor," he said with his customary cheer.

"Ah, Billy, do you have something to report?"

"I do." He looked so smug that I laughed.

"A shilling if it's good," I said.

"It's good," he said.

He sat cross-legged on the floor and told his tale.

"After you and the doc left the market, I took my position, just as we'd planned. That Arab, whatisname, Bashir, 'e didn't wait long. As soon as 'e reckoned you'd gone 'e asked the chap at the next stall to keep an eye on things and 'e went into the pub."

"He didn't see you following him?"

"Not he! Intent on 'is business, weren't 'e? Anyway, I follows 'im in and 'e makes a telephone call. 'e spoke to someone called 'habibi' and said that two gentlemen 'ad been by inquiring about the coins. 'e said 'e'd told you everything they 'ad planned and you'd be along to Mr Bramley's for more information. The Arab asked when 'e'd get paid and then 'e nodded and repeated it, seven o'clock in the Five Crowns."

"You should have come to get me," I said. "There was ample time for me to get there and see who paid Bashir."

"Not to worry, Mr 'olmes. It's all in 'and. Cor," he said to Watson. "Where's the trust, eh?"

"I'm sorry, Billy. You've never let me down before, and I have not forgotten the great debt I owe you from last year."

Mollified, he grinned and said, elaborately, "Sooo, if I might go on with my tale, Mr H?"

With a wave of my hand, I signalled he might continue. Watson managed to stifle a chuckle.

"I 'ad Tommy and the others standing by and I left them with Bashir. Then I 'eaded up to Holloway. I got cousins up that way and I got them working on finding out about Bramley and Sons. They'll send word if they learn aught.

"Then after a spot of dinner—my Aunt Mable makes the best gingerbread—back I comes to t'Angel. It was closing-up time by then and Tom-Tom said Bashir 'adn't made a move from 'is stall since I left. We decided Tommy would stick with Bashir and I'd keep an eye on the bloke what he was meeting.

"So it's almost seven o'clock and off our friend goes to the Five Crowns. Me and Tom-Tom followed taking care 'is nibs didn't spot us.

"Down 'e sits in the pub and in comes a man you'd know, Mr 'olmes."

"Let me guess," I said. "A tall, fair man?"

"Ha! I knew that would get you all excited. But you're wrong."

"Wrong?"

Watson spluttered. It might have been laughter. I was too astonished at Billy's tale to pay much heed.

"So who was it?"

"A man who ain't no Frenchman, if you get my drift."

"Watteau?" I said.

"'Cept that's not the name 'e's using. 'e's Flaubert this week."

"How did you recognise him?" Watson said. "How can you be sure it's the same man?"

"Mr 'olmes gave me 'is picture ages ago. You said 'e'd be back and you was right."

"Watteau," I said. "I owe that gentleman… Damnation! I could have had my hands on him."

Billy hadn't lost his smug expression and I realised my distress was premature. "Well?" I demanded. "There's more?"

"Heaps!" He grinned, winked at Watson and added, "Reckon my shilling's safe enough." He chortled and I could not help but laugh. He continued his tale.

"As I said, me and Tommy 'ad arranged that 'e would follow Bashir and I'd keep watch on the bloke 'e was meeting. Sure enough, after 'anding over a wad full of notes, Monsoor

Whatsisname gets up and leaves. I follows behind. Not too close, but I didn't let 'im out of my sight neither. I reckoned 'e'd get a cab and I started to wish I'd sent Tommy back to you, Mr 'olmes, but 'e didn't do that. Get a cab, I mean.

"Nah, 'e goes down the Pentonville Road and waits in Claremont Square. It weren't a nice night for a wait but 'e didn't 'ave long. A few minutes later along comes Bashir. I was 'iding in the trees and neither the Frenchman nor the Arab spotted me. I couldn't see Tommy, but I knew 'e weren't far away. Just as the Arab drew level with Frenchie, Watteau or whatever 'is name is steps out and shoots the poor bastard dead."

"What?" I cried.

"Good God," said Watson.

"See, I thought that would put the wind up you." Billy was remarkably calm. Strange how the young are immune to things that horrify adults.

"At that," Billy continued, "the fake-Frog spotted Tommy and I saw 'e was thinking about firing at 'im. Leave no witnesses. 'Course, Tom-Tom was too far away to see the bloke's face, but I don't reckon a man like that would be the kind to take a chance.

"Anyway, Tom-Tom starts running towards us and… Well, I 'ad no option, did I?"

"What did you do?" Watson sounded as breathless as I felt.

"I jumped on top of the villain and managed to knock the pistol out of 'is 'and. Tommy blew 'is whistle and 'e 'elped me get the man to the ground and we sat on 'im."

Billy chortled so hard at the recollection that tears of mirth streamed down his grubby cheeks. "Oh, you should 'ave seen 'im, Mr 'olmes," he said. "What a conniption 'e made!

"Anyway, no more than a minute later a bobby comes along, Keller by name. Not someone I know but 'e did 'is job right enough. I tells 'im Mr 'olmes 'as been looking for this bugger, begging your pardon, sirs, and would be glad to know 'e was in flowery dell."

"Flowery what?" Watson said.

"Flowery dell: prison cell," I said. "Where is he now? Watteau?"

"They're 'olding 'im in the Islington Police Station. Tommy stayed to keep an eye on things. I said I'd come to fetch you. Thought you might want to see the villain for yourself, Mr H."

"You have excelled yourself, Billy. You and Tommy both. But what a risk you took. Here—" I handed him a guinea. He looked at me with a triumphant grin. I suppose he was entitled.

I rose and fetched my coat. Watson said, "What happened to Bashir, Billy? Are you sure he's dead?"

"Dead, sir; dead before 'e 'it the ground, I reckon. Most of 'is head was blown off."

"I am sorry to hear it. I rather liked him, despite everything. Do you want me to come with you, Holmes?"

"Thank you, Watson, but I doubt there's anything you can do. No, there is something. I would appreciate it if you would call Beatrice. She will be glad to know this fellow is behind bars."

"Yes, of course. But are you sure you don't need me to come along?"

"It is a filthy night, my dear fellow. I'll be perfectly content if you will just let Beatrice know what's happening. She does not like it when I exclude her from important news, and this is exceedingly important."

16

A short while later, Billy and I arrived at the police station in Stoke Newington High Street. It is a big, red-bricked building with a decidedly institutional air.

I did not know the policeman at the desk but he recognised Billy at once. "Ah, you came back, did you, lad?" he said. "There, that's sixpence I owe the sergeant." To me, he said, "Are you really Mr Sherlock Holmes?"

"I am," I replied. "I understand you have a man in custody. He speaks with a French accent and this evening he killed an unfortunate merchant from the Chapel Street Market. I should like to see him."

"I'll fetch the sergeant," the man said, springing to his feet. "Please take a seat, Mr Holmes. Is there anything I can fetch you? A cup of tea?"

"Nothing, thank you. Just the prisoner."

The policeman hurried away and returned with his sergeant. The senior officer, a cyclist with a new baby and a red-headed wife, was about forty years of age and bore a capable air.

"Mr Holmes," he said, shaking my hand with great enthusiasm. "Well I never! Do you know, when this young chap—" He ruffled Billy's unruly hair much to my young friend's disgust. "When this young chap said Mr Sherlock Holmes was a friend of his I had my doubts. Yes, indeed I did. But he seemed very particular and since he and the other boy had caught a cold-blooded killer I was prepared to give him the benefit of the doubt."

"Yes, thank you, Sergeant. Tell me, have you spoken to the prisoner?"

"I've tried, Mr Holmes. He claims not to know any English and I'm afraid I never learned French."

"He is not a Frenchman. He is Canadian. It is my belief he murdered an entire family. I would like to see him."

"Yes…" The policeman hesitated, obviously uncertain that some upstart consulting detective might dismantle his case.

"Congratulations on the new baby," I said. "Your first?"

"Yes! By Jove, yes indeed it is. But how on earth…?"

"You have a small creamy stain on your left shoulder. The result of an infant's posseting, I perceive. Fathers tend to be much more likely to look after their first born than later children, though there are exceptions, of course."

"Why you are everything I had heard, Mr Holmes. Indeed you are. Yes, of course you can see the prisoner. This way if you please."

"Billy, you stay here. I am sure the sergeant will need you to sign a statement, but I may need you again in any case. By the way, Sergeant, where is the other boy, Tommy?"

"He is having some tea and biscuits in the back. You want to join him, lad?" he said to Billy.

"Cor, rather!"

"Good lads," the sergeant said as he led Billy into the break room to reunite with his old crony. "What a risk they took though, bringing down an armed man like that."

"They are resourceful fellows," I said. "They have proven their worth to me countless times."

There came the sound of boyish laughter from the break room, and I thought how tickled the boys would be to tell their friends they'd been treated with such friendliness by the Regular police force.

I followed the policeman down into the cells and there was Watteau with a smug grin on his waxy, yellow face.

"Well," I said. "I thought we'd meet again some day. How kind of you to accommodate me and come here, Monsieur. You saved me infinite pains."

"Mr Holmes," he said genially. "Why aren't you dead yet?"

"I am not so easy to kill. It is your own mortality that should concern you. Your time on this planet is running out. Caught red-handed with the weapon still hot. Brought down by mere boys, tut, tut. The press will pillory you and then the hangman will have his turn."

"I should have killed you in Bitterne."

"You would not have succeeded. Many men better than you, deadlier than you, have tried and failed."

"It is all right. I've caused you pain. I wounded that pretty Lady Beatrice and that, in turn, wounds you. Oh, you have no secrets from me, Mr Meddlesome Holmes. I saw the way you looked at each other. I know I can do worse things to you than merely end your life."

The implication stabbed my heart like a shard of ice. I held my indifferent face, however, and said, "Why did you kill the Arab?"

"He was of no further use."

"Come now, that is not a reason."

"It is the only reason I shall give."

He turned his back and refused to say any more. At length I rose to leave. As the officer unlocked the cell door Watteau said, "You are responsible for the deaths of many people I esteemed, Mr Holmes. It is because of you that my old friend Albrecht Porlock hanged, leaving his wife without a husband and his children without a father. For shame. Your interference destroyed an organisation that would have paved the way for a new world, a better world. Only an Englishman would have such hubris as to think this mighty British Empire is without flaw. You will pay for your interference. Enjoy those boys and that lady while you can."

I would not give him the satisfaction of lunging at him. I would not afford him any satisfaction at all. But I swear by God I would have ripped his throat out in an instant if I had not managed to keep the tightest hold of my emotions.

No.

I would not give him the satisfaction.

At the sergeant's invitation, I joined the boys in the break room. I was shaking with anger and I needed to get my temper under control.

Tommy and Billy grinned at me when I came into the room. "We did all right, didn't we, Mr 'olmes?" Tommy said, his mouth full of a jam sandwich.

I forced a smile and agreed that they had both done exceptional work. I gave Tommy a coin and his grin got even wider. "Cor! Thanks, Mr 'olmes!" he said.

"Two fine young men, Mr Holmes," said the sergeant. "They're a credit to their parents and to you, too."

The desk officer came in and said, "There's a lady here, Sergeant. Says she's a friend of Mr Holmes." The policeman stared at me as he spoke as one might stare at a two-headed donkey.

"A lady? Alone?" the sergeant said.

"That will be Lady Beatrice," I said. "Sergeant, you have been so accommodating. May I prevail upon you a little further?"

"Anything you need, Mr Holmes," said he. For a moment, I was reminded of friend Watson.

"A room where I might speak alone with the lady."

"Of course, of course. There's an office..."

Moments later, I was sitting in the cramped dingy room with my wife.

"I want to see him," she said.

"It is out of the question."

"It wasn't a request. Sherlock—"

"It is not a debate. I said no and I meant it."

She glared at me with as much anger as I've ever seen her show. She is not a demonstrative woman as a rule. Well, there have been exceptions; but she shows her heart only rarely and then only to the people she trusts absolutely.

"You must trust me," I said. I reached to take her hand but she snatched it away. She rose and paced, though the room was too small to allow more than three strides.

"You will own I have only your best interests at heart?" I said.

"Yes. And you will own we have a contract in which you agreed never to restrict my actions?"

"I know. Forgive me."

Something in my tone held her and she turned to look at me.

"You're frightened," she said. She sank into the chair and took my hands in hers. "My dear, I am the one who should ask forgiveness. I've never seen you look so distressed. Come. I will hear your argument."

I related my conversation with Watteau verbatim.

"You think I am at risk then?" she said. "I and the boys?"

"Yes."

"Then this whole business of the coins and murders in Hatton Garden is altogether darker than we supposed."

I did not reply.

"Sherlock?"

"I feel manipulated," I cried.

"By me?"

"No! Good God, no. But all through this case I have felt I was being fed pieces of information in order to lead me in a certain direction. The whole thing is still too murky for me to determine who is behind it."

"Watteau's involvement is chilling. Yes, I understand."

"Beatrice, I promised the Queen that I would never let you come to harm. I wish I could guarantee your safety." I sighed then said, "I do not suppose I could persuade you to stay in Windsor...?"

"Good heavens, no, never again." She smiled and settled back into silence. Then, after a few moments reflection said, "What if I left London for a time?"

"France is no safer. The violence has not abated."

"No, not France. Sussex. I have a cottage there."

"Really?"

"My dear Sherlock, I gave you a complete inventory of my property when we decided to marry. You did not read it."

"It was not important. But you would go?"

It seemed altogether too easy. My wife is not one to give in without a fight.

"My presence in London can only distract you. I might end up getting you killed. No, I shall bury my pride and go to Sussex, and I shall bring those boys with me."

"Boys?"

"Billy and Tommy. I owe them a great deal, Sherlock, and they are no less at risk than I am. Besides, the sea air will do them both a lot of good. Their mothers will not mind, will they?"

I released a long breath. "Thank you. Your capacity for surprising me seems infinite. I confess I shall be immensely relieved to know you are safe. As for their mothers, I doubt they will even notice the boys are gone. Billy and Tommy spend half their lives on the streets, as it is. I shall take care of the families, in any case.

"How soon can you go?"

"I can leave in a day or two, but the boys will be needed for the trial, won't they?"

"Yes. I shall see if I can get the case expedited… It will still take a few days to arrange, though."

"The boys can stay with me in Wimpole Street," Beatrice said, "Until we're ready to leave for Sussex."

"And by your leave I will stay with you, too."

"You do not even need to ask, my dear. Come, let us tell the boys. I hope they will not be too upset."

Upset? Ha! I thought they would deafen me with their cheers and hurrahs. The policemen chortled at the boys' exuberance and I could not help but smile.

"And stay with you, miss? In that fancy house in Wimpole Street? Really, miss? Cor!"

Watson was half-asleep when I telephoned. Though I told him to stay at home, he insisted on coming to Wimpole Street, bringing his weapon and mine to ensure our friends' safety. Just a short while later, we all gathered in my wife's house.

The boys were on the very best behaviour; they were too awed to be rowdy. They had a bath without demur (I suspect astonishment at the sight of clean water rendered them mute), put on the nightshifts that had been found for them, and drank cocoa. Only after they had been bundled off to bed did they begin to giggle.

What Beatrice's staff made of her bringing two filthy street urchins into her home I can only guess, but they made no comment in my hearing.

"It is kind of you to take care of the boys like this, Beatrice," Watson said in a drowsy voice after a late supper. "They have little enough joy in their lives. If it were not for Holmes I do not know what would become of them."

I waved away this tribute. "We have a mutually satisfactory arrangement," I said. "The boys have often proven themselves of immense help in my work and I pay them fairly, I hope. Their home lives are... well, less than satisfactory.

"Billy's mother tries hard but with six children and no husband she finds it very difficult to make ends meet. Billy has a good brain and would do well in school, but he must help support his brothers and sisters and so his education is almost non-existent. That he can even read is a tribute to his own determination."

"And Tommy?"

"Tommy's case is even worse. His mother is a prostitute and he never knew his father. Oftentimes he cannot go home because his mother is entertaining one of her clients. Yet of all the boys, his is the kindest heart..."

I said nothing more. I could have told Beatrice that Tommy has a special regard for her. I suspect he harbours a fantasy that she and I will one day adopt him. I wonder what she would make of such a dream.

Watson at last went to bed. I believe he enjoys sleeping in what Beatrice calls 'John's room'. It suits him, somehow, with its cheery rose wallpaper and charming view of the back garden.

We decided he would look after my wife and the boys while I conduct business elsewhere. It is only for a few days, I hope.

Wednesday 4 May 1898

This morning after breakfast, I took a cab to Whitehall. It has been some time since I saw Mycroft, nor have I heard from him. That is not unusual, of course. I suspect events in Africa have been keeping him busy.

Gillespie greeted me with his customary warmth. "Come in, come in, Mr Holmes," he said. "Let me take your coat. Such a damp and gloomy day it is. There now, that's better... He's not engaged at present. You may go straight up. Shall I bring you up some coffee?"

"That would be most welcome, thank you."

Mycroft was on the telephone when I entered but he waved me to the armchair by the fire. His voice was civilised, calm, evenly measured. He was, in other words, furious.

He hung up the receiver at last and spluttered. "Insufferable incompetents!" Then, calmer, "Hullo, Sherlock. How are you this misty morning?"

"Better than you, I fear, dear brother. South Africa?"

"Egypt. But never mind that. Did you have a pleasant night in Wimpole Street?" He sat in the chair opposite me with a suppressed groan and eased his right leg onto the footstool.

"I thought I had brushed away the last of Mme Chabon's croissant crumbs from my waistcoat," I said.

"Almost. Ah, I wish you had thought to bring me some. Your wife has the best cook in all of England. If I were a marrying man I'd marry Bella Chabon."

"I shall ask Beatrice to invite you to dinner to atone for my thoughtlessness, Mycroft."

"That would be a most welcome courtesy, indeed."

"It may be a while, however. She's leaving for Sussex as soon as possible."

"Sussex? Why in God's name would anyone want to go to Sussex?"

"She has a cottage there."

"But she's not going for her health... Come, Sherlock, what has happened?"

I said, "Wait until Gillespie has delivered the coffee and then I shall tell you all. You have a little time?"

"A little."

We discussed politics for a few minutes. Emin Pasha, Madhist, Spain... Then there was a knock at the door and Gillespie entered with a large tray.

As soon as he'd left, the coffee poured, the bread buttered, and Mycroft finished grumbling about the demerits of plain bread compared with croissant concluded, I reviewed recent events.

My brother listened intently and did not interrupt. He waited until I was finished before saying, "Well, my influence over the legal justice system are not as potent as you seem to think. Still, I shall speak to some people and see what I might be able to arrange. I perfectly understand why you are anxious for your wife's safety. Still, I would have thought those boys could look after themselves."

"Perhaps, but Beatrice is fond of them, and it would distress her if they were hurt. She has already suffered at the hands of that gang, Mycroft."

"Yes, yes, I know." He shifted his position again and it was obvious he was in some discomfort.

"Have you seen a doctor?" I asked.

"Why? He would just tell me I have gout. Probably urge me to take a little rest. As if I can loaf about like a shop clerk."

"I do wish you'd..." I began, and then bit my tongue.

He met my eyes and said, "Careful, Sherlock. That comes perilously close to brotherly love."

"I apologise," I said, smiling. "I cannot imagine what I was thinking."

I made myself swallow my other expressions of concern. Truly, my brother looked unwell. Seeing him in such obvious discomfort unsettled me and for the first time I thought about mortality, Mycroft's mortality, and the thought quite froze my joints.

With his assurance that he would see what he could do about Watteau's trial, I left. Gillespie handed me my coat and said, "I don't suppose you could get him to take a holiday, Mr Holmes? He's worn out, for all he protests he's perfectly well."

"I could not even persuade him to see a doctor. But never fear, Gillespie. I have an idea."

I returned to Baker Street and read the response to a telegram I sent last night. Michel Watteau of Ontario is wanted by the Canadians in connection with five murders. The French and the Americans also have charges against him. I harboured a brief and, I confess, grotesque thrill at the thought of that creature facing the guillotine. Then I remembered what passes for justice in today's France and shuddered.

Why has he come back to England? Is it only to punish me? No, there is something else, something more sinister. I thought about returning to see him in the cells, but it would only make me seem weak and give him the advantage. No, I must trust to my own wits.

It was almost two o'clock by the time I returned to Wimpole Street. The door was opened by an unfamiliar youth. I stared open mouthed for several seconds. "Tommy?" I said at last when I recovered the power of speech. "Good God!"

"Look smashing, don't I, Mr 'olmes? 'er ladyship took me and Billy shopping. All new threads she got us."

"And haircuts. Well, well, you had a handsome face under all that grime, Tommy. I never knew."

"Me neither."

The combination of haircut and smart clothing somehow managed to reveal Tommy as a small boy. How curious; I never thought of him that way before.

Billy was sitting on the sofa reading a book. He was so engrossed he did not even notice me.

Beatrice was writing a letter. She signed her name before coming to greet me.

"I am sorry your brother is still under the weather," she said.

"A clever woman must be the most dangerous creature in all of creation," I said, laughing. "You are quite right. Mycroft has not improved and I am concerned about him. Perhaps you might invite him to dinner before you leave for Sussex? It would lift his spirits, I think."

"Certainly. He may join us tonight if he is free. Would you like to telephone him?"

"Thank you, I shall."

As I dialled the exchange I said, "I see you have been shopping. I hope you were careful."

"I was. Dr Watson is a perfect bodyguard, though I fear those boys rather wore him out."

It has been a long, if pleasant enough day. I have decided I quite like staying at Wimpole Street. The staff are pleasant and helpful, the house quiet and well ordered, and my wife is an excellent hostess.

"I feel quite the queen bee," she said this evening as we sat down to dinner. "Surrounded as I am by all these handsome gentlemen."

Mycroft can be a charming guest when he puts his mind to it. He very much likes his new sister and not only because of the quality of her table. We discussed a great many things such as the current state of the military, the merits of electric light over gas, and the reviews of Strauss's latest, *Don Quixote*.

Beatrice was careful to include the boys in the conversation and I was very surprised to hear Billy say he would like to join the army as soon as he is old enough.

"And what would you like to do in the army, young man?" Mycroft asked.

"I'd defend the Queen," said the boy, "and my country. I should like to plan an attack and lead men into battle."

"You would need to be an officer," Watson said. "Tommy Atkins—common soldiers—do not do much in the way of planning."

Billy looked crestfallen. "Oh. I don't think I could be an officer. You need to be able to buy a commission, don't you?"

"If you need to be commissioned, Billy, I am sure it can be arranged," Beatrice said. "But you will need to study hard, too."

He stared at her in awe. I was reminded of a picture book I had as a child: Ali Baba beholding the treasure in the cave. That was Billy at that moment.

"What about you, Tommy?" I said. "Do you mean to follow your friend into the army?"

He shuffled uncomfortably in his seat for a moment before saying, "I'd like to play the piano, Mr 'olmes. Lady B 'as been teaching me this afternoon. It's smashing!"

"Tommy has an excellent ear," Beatrice said. "I think he will make a very good pianist. You shall have more lessons when we go to Sussex. And you, Billy, shall have plenty of books."

"Thanks awfully, miss," Billy said.

They turned their attention to their plates. Though utterly bewildered by the assortment of knives and forks, they followed my lead and did far better than I would have expected. How easy it is to change a life. A little caring, a little thought, some soap and clean clothes. The change in these boys seemed almost miraculous and yet, now I think about it, it is not so strange, really.

"Speaking of military matters," Mycroft said. "What news from France? Have you heard from your friend Zola, Beatrice?"

"He has appealed his conviction. Now we wait. He is distressed but resolute."

"I hope the courts will come to their senses," he said. "But I am not optimistic."

"On the subject of trials, what news of a court date for Watteau, Mr Holmes?" Watson said.

"I had a word with some people. We have been able to arrange it for this Thursday, the fifth. At least the trial should be short and the boys' testimony will be fairly swift."

"We can be ready to departure for Sussex as soon as the boys have given evidence," Beatrice said. "I hope you will not mind staying here until then."

"We'll cope, miss," Billy said with a cheeky grin.

"That's splendid of you," she said in the same spirit. After a pause she added, "You know, the cottage is not very far from the sea. It is so quiet and peaceful there. I wonder—forgive me for asking—but I wonder if you might be willing to come with us, Mycroft?"

"Me? To Sussex? What on earth for?"

"For a holiday. Peace and quiet and Mme Chabon's good food. I promise you'd be very well looked after. Frankly, you'd be doing me a favour."

"Would I?" Mycroft looked sceptical. "How so?"

"Well, your brother will be here working on his case and I would rest easier in my mind if Dr Watson were with him. On the other hand, I would feel much safer knowing there was a man at hand in Sussex. I have my father's valet, of course, but he is very old. Would you consider it, at least?"

"Well… it is a very busy time," Mycroft began.

"I had a telephone installed just last month, and there is a study. You could still handle any crisis that might occur, and the trains to London are regular should you need to return." She took a sip of wine before adding, casually, "I know Mme Chabon would love to try some of her recipes on a man of your palate. Just yesterday, she said she wanted to make a lamprey à la bordelaise. I confess I do not care for the dish myself, but she would be dearly love to make it for you."

"No, it is not for everyone," Mycroft agreed. "The sauce is made from the blood of the lamprey."

"She spoke of cherries clafouti for dessert."

"Well," said Mycroft with a little lick of his lips. "If I can be of service. After all, what's a brother for?"

17

Thursday 5 May 1898

This morning Billy and Tommy gave their evidence. Mr Justice Mellors was not pleased at the proceedings being rushed, but a well-placed word from the right official moved things along and His Honour kept his sermonising to a minimum.

The crown prosecution in the form of Sir Peter Huggins managed to slip in the suggestion that should the English courts fail in their duty, the Canadians would be happy to do show us how things should be done.

"We do not care about Canada," declared the judge.

"Surely," said Sir Peter in his silkiest tones, "the murder of a pregnant woman should outrage the entire world, My Lord."

"Never mind that," the judge said with a malevolent glare at the accused. "Get on with it."

And so it all went very swiftly indeed. Billy gave his evidence calmly and without the relish I half-expected of him. Clearly and concisely, he told the court that he happened to be returning from the Chapel Market by way of the Pentonville Road. Then on Claremont Street, he witnessed the accused shooting a man dead with no provocation whatever.

"How do you know the man you observed was the accused?" Huggins asked.

"Because we jumped on 'im; me and my mate Tommy."

A chorus of oohs and "Stout lad!" echoed through the chamber.

"And what happened then?"

"Tommy 'ad a whistle, sir. 'E blew it loud and a bobby... er, policeman came and put 'is nibs under arrest. Then we went back to the station and gave our statement."

The defence did not even bother to question him. Billy was discharged with a commendation from the bench, told he was a fine example of today's youth, and his parents should be proud of him.

Next came Tommy, more nervous, pale beneath his freckles, but he, too, delivered his testimony with calm and assurance. He had little to do but corroborate Billy's testimony, and then he too was commended and dismissed.

The only other witness for the day was Constable Keller. He related that he had been alerted by the sound of a whistle. "The man was dead, your honour," he said. "With his brains all over the pavement."

The judge looked queasy; Huggins did a poor job of concealing a smile, and the remainder of the proceedings have been adjourned until tomorrow.

Beatrice and I took the boys to the Savoy for a late lunch as a reward.

After the splendour of Beatrice's home and table, the boys were not at all awed by the Savoy. They were allowed to order what they pleased and, though understandably giddy, behaved remarkably well.

"What shall you do next, Sherlock?" Beatrice asked as we left the Savoy. "Do you have a plan?"

"I shall return to Demosthenes Jones. If the Egyptian was paid to send me in one direction, it is possible that Jones was, too. I also want to go back to Camden Town to see if I have missed anything. Finally, I need to see if there have been any developments in the diamond district."

"You will be careful?" B said. "Forgive me; foolish question. I know John will not let any harm befall you."

"You may count on me," Watson said. He stepped back apace, presumably to allow me to bid farewell to my wife in some tender fashion.

I shook Beatrice's hand and she squeezed my fingers. "Will you write to me of all that is happening? If not for my concern then at least for my curiosity."

"I shall. And if Mycroft becomes a bother let me know and I will find some reason to hasten his return to London."

She treated me to her deep throaty laughter that always makes me smile. I handed her into the carriage. Billy said, "I'll take care of the lady, Mr 'olmes, never fear."

"*We'll* take care of the lady," Tommy amended.

"I don't doubt it. Mycroft will meet you at Victoria."

The cab sped off leaving Watson and me standing on the Strand on a damp Thursday afternoon.

"You all right, Holmes?" Watson said.

"I was remembering our friend Collins who died not twenty feet from this very spot... We have lost some good friends over the years, Watson."

"Given the nature of our work, not nearly as many as one might expect. Collins's widow is doing very well and his children are thriving. Come. Let us not linger here. We have work to do."

We took ourselves off to Soho to see Demosthenes Jones. He looked up with his usual bland face. "Ah, Mr... Holmesss," he hissed. His eyelids were sunk lower than usual and he reeked of hashish.

"I think you know why we are here, Jones," I said.

"I'm sure I do not, Mr Holmesss," he replied. He puffed on the hookah and offered the mouthpiece to me, shrugged at my reaction, and resumed puffing.

"Your friend the Egyptian is dead. Murdered."

"I know no Egyptian," he replied.

"Know no Egyptian!" Watson spluttered. "Why, man, it was you who sent us to him. Bashir of the Chapel Market."

"Oh, that fellow. I don't actually know the man, you understand. I just heard his name."

"He was murdered because someone paid him to lead us on a merry chase for non-existent treasure. That same person paid you, too. Can you not see your peril?"

His dull eyes barely registered my words. I kicked at the hookah and sent it flying through a tawdry beaded curtain.

"Here, here, no reasson to get upsset, Mr Holmess," said the man.

"Your life is at risk. Don't you see that?"

"Who'd want to hurt me? I don't know nothin'."

"Who told you about Bashir? Answer me, who was it?"

But he was too far gone to reply.

"Leave it, Holmes," Watson said. "You won't get any sense out of him in this state. Best come back early in the morning before he's started smoking." He coughed and covered his nose and mouth with a handkerchief.

We stepped out into the busy streets. I glanced at my pocket watch.

"It's five o'clock," I said. "I feel we have wasted the whole day."

"Not so. The trial took up hours, and then you had to say a proper goodbye to your wife. I do hope those boys won't wear

218

her out. They are on their best behaviour now, but heaven help her once their natural exuberance re-emerges."

"Perhaps," I said. "I would like to do my own reconnaissance of Camden Town. I should like to check in on Hatton Garden, too, but that can wait until tomorrow."

We crossed Leicester Square and began our walk back to Baker Street. At the corner, I hesitated and looked back.

"Holmes?" Watson said.

"I wonder if I do right to leave him… Perhaps I should stay here and keep an eye on the man."

"Surely if he were at risk they'd have killed him by now?"

"Perhaps… Little of this case makes sense to me, Watson. It feels like…"

"Like?"

I shook my head. "As if there were a dozen men making decisions and each pulling in a different direction. One man I can match but playing chess with a dozen all at once, each with a different style and set of skills…"

"It's a puzzle," he agreed. "But you'll solve it, Holmes. The man, indeed, I should say the army has not been born who could defeat you." He patted my shoulder in a brotherly manner. "If you'd been at Balaclava in '54 the outcome might have been far different."

"I think Mycroft would have served them better. Ha! I wonder how he'll do in Sussex with two unruly boys and a tiny cottage."

"The boys probably won't spend much time indoors, Holmes. Beatrice will have them out on the beach if I am any judge. I think Mycroft will do very well indeed. The break will do him a great deal of good."

"True. He has been looking very poorly. But what am I to do about Jones?"

"Well, you cannot stay here. You are too recognisable. Surely he's safe enough for the moment? You can return later in disguise if you wish. Or I can stay here. I'm not as obviously recognisable as you are."

That was something.

"You would not mind?" I said. "There is a restaurant just across the street from Jones's shop. You could sit there, have dinner, and keep watch. I'll come back to replace you as soon as I've changed."

"Yes, all right... No. No, Holmes, that makes no sense. Go on to Camden Town and do whatever you must. I'll be all right here for a few hours. I shall follow Jones when he leaves. Don't worry; I'll keep a good distance. I have learned something from watching you, you know."

"Of course you have, that is not the issue."

"But something worries you. What is it, Holmes? I can see on your face that you are troubled."

"Watteau said or implied that the people I care about are most at risk. Really, I wonder if it might not have been wiser if you had gone to Sussex with the others."

"Oh, for goodness sake." He stood facing me with his most determined face set. "I'm a grown man, not a schoolboy nor a woman nor an out of condition older man. I am a soldier."

My impulse to laugh did battle with my urge to salute. I managed to do neither. "Of course you are, my dear fellow. Very well, do you go on to the restaurant and keep an eye on Jones. I shall follow your suggestion and go to Camden as soon as I have changed. Please, be careful."

"Of course. And you, too."

In Baker Street, I found a group of the Irregulars. I called Kevin over and said, "I have a job, if you boys are interested?"

"Whatever you need, Mr 'olmes."

I gave him his instructions and nodded. "Right you are, sir."

"Good lad. Here's a little money, just in case."

Two hours later, I was sitting in a small public house in Camden Town enjoying a glass of bitter. The place was soon full and I kept watch as the groups formed, changed, reformed. After an hour, I had selected a small group of working men dressed, like me, in flat caps and stout working gear. The man who was the apparent leader of the group was holding forth on the disgraceful matter of immigration.

"Coming over 'ere," he declared. "Stealing our jobs, robbing us blind. Some of 'em look like soot, the colour of 'em."

"Not in a region like this," I said. "Surely Camden is for Londoners. You wouldn't find foreigners in parts like this, surely"?

"You think not, Mr—?"

"Stout," said I. "John Stout at your service."

I tipped my hat and bowed slightly. Men like that enjoy good manners even though they often have little enough themselves.

"You see," said my new friend. "That's 'ow an Englishman behaves. Proper respect. Not to contradict you, Mr Stout, but you'd be astonished at the newcomers we 'ave, right 'ere in Camden."

"No," I said in a properly aghast tone. "You do astonish me, Mr—"

"Blessed, Sir. Jabez Blessed at your service." He doffed his cap and bowed in a stately manner.

"Pleased to make your acquaintance," I said. I turned my chair slightly towards them and, at their gesture, pulled it over to join in the group.

"I thought about moving to Camden Town," I said. "Don't at all like the way things are going in Hackney. Came here tonight to take a gander. I am disappointed, very disappointed..." I shook my head in sorrow. I was half-afraid I'd overdone it but the men were too much in their cups to notice.

"Well, it's the way this city is going, ain't it?" said another man. A hefty labourer with splinters in his fingers and huge callouses on his hands and arms. A former blacksmith and now a carpenter.

"It's never been much different, Bert," said Blessed. "But it's getting worse."

"Are there many newcomers in this district?" I asked. "I thought Camden was a stable, well-settled area."

"Some parts of it, Mr Stout. Some parts of it. But around the fringes... Do you know we've got an African living here now?"

"Probably got tired of the desert," said Bert. All the men hooted.

"Well, that's exotic, that is," I declared. "Well I never. What's an African doing in these parts, eh?"

"Up to no good, I'd say."

"Does he come in here?" I asked. "Is he sociable?"

"Not he. Don't drink. Some religious thing, I hear."

"Still," said Bert. "He's pleasant enough, I will say. Polite and keeps himself to himself."

"Well, that's something," I said. I wiped my mouth with the back of my hand and ordered another round for my new friends. Oh, they were so happy to include me in their little coterie. Any

Englishman can be had for the price of a pint. Half a pint if his straits are bad enough.

I stayed another couple of hours, insisted on buying yet another round, and finally made an exaggerated stumble out the door a little past eleven. A shame Mr Amun did not frequent the public house. I hoped Watson had had a better evening.

Not until I reached Baker Street did I realise anything was amiss. Kevin was on the doorstep and he sprang up the moment he spotted me.

"We've been searching all over for you, Mr 'olmes," he said.

"Why, what has happened?"

"It's Dr Watson, sir. 'e's been attacked."

18

Kevin and some of the other boys had managed to get Watson back to Baker Street. Mrs Hudson telephoned Stamford from St Bartholomew's Hospital, and he was tending my friend when I tumbled into the living room.

"Watson!" I cried. "Dear God, what has happened?"

"Nothing much," my friend replied. He tried to give me a grin, but winced. There was a stomach-churning amount of blood around his head and neck.

Stamford said, "Sit down there, Mr Holmes. I would not have thought you were the sort of man to be squeamish at the sight of a little blood."

"A little," my mouth was so dry I could scarcely speak. "A little, do you say?"

"It looks worse than it is," Watson said. I know him too well to be fooled by that stoic tone.

"That is true," the surgeon said. He finished treating the wound, a gash on my friend's left parietal area, and applied a clean bandage. "Good thing you were wearing a hat," he said. He and Watson laughed. Laughed!

"Oh come, Holmes," Watson said. "You need not look so stricken. It is a cut and it has bled a fair bit, but no real harm done. As you see, I am alert. I have all my faculties… What was your name again?"

"Most amusing," I lied.

"I am afraid your friend's sense of humour has failed him for the moment," Stamford said. He rose and put his instruments back in his medical bag. "If he were any other man I'd say he was worried about you. Well, I shall head off, if you don't mind.

My wife doesn't like it when I'm out too late." He squeezed my shoulder. "He's really not so bad, you know, Mr Holmes. I shouldn't worry. A dozen stitches, no more."

"A dozen…"

"Good thing I have such a hard head, isn't it, Stamford?"

"Always knew you were hard-headed, Watson," the other replied. "Now we have the evidence of it. Hard evidence, you might say." He cackled. "Yes, well, I must be off. Give me a call if you need anything. Cheer up, Holmes. It could be much worse, you know."

"I do know."

After he left, Watson and I sat in silence for several minutes. He was lying back with his eyes closed and a compress on his forehead.

The door opened and Mrs Hudson flittered in. Not an easy thing to do with a full tea tray, but she managed.

"What is this city coming to?" she demanded, "When a respectable gentleman cannot walk down the street without being accosted by vagabonds and varmints."

"Varmints?" Watson opened one bloodshot eye to look at her. "You've been reading those Western stories again, haven't you, Mrs Hudson?"

"Ooh!" She set the tray down on the table with a clatter. "You're as bad as he is," she said. I could not tell if the admonishment was for Watson or for me, but we both said, as on cue, "Thank you."

She fled, her hands over her ears to try to block out the sound of our laughter.

"Cup of tea, Watson?" I said. I poured and handed him the cup.

His hand trembled slightly as he took it. The first sign of how traumatised he really was.

"Steady, old chap," I said. I helped him with the cup and, after a few mouthfuls, he was able to manage on his own.

"You might find a cup beneficial yourself," he said at last. "Or perhaps you've had enough beer to satisfy all thirst?"

"For at least a week," I agreed. I refilled his cup and said, "What happened?"

"Well, I stayed in the restaurant for a couple of hours then around half-seven I saw Jones leave. It was dark enough and there were still plenty of people about so I was sure he had not spotted me. I followed at a distance, though, just to be safe.

"He was obviously under the influence of his drug and meandered all over the street, bumping into people... I half-thought I should take his arm and lead him home, but we had agreed I should merely follow so I hung back."

"Good thing, too," I said. "I very much doubt this was Jones's first time to stagger home in that condition."

"True. In any event, he reeled up Shaftesbury Avenue then turned, first onto Coptic Street and then at Montague Street. It was still busy but it got quieter as we walked. I kept pace about thirty feet behind him. Do you know how hard it is to walk so slowly?"

"I do."

"Oh. Yes, of course. Anyway, at last Jones turned onto Woburn Walk and that is when calamity struck."

Watson took a breath and I refilled his cup. I bit my lip to stop myself from hurrying him on. He gave me a watery grin and said, "Poor Holmes. I must look wretched indeed to warrant this sort of patience."

I said, "Long experience has taught me not to bother trying to hurry you, Watson. Nothing more."

He chuckled, then winced and held the compress against his head for a moment before continuing. "Woburn Walk... That is such a delicate little thoroughfare; you know it well, Holmes. I remember thinking it was a rather more elegant residence for a man like Jones than I'd have suspected. That's the last clear thought I do have. It's all a bit of a jumble...

"I remember a man leaping out of nowhere—I think he must have been following me as I was following Jones—and I heard the sound of a gunshot. Everything turned red and Jones collapsed like a broken marionette. Then what...? Oh, I remember I gave a cry and lunged at the assailant. I don't think he expected that for he dropped his weapon. I had him. I had my hands on him, Holmes..."

The tremor became more pronounced but this time it was from fury.

"Who was it, Watson? Did you see his face?"

"Oh yes, I saw him clearly enough, Holmes. That is something I shall never forget. It was Rickman... The fellow who calls himself Rickman. He's a big chap. Well, you remember, and he easily knocked me down to the ground and began kicking me."

He rubbed his head. I swallowed my fury. I swallow it again now, remembering. Fury will not help my friend, not yet. But the time will come.

"He would have finished me off, Holmes, I have no doubt of it. I remember his boot in my face and the pain and feeling sick. I remember thinking I must have a concussion... Silly, that. A doctor diagnosing himself." His laugh was void of all humour.

"I'm surprised he did not finish the job…" I said. "Forgive me. I meant—"

"No need to apologise, Holmes. I know what you meant. There's no doubt in my mind that he fully intended to kill me and would have done so if Kevin hadn't shown up. That boy… Oh, you should have seen him, Holmes, you would have laughed."

"I doubt it."

"Poor Holmes. Sit down please; it hurts my neck to look up at you. That's better. Well, Kevin arrived out of nowhere—I assume he was keeping an eye on me? Yes, I thought so. He blew his whistle and then he pulled out his catapult and hit my assailant right on the head with a stone. The villain howled and bolted. It was such a sight…" He laughed, a proper laugh, followed by a groan.

"The commotion drew people out into the street. No one did anything, of course, though I think someone must have gone to call the police, or perhaps they heard the whistle…

"What then…? I cannot really remember. The next thing I recall is Lestrade asking me if I was all right…"

"Rickman?"

"Fled, I gather. Lestrade was pretty hot about it, too. 'You had your hands on him, Doctor…' he kept saying. I'm not sure what point he was making."

"I hope he wasn't blaming you for Rickman's escape."

"No… I don't think so. Does it matter?"

I bit back the retort that sprang to my lips and said mildly, "No, not at all."

He gave me a look and I saw that, even wounded as he was, his faculties were intact. "It would be unfair, that's all… What is Jones's condition, do you know?"

"Dead."

Watson finished the last of the tea, tried to put the cup back in the saucer, and failed. I took the cup from him and. without looking at him, said, "Why did you not send for me?"

"Why? There was nothing you could have done. I'd already failed…"

"Failed? My dear fellow, how can you say so?"

"You gave me one job, Holmes. Keep Jones alive. Jones is dead. Ergo, I failed."

"You identified his killer. You were able to give an account to Lestrade. Most importantly of all, you stayed alive."

He shook his head. For the first time in our long association, I saw my friend was at the end of his tether. He would not weep. He is, as he often reminds me, a military man. However, his nerves are shattered. I fear he shall relive the battle of Maiwand tonight in his nightmares.

I settled him in bed, tucked him in like a Nightingale, and offered to stay with him.

"Oh, do go away, Holmes," he said crossly. "I am not a child. A good night's sleep shall set me to rights."

And so he sleeps. I have left his door ajar and have made up a bed on the couch in case he should need me during the night. But first, I went downstairs to the hallway and made a telephone call.

19

Friday 6 May 1898

It has been a long day and I am weary but I shall write a few notes before I lie down to sleep.

This morning after breakfast, Watson and I took the train to Sussex. Beatrice was delighted to have us join her little party, and sent a carriage to collect us at the station.

After so much talk about 'the cottage', I was astonished to find it was, in fact, a large fifteenth-century manor. Richard the Third had not met his fate on Bosworth's field when this building was erected.

"Why on earth do you call it a cottage?" I said. "It is as stately a home as any I have ever seen."

"It was my father's name for it. A jest. I suppose it stuck."

My wife has a knack for timing; for knowing when a thing may be done and when it should not. This talent was very much in evidence upon our arrival. While my instinct would have been to bundle Watson off to bed, Beatrice suggested luncheon in the morning room. And so we sat, B and Watson and Mycroft and I, with excellent food before us and the sparkling sea in the distance. We sat and talked about civilised things: music, art, and history.

"Elizabeth slept here before she was queen," Beatrice said. "So did Sir Walter Raleigh—though my father assured me it was not at the same time."

"It is a charming building, Sherlock," Mycroft said. "I have not had a chance to explore the whole thing yet. Perhaps you will join me later?"

"I should be delighted," I said, "But Beatrice may prefer to give us the grand tour?"

"I shall do nothing of the sort," she said. "Half the fun of exploring a place like this is the unexpected discovery. My presence would rob you of that. Besides, I promised the boys I'd take them to the beach."

"Where are those boys?" I asked.

"Tommy is practicing the piano. He has a natural talent, Sherlock. I really cannot believe how quickly he has mastered the basics. And Billy went horse riding with young Jessup, the groundskeeper's son."

"Horse riding? Those boys will never be able to readjust to London after all these treats."

Her eyes stared out the window towards the clear grey water. "Then I shall have to readjust London to accommodate them."

The rest of the day passed very pleasantly. Watson took a long nap and seemed much improved when he awoke. Mycroft and I spent several hours exploring the house, and vastly entertaining it was, too. Not once did he limp or seem unwell. He easily kept pace with me as we climbed staircases, examined the gallery, and discovered the many nooks and crannies that seem to exist merely to entertain small boys. Or grown men who have retained much of their childhood.

As we explored the garden—I was astonished that my brother did not protest either the fresh air or the exercise—I told him about the recent happenings in the case.

"Beatrice told me when you called," he said. "Thank heaven your friend Watson is such a stout fellow. A lesser man might not have survived."

"True, though I doubt he sees it that way."

"Are you sure… Forgive me, but are you sure bringing him here was the wisest course of action?"

"He needs time to recuperate. Not to mention I need to know he is safe."

"He is a military man, Sherlock. Safe is the last thing he would ever want. He and your wife have that in common. I must say, I was surprised enough that you persuaded Beatrice to leave the city. She is not a woman who likes sitting idle, I think."

"No, she is not. But how can I work, Mycroft, if I am forever worried about the people I—" I broke off and amended, "The people who matter to me?"

His shrewd eyes softened. "Don't misunderstand me, brother dear," he said. "I am not criticising. I'm just a little concerned these people who, yes, love you, will set their own feelings and interests aside to accommodate you. They came here without demur because they would not cause you a moment's worry."

"It is not forever," I said. The garden was a pleasant sight. Forget-me-nots blanketed the ground almost to the water's edge; roses and sweet peas and lilac presented a sight far too jolly for this dismal conversation.

We headed for the folly and sat there for a while listening to the sound of the trees and the distant gurgle of the sea. I would never admit such a thing to Watson, but there are times when the peace of the country is preferable even to London.

"Well," I said. "I shall give Watson a few days to rest then he may return to the city if he wishes."

"You might consider staying here, too, my dear fellow," Mycroft said. "Do you think you're the only one to worry about the safety of his loved ones? Would it hurt so much if you were to stay a short while?"

I pondered aloud: "Lestrade is scouring the city for Rickman. I spoke with Glaser last night and all seems quiet in Hatton Garden. He and young Stevens have developed a bond and I have no doubt they can keep the diamond district safe without my help. No, you are right. A few days away from London should not hurt. Furthermore, I concede that Watson would probably feel less guilty if I were to stay here, too. I do not suppose Beatrice will mind."

Mycroft grinned at me. "I dare say the girl can put up with you if we can."

Both Watson and Beatrice managed to keep their relief at my change in plans to little more than a ripple. "Do you good, old man," Watson said. "You've been looking a bit peaked. A break will set us both to rights."

Beatrice smiled and said, "Whatever you like, my dear." Something in the way she said the words made me realise she and Mycroft had planned this between them. I hate being managed, even when it is for my own good. Still, I have been out-manoeuvred and by experts. I can only bow in the face of such expertise.

As I made my way down to the dining room, I spotted a familiar face. "Daisy?" I said. "I did not expect to see you here."

"Oh, hullo, Mr Holmes," she said. "Her ladyship called and asked if I'd like to make a bit of extra money helping out here for a few weeks. It's a larger party than she is used to and she was glad of the help. Good for me, too, sir. With Maurice and me saving for the wedding the little extra is a big help."

"I'm sure it is. When are you and Stevens getting married?"

"This August, Mr Holmes; I do hope you'll come to the wedding, you and her ladyship." We reached the main hallway and she indicted the great double doors to our left.

"Well, here we are, Mr Holmes. That's the dining room through there."

As I turned to leave she added, "By the way, I wanted to thank you, sir."

"Thank me? For what?"

"For suggesting Maurice to Inspector Glaser. He's learning ever so much and he idolises the inspector. 'Smartest man in all of England saving Mr Holmes himself,' he said."

"Glaser seems quite taken with your fiancé, Daisy. I'm glad the arrangement is working out for both of them."

Saturday 7 May 1898

Beatrice's old friends Edward Davenport and Julia Simms from Rillington Manor arrived this morning. B had invited them for the weekend before I invited Watson and myself. It is fortunate this 'cottage' has so many bedrooms.

I never had the pleasure of meeting Davenport at Rillington Manor; he had been discharged long before I arrived to investigate that sordid case. Beatrice says her friends are greatly improved in health and appearance. "Life at Rillington Manor was difficult, I know," she said. "But were it not impossible outside a story book I should vow they are both ten years younger."

Mr Davenport's tavern has been doing excellent business and he has been able to hire three men. Miss Simms tends to the lodging side of things.

"I cannot think why I did not leave service sooner," the former butler told me. "Of course, none of it would have been possible without Lady Beatrice's assistance. She gave me the money to set up my business. She is the kindest woman in all the land. Always was, even when she was a child."

They are both intelligent, well-informed people and have known B all her life. It is obvious there is a great deal of affection among them.

Over dinner, we enjoyed as lively a conversation as I have ever experienced. B, in green silks, is delighted to have all her friends under one roof.

"May I ask about your work, Mr Holmes?" Davenport asked. "I confess I was very jealous when Julia told me all about your case at Rillington Manor—though I was well out of that place, to be sure. All the same, I should have loved to see you work."

"Thank you," I said. The man really is as bright as Watson told me. "It was not a particularly challenging case, though there was little enough to go on at the start."

"Holmes's new case is not without interest," Watson piped up. "'The Case of the Camden Poltergeist', I call it."

"What's a polter... pol... that thing?" Billy said.

"A poltergeist," Julia said, "is a mischievous spirit. They move objects."

"A ghost," Tommy said, indifferently.

"Have you ever seen a ghost?" Davenport asked him.

The boy shrugged. "London's full of 'em."

"Indeed," Julia said. "How did you get involved in such an odd case, Mr Holmes?"

"All of Holmes's cases are odd," Watson said. "Or he wouldn't be interested. But this one came by way of a friend of Mr Mycroft Holmes."

"Good thing he knew you then, Mr Holmes," said Tommy. "If you had to look into every haunting in London you'd never have a day off."

We all laughed and there followed a conversation about famous hauntings around the city. Julia Simms is something of an expert on the subject. After a very short time it became tedious.

"What news from France?" Watson asked B, seeing me flag. "Have you heard from your old friend, M Zola?"

"He writes now and then," she said. "His second trial is due to start in a couple of weeks."

"And this time they will be sure that the charges stick," Mycroft said. "It is a damned mess. I beg your pardon."

She waved away his apology. "No, you are quite right: it is a damned mess. There is blood on the streets of Paris, indeed all over France, and in the meantime, Captain Dreyfus languishes on Devil's Island."

"Devil's Island, miss?" Billy said. The name of that wretched place had caught his imagination.

"It is a dreadful place," Watson said in a fiendish voice. "An island in French Guiana. It is a gaol with the most terrible conditions. Prisoners are treated as little more than animals."

The two boys stared with open mouths and wide eyes.

"A terrible place for a guilty man," Beatrice said. "But how much worse when the man is innocent?"

"Who, miss?"

"Alfred Dreyfus. It is complicated... Well, you are intelligent young men. I shall try to explain." She set down her fork and sipped a mouthful of wine before continuing.

"The French had reason to believe there was a spy selling their secrets to other countries. Captain Dreyfus was an officer in the French army and suspicion fell on him."

"Why him, miss?" Tommy said. "There must have been some reason he was suspected."

"There was," I said. "He is a Jew."

The boys looked at me blankly.

"Your confusion is understandable," Mycroft said. "It is a stupid reason—no reason at all, in fact. But based on little more than the man's religion, Dreyfus was arrested."

Tommy and Billy exchanged a glance.

Julia said, "You mustn't worry, boys. Such a thing could never happen here."

Billy gave her an amused look and said, "'Course it could."

After dinner, we adjourned to the music room. Beatrice played for a while and then asked Tommy to play.

I gritted my teeth and gave my wife a reproachful look. All very well to encourage the lad, to teach him the rudiments of music, but did we have to be subjected to his plonking? I was, however, pleasantly surprised by the boy's skill. Clumsy and uncertain he may be, but I could see the promise my wife recognised. I just wish he had played another tune. *Amazing Grace* is not a happy song for me. In my childhood, it represented those wretched Sundays in a dreary church away from those things a boy would prefer to do: climb trees, steal eggs, and torment his brother. Later, the organist played it at my father's funeral and I have detested it ever since.

The words of the song came back to me:

I once was lost but now I'm found
Was blind, but now I see ...

I wonder what made Beatrice select that particular song. Does she know how well it applies to me? No, she has never seen me as lost or blind. I glanced up and saw her bright eyes studying me, anxious for my approbation of her student; amused at my reverie. I smiled and thought again of one verse:

Yes, when this flesh and heart shall fail,
And mortal life shall cease;
I shall profess, within the vale
A life of joy and peace.

Well, something to aspire to, anyway.

The last notes ended and we made a show of applauding appreciatively.

"This in one week, Sherlock," Beatrice said. "Can you imagine?"

"You are a music prodigy, Tommy," I said.

"I can't read the notes yet, but I'm learning, aren't I, miss?"

"You are. Most certainly you are." She beamed at him and he blushed. "He is a very diligent student, you know. He practices for hours every day."

Billy yawned. "Can we go and say goodnight to the horses now? C'mon Tom-Tom. Race you to the stables."

Monday 9 May 1898

The Davenports returned to London this morning and Mycroft removed himself to Beatrice's library to work. Watson took the boys out for a hike along the coast: "Good sea air. It'll do us good," he said.

B and I spent an enjoyable day talking, walking around the garden, and being alone together as has happened so rarely since our return from the Continent.

Such joy.

20

Monday 16 May 1898 - London

Watson and I arrived back in Baker Street a little after two. He is in much better spirits and has completely recovered from his injuries. I left him to unpack and indulge Mrs Hudson's need for gossip, while I took a cab to Scotland Yard.

In recent years, I have observed a marked change in how I am greeted by the detectives and policemen there. When I first began work as a consulting detective, the policemen were suspicious and comments were disdainful. Now when I enter I hear, "Oh, Mr Holmes, how good to see you... Fetch you a cup of coffee, Mr Holmes? What can I do for you, Mr Holmes?" Watson finds this delightful, of course, and says it shows how highly I am esteemed by these men. All the same, it is a little embarrassing. What is worse than the, yes, sycophantic greetings are the whispers: "That's Sherlock Holmes, that is..."

Today I reached, as Watson might say, a new high in lows: One young upstart at being told who I was declared, "Really? That's Sherlock Holmes? I thought he was just a myth."

A myth! Ha!

I hurried through the aisle of desks and chairs to Lestrade's dingy office at the back. The inspector was on the telephone when I entered the room, but he waved for me to come in and take a seat. A moment later, he set down the instrument and shook my hand.

"Nice to see you, Mr Holmes. Can I get you some coffee?"

"Thank you, no. You look well, Lestrade."

"So, you'd like an update on that Rickman chap, I suppose?" Lestrade said. "Well, I'm sorry to have so little to report but the fact is I have nothing new to tell you. The fellow has vanished. Completely vanished. I suspect he's done a bunk and fled the country."

"Why do you think so?"

"Well, we have the entire Metropolitan force looking for the man. Someone like him, with such a distinctive appearance, surely cannot hide forever."

"Any man can hide in a metropolis of this size if he chooses, Lestrade. He may well be lying low until the hue-and-cry have died down."

"Perhaps. We shall not forget him though, of that you may be sure. If he is still in London we will find him." He opened a tin of biscuits, offered me one which I declined, and closed the lid. "I hope Dr Watson is feeling better?"

"He is much improved, thank you, Lestrade. I shall pass on your regards to him. Tell me, what news from the diamond district?"

"Nothing much. Glaser has it all in hand. He always does, of course. He wants to keep young Stevens permanently, but I don't know."

"You have other plans for my young friend?"

"The boy has the makings of a star and no mistake; seems a shame to waste him on the Jews. I want him to get as much experience as he can and he'll learn a lot from Glaser. But he'll be quite an addition to my own team in due course. Of course, Hill has his eye on him, too."

"Leave the boy in Hatton Garden for now, Lestrade. All my instincts tell me Rickman's interest in that area has not ended.

There will be more developments and you may be very glad to have two such exceptional policemen on hand when they occur."

"If you think so, Mr Holmes, then I shall of course take your advice." His narrow eyes glinted. "Any mistakes I've ever made in my career have been because I did not listen to you. Well, at least I've learned from those mistakes, eh?"

Belatedly I realised he was looking for approbation. I am not good at spotting these things and usually Watson has to give me a nudge. However, this time, and I think it is to my credit, I saw exactly what he was after.

"We have both benefited from our long association, Inspector," I said genially. I feared to say any more. As it was, the man looked like he might float away, so puffed up was he at my words. I anchored him with another question.

"What news of Watteau? I understand the jury convicted him in less than half an hour?"

"Closer to ten minutes, I should say. He is in Newgate and will face the hangman next Tuesday."

"I would like to see him."

"Of course, if you wish. But is it—forgive me—is it wise?"

"I will not rest easy in my mind unless I try. I have no great expectations of his cooperation, but perhaps he will surprise me."

"He's a villain of the worst order and no mistake." Lestrade stood up and put on his coat. "Come on then," he said.

"You mean to come with me?"

He looked surprised. "Of course... Oh, if you'd rather I didn't—"

"No, not at all... That is to say, I know how busy you are. But I should be delighted to have your company, Lestrade."

He was still so enlarged by my compliment he took my assent at face value.

And Watson thinks I have no social graces.

It did not take us long to reach the prison and, thanks to the inspector's presence, gained entry easily enough. There was none of the customary wrangling about whether I had any right to visit a prisoner. I must say Lestrade seemed happy enough merely to be my attendant. He has, after many years practice, learned to melt into the background and let me work. As he said, we have come a long way since the early days of our association.

We were led through the sour and fetid warren of corridors to Watteau's cell. It is as dismal a place as any on earth and I might pity any man who finds himself in such straits. Under normal circumstances.

This man neither warranted nor wished any sympathy. He was sitting on his cot reading the Bible with a sardonic expression on his yellowish face.

"Oh, if it isn't my old friend, Holmes the busybody," he said as I entered. "And who are you, sir?"

"I am Inspector Lestrade of Scotland Yard," said the policeman.

"He is my friend," I said. (I shall probably never hear the end of that.)

"Well, Monsieur," I continued. "So you face the hangman?"

"In time. Anything might happen. I might die in my sleep." He smirked at me. Really, he had no fear whatever. In other circumstances, I might admire his stoicism.

"Do you come here to hound me again for answers, Holmes? You shall have none from me, I vow."

"It was merely an act of charity," I said.

"Charity?"

"To give you the opportunity to clear your conscience before you meet your Maker."

"I do not believe in such things."

"A Maker? Or conscience?"

He smirked again. "Either one. Still, I am bored and happy to entertain you. I will not tell you who hired me, or what I was to do, but we may discuss other matters. Art…"

"Jewels."

"Ah, jewels… I do rather like a well-cut diamond. There is a newer cut becoming popular, the round brilliant. Are you familiar with it? Your Jewish friends could explain it to you. I am no jeweller but I dabble… New tools allow for greater precision. You might say jewellers are now doing for gemstones what you have done for police work." He laughed. "Some prefer the old European cut but I find it flattens the stone and does not allow for the same brilliance as this newer variant."

"Is that how you expected to be paid? In diamonds?"

"Paid? Who said anything about payment?"

"You did. You said you had been hired. One does not accept a job without first negotiating payment."

"Oh, very good! Very clever. I tend to forget, you know. I think of you as just an ordinary man but you are really nothing of the sort, are you? Not like the lapdogs who follow you around." He gave Lestrade a mocking smile. Lestrade, to his credit, did not react.

"Not that you're as clever as they think you are," Watteau continued. "You're not even as clever as you think you are."

"And yet here you sit in gaol awaiting death."

"Enjoy your freedom and your life, Mr Holmes."

There was something sinister in the way he said it, and I was revolted by his malevolence. I kept my features in check, however, and said mildly, "I do and I shall. Sadly, you shall enjoy neither."

As I reached the door, a thought struck me. I turned and said, "You are dying in any case. That is why you can face the hangman with so little regard. Why you offered no defence at trial. What is it? Liver failure?"

"Cancer." For the briefest of instants his stoicism failed him and I could smell his terror.

"Of the bowel?" I asked.

"It started there but it has spread. I am rotten inside, but then I think you knew that."

I cannot, even now, explain why I said it. The words spoke themselves. "Is there anything you need?"

He shook his head. The cell door was unlocked and he said, suddenly, "You should not have gone to France, you know. You make people nervous. Do be careful, my old friend."

With that, he turned his back and picked up his book.

As we left the wretched building Lestrade said, "You cannot take anything he says to heart, Mr Holmes. It's all bluster."

"Is it? And yet Watson only narrowly evaded death no more than a week ago. I have missed something."

"You?" The inspector could not have sounded more astonished. "I find that hard to believe, Mr Holmes." I was too deeply engrossed in my thoughts to pay him much heed. His yammering was just enough to irritate. Not for the first time I appreciated Watson's capacity for silence.

We reached Baker Street and I hopped out. I was halfway up the steps to the door when I realised I should pay Lestrade some compliment for accompanying me.

"Ah, thank you, Inspector," I said, returning and shaking his hand. "I very much appreciate your assistance."

"My very great pleasure, as always, Mr Holmes. May I ask what will you do next?"

"Next? I shall think. Goodbye."

Tuesday May 17 1898

I have not been to bed. All night I sat with my knees to my chin and my pipe dangling from my lips, yet no progress have I made.

There is a piece of this story missing. Some piece that ties all these strange events together: the Camden Town 'poltergeist', the murders in Hatton Garden, the deaths of Bashir, Jones, and Kidwell. In addition, what of the coins? No reputable Egyptologist believes in their existence and yet they seem to be at the heart of the mystery. Then, too, there's Watteau's hint about France. *You should not have gone to Paris. You make people nervous.*

Why should I not have gone to Paris? Whom do I make nervous? Those words seemed sincere insofar as anything that villain ever said could be called so. Certainly more than his well-practiced comments about diamonds. These are the puzzles that perplex me. Just when I think I have snatched them by their shrivelled spines they crumble into nothingness.

Why did Watteau put so much emphasis on diamonds? Almost I feel I am being lured to Hatton Garden, but for what purpose?

Where was I last sure of anything? Before Watson was injured… yes, I should go back to my thoughts of that period. I lost my way when I came back from Camden Town and saw all that blood. I shudder now to remember.

What did I learn that night? What was it that Watson's injuries shook out of my brain?

There was the African gentleman who moved into the area, who is so genial but so mistrusted for no better reason than his race. Tommy was right: England is just as capable of bigotry as any other nation.

I must see what I can learn about this gentleman, Mr Amun. And there was someone else new to the area, oh yes, the pretty blonde widow. If only Beatrice were here, she would do a fine job of following that particular lead. Heaven keep me from widows!

No, I must let Beatrice stay where she is, at least for the moment. At least I know she will not complain about her exile. Once she has committed to a thing she sticks with it. I received a letter from her this morning. She and Mycroft spent much of the day at the beach. The weather is pleasant and the fresh air is good for the boys. Quite a domestic arrangement they have there, with their food and long walks and intimate conversations.

Tommy continues to improve on the piano and Beatrice suggests I might teach him the violin, too, when they return to London. Me, teach violin? Does the woman not know me at all?

She has gifted me with a photograph, and a stunning work it is, too. She took it one morning when I was sitting on the Downs looking out towards the sea. I must have been completely lost in thought for I had no idea she had photographed me. The image is clear, beautifully framed, and precise. Watson, taking it from me, whistled and said, "If there was ever any doubt how that woman feels about you, Holmes, you have your proof right here."

"Whatever do you mean?" I said.

He smirked. He never lets me forget that he has an understanding of women that I shall never attain. "She has

246

captured you at your finest: The light on your face makes you almost handsome."

"Almost?"

He laughed and handed the picture back to me. "Where shall you hang it?"

"In my bedroom." He said nothing but I think he understands there is in that photograph something naked in my expression that I would not want visitors or strangers to witness.

In the normal course of events, I should like Watson to follow up on the widow, but I am reluctant to let him out of my sight. I think today we shall visit the diamond district and see if there have been any developments. Yes, overall I think that is the best course.

Wednesday May 18 1898

Watson is sleeping. Only nine o'clock and he is in bed. I forget sometimes that other men get weary. I am fortunate in my constitution.

We ended spending the night in Hatton Garden. The rabbi was delighted to see us, shook our hands, and commiserated with Watson over his injuries.

"You have not given us any new tales for some time, Doctor," the rabbi said. "I do hope you have not given up your writing."

"Not at all," Watson replied. "But in recent years Holmes has been engaged on cases that tend to be far more sensitive than in the past. There are stories and I have written them, but they cannot be released until certain parties are no longer with us."

"'Discretion shall preserve you; understanding shall keep you,'" said the rabbi.

"Proverbs," said Watson. "I remember from Sunday school. Wise words."

"And plenty more where that came from," the rabbi said, smiling.

Glaser and I sat in the corner discussing our work. Things had settled down and were quiet enough, beyond the usual petty crimes. We had been speaking for more than a few minutes when the rabbi's wife said, "David, have you told Mr Holmes your news?"

"My news? Oh." He flushed. "Yes. Rivkah and I are to be married."

"*Mazel tov*!" I said.

They all chortled. The rabbi said, "Are you sure you're not Jewish, Mr Holmes?"

"When is the happy day?" Watson asked Glaser.

"August eighteenth," Rivkah said.

The rabbi poured wine and we drank a toast to the happy couple.

"Where is dear Beatrice this evening?" Miriam asked.

"In Sussex…" I did not want to alarm any of our friends and so said no more.

"We hope you'll come to the wedding," Rivkah said at a nod from Glaser. "You and Beatrice and the doctor."

"We shall put it on our calendar," Watson said. He made a note in his journal then said, "Do you know, Holmes that's three weddings we shall attend in the same week."

"Three?"

"Yes, there's Daisy and Maurice Stevens on the fifteenth; Miss Simms and Mr Davenport on the sixteenth, and now David and Rivkah on the eighteenth."

"Oh, good grief," I said.

"An abundance of joys," Miriam said.

"You do not care for weddings, Mr Holmes?" the rabbi said, his eyes twinkling.

"Holmes doesn't care for social engagements, generally," Watson said.

"Oh." Rivkah looked crushed.

I hastened to say, "That is true as a rule, but I shall be very happy to attend the festivities of your nuptials."

"I've never been to a Jewish wedding," Watson said. "Is it very different?"

The conversation turned to things matrimonial and I sank back into reverie.

Later, Glaser took me aside and said, "You are worried about Beatrice?"

I admitted as much and told him everything that had happened since I had last seen him.

"I understand your concern," he said. "It's wise to have her stay in the country for a time. You do not think Lestrade is right, that Rickman has fled the country?"

"All my instincts tell me Rickman has not yet completed his task, whatever that may be. Watteau's smugness suggest this is not yet over."

"Watteau... When does he hang?"

"Next Tuesday, the twenty-fourth." I tried and failed to suppress a shudder.

"You are required to attend?"

"Required? No; but I feel a sense of obligation. Perhaps it is unworthy of me, but I will not rest easy until I see him hang from the end of a rope. I have not forgotten the great misery he inflicted. No, I must attend."

"And Beatrice? How long shall she stay in Sussex?"

I fought down a truly irrational annoyance. The man was not prying into my private affairs and yet I felt irked.

"Until I deem it safe," I said.

"Mr Holmes, if I have offended you—"

"You have not. Forgive me. I am concerned for the safety of my friends, for Beatrice, and even for those boys who have no idea what risks they take... I mean no discourtesy, Glaser. It is simply my way."

"I understand. I hope you know you can count on my help at any time."

"Thank you. I shall keep it in mind. Now, you were telling me what has been happening here."

"We trudge along the same as always. The same pickpockets, the same drunks, the same brawls. Only we do not have Mordechai or Bing..."

"There have been no thefts—major thefts, I mean?"

"No, nothing. We have been extra vigilant ever since those murders. The merchants are very careful with their merchandise, although you would not think it to see the cavalier way they conduct business on the street or in cafés sometimes."

"What happens to the gems when people go home at night?"

We sat by the window looking out into the street. Even off-duty Glaser never relaxed.

"Well, many of the merchants live above their workrooms. Not all, of course. Mordechai used the entire building for work: one floor for working metals, one for gems, one for design and so on, but he was exceedingly busy and energetic in his craft. He was one of life's learners and never happier than when he was discovering something new.

"But to answer your question, the windows are blackened out, as you observed, and are covered with bars. There's also the vault where the gems and metals and dust are locked for the night."

"I'm sorry, did you say dust?"

"Gold dust," he said, smiling. "Nothing goes to waste. That wasn't just Mordechai being parsimonious; it's standard practice for the jewellers. The dust from engravings and filings are all carefully swept up at the end of the day and are melted into pieces of gold."

"Extraordinary," I said. "You're a font of information, Glaser."

"Not really," he said. "I only know what I do from hearing Mordechai and Daniel talking about it over the years."

As if on cue, the door opened and Solberg came in carrying three glasses of wine. "Talking business, eh? I thought as much. Here, in case you get thirsty."

He handed us the glasses and we sipped the excellent vintage.

"So you and Glaser shall be related, Mr Solberg," I said. "How shall you like having a policeman for a son-in-law?"

"A policeman?" he said. "Not so much… But David? Ah, David is a joy. Listen, if it were up to me he'd have an honest job, but a policeman is what he is and I must accept that."

The two old friends laughed together. It was obviously a very old joke between them.

"My daughter loves him and he makes her happy, that's all any father cares about. Besides, he's the closest friend I have in the world so what more could I wish?" He hugged his friend and kissed his cheek.

"Just as long as you don't expect me to call you 'papa'," said Glaser.

Thursday 19 May 1898

I spent the morning with the Irregulars and then visited Scotland Yard. Lestrade was out but Hill assures me they are doing everything they can to locate Rickman. He shares Lestrade's opinion that the man has fled the country.

I returned home to a telegram from Mycroft. "Urgent business demands my return. Will call."

Impatient, I could not wait for him to telephone me and so I left a message with Gillespie asking my brother to contact me the instant he arrived. I tried telephoning Beatrice but she went out with the boys early this morning. Mr Fallon assured me her ladyship was in excellent health and would call me as soon as she returned.

Watson said, "He would not have left Beatrice unless he were assured of her safety, Holmes. You knew he could not stay in the country forever."

"I know, I know—" Still, I fretted and paced and fretted some more. Finally, a little after two o'clock, I heard the telephone ring and I leaped down the stairs to answer it.

Mrs Hudson gave me a reproachful look but I shied her away.

"Mycroft—" I began, but he forestalled me.

"She is perfectly safe, Sherlock, calm yourself. Surely you did not think I would just abandon her without first seeing to her welfare?"

"No, but—"

"But, nothing. I am sorry; I was rather enjoying myself and I did not take too kindly to having to return. Still, there are urgent matters that demand my attention. I can say no more than that, at least not over this contraption. I must also review some funeral arrangements. No, no, nothing that need trouble you. Lord Gladstone: We have been expecting it.

"As for Beatrice and those boys, they are all perfectly healthy and in excellent spirits."

"But are they safe, Mycroft? Fallon is a fine man but he is nearly as old as Gillespie…"

"I would stake Gillespie against any dozen men," Mycroft snapped. "And so would you. Those old soldiers are a treasure beyond all counting, as you yourself ought to know."

"Yes, but—"

"Beatrice keeps a gardener and a man for the stables. I have spoken to them and asked them to keep an eye on things. I have also had a word with the local constabulary and they are to check in twice a day. I really think you are worrying unnecessarily, Sherlock. The girl is no hothouse plant who will shrivel up in a tender breeze. She's very capable and, I may add, running out of patience with your mollycoddling."

"Mollycoddling!"

"Quite. Now, I really have to get back to work. This situation is very pressing. Goodbye, Sherlock."

With that, he hung up the phone, leaving me listening to the burr on the line.

21

Watson has been urging me to go for a walk. I think my pacing is getting on his nerves. I really cannot blame him, but I dare not leave the house. I am coiled with apprehension. I loathe this. This is precisely the sort of thing I feared all those years when I held the fair sex at bay.

At length, Watson left. I asked where he was going but got nothing more than a snappish, "Out!" for my pains. I do not know why I put up with him sometimes.

At last, at precisely seven o'clock, the telephone rang and I fled down the stairs to answer it.

"You telephoned?" Beatrice said, her voice full of laughter and disregard for my agonies.

"You are alive then," I snapped. "I had visions of terrible things."

"Why, Sherlock," she said. "You sound cross. Do you have an upset stomach?"

"Do I—what?"

"Because some mint tea will settle your digestion. Mme Chabon swears by it."

"Beatrice—"

"There are chemists' remedies, too, I believe…"

"Beatrice!"

"Yes?" she said mildly.

I took a deep breath and tried to even my voice. "I was worried about you. And the boys, of course. All of you."

"That's very sweet."

"It is nothing of the sort."

"You're right. You should be ashamed."

"Ashamed?"

"Well, I don't know what you want me to say." Now she was starting to sound vexed. "Really, Sherlock, your vanity, even by general male standards, is truly quite extraordinary. Do you have no faith in your brother? In me? I am not some doddering old fool, you know. I have sense and instincts and, when all else fails, I can run rather quickly."

I took a breath and released it slowly. "I am sorry," I said. "I did not mean to sound…"

"Like a caring husband?" she said, finishing my tardy sentence. "My poor dear. I suppose I am still not used to having a husband. It is not as if we have been married so long, though. You must give me some time to adjust. Besides, our agreement never allowed for affection."

"I know." I suddenly felt exhausted. "I apologise for that. It rather crept up on me."

"Silly goose," she said. Her laughter gurgled through the receiver and I suddenly felt lighter, freer than I had in some time.

"You forgive me then?" I said.

"For caring what happens to your wife, not to mention those boys of whom you are so fond? Do not try to deny it. There is nothing to forgive. Indeed, it is I who should apologise. I should not have been so cavalier with your feelings. Now I shall tell you something that will ease your mind, I hope."

"Yes?"

"I have not been idle as you seem to suppose, nor do I take my safety nor that of my charges lightly. To that end, I have sent several telegrams and the upshot is Miss Simms and Mr Davenport have agreed to stay with me for a week or two."

"Ah, that is good news. Davenport is a sturdy fellow. I am very glad to hear it."

255

"And there's more: Daisy has agreed to stay with me until her wedding. And," she paused for dramatic effect. "I spoke with David and he says he can spare Stevens for a few days. He says he owes you a favour or three."

"Oh, that is excellent. Very well done, Beatrice. I confess I feel a bit of a fool. I should have realised you would have it all in hand. When do your friends arrive?"

"Miss Simms and Mr Davenport arrive tomorrow morning. Stevens will be here on Saturday. Still, I should very much like to return to London. I suppose there's no chance of that?"

"Not yet," I said. "Lestrade is convinced Rickman has left the country. There has been no sign of that gentleman since he attacked Watson. Still, I should like to be certain before I risk anyone else. Come to think of it, I let Watson go out a while ago and I have no idea where he's gone."

"He'll be playing billiards with Stamford," she said. "I imagine your anxiety made you fractious."

"Fractious?" I said. "Not I."

"I must be thinking of another Sherlock Holmes," she teased. "Still, it would be nice if you were to apologise to him when he returns."

"Apologise? Whatever for?"

"For behaving in such a way that drove him out into the night. He was obviously cross."

I held my silence as my mind struggled between replaying the early evening with Watson and how my much-too-clever wife had perceived what had happened. She gave me several moments before saying, "He always tells you where he is going, Sherlock. That he did not do so this time suggests you were behaving in a rather fretful manner. You certainly seemed vexed when I called."

"I suppose you may have a point," I conceded.

Watson returned around eleven o'clock. He had, indeed, been playing billiards with Stamford. The chalk on his fingers and around the waist of his coat where he leaned against the table were sure signs.

"Well," he said as he hung up his coat. "I take it B is safe?"

"Yes, she is. I cannot imagine why I allowed myself to get so fraught. I am very sorry, Watson. It was wrong of me to take it out on you."

He blinked, sat down, poked the fire, and said, "She told you to apologise."

We looked at each other and laughed.

"Serves you right," he said.

"Serves me right?"

"To end up with a wife who so able for you."

I said, ruefully, "You are quite correct. I remember the Queen once observing that Beatrice would not be content unless she married a man at least as smart as herself. Beatrice replied that she thought she had overshot the mark. Now I think about it, though, I believe she did nothing of the sort."

"You are no longer anxious about her safety?"

"Well, less so, anyway. Mr Davenport and Miss Simms will be staying with her for a few days."

"Oh, that is good news. I am delighted to hear it. Davenport is a thoroughly reliable gentleman and well able to handle any crisis. It will be nice for Beatrice to have some company, too."

"And there is even better news: Stevens is to join them for a few days, too. I'd trust that young man over half of..."

"Half of?"

"I was about to say half of Scotland Yard. That would have been true in the old days but not so much in recent years. While there are still some fools like de Vine, the worst of them have left or have gained some sense. Even Lestrade."

"Now, now, Holmes. You always said Lestrade was one of the best."

"That was not saying much... But, no, you are right."

"Well, you told him he was a friend," Watson said. "He has mentioned it twice to me since. I suspect all of Scotland Yard has heard it by now." He chuckled.

"I shall never hear the end of it," I said.

"After all the help that man has given us over the years, I should say it was a very small reward. Well, I'm off to bed." He rose and said, "By the way, aren't you worried about Mycroft?"

"All of the government offices have secret means of egress. Anyone watching for him outside his building will be in for a long wait. I have also asked Gillespie to arrange an escort for him to and from his apartments. He is not happy about it, but I cannot help that. Oh, and I would appreciate it, my dear Watson, if you would not go wandering about on your own. You've already given me one bad scare."

"I don't need an escort?"

"As you never tire of reminding me, you were a soldier. You might keep your revolver handy, though."

Saturday 21 May 1898
A letter from my wife arrived this afternoon. She says,

My dear husband,
You will be pleased to know Mr Davenport and Miss Simms arrived this morning. I am pleased the weather is so congenial for their visit.

Mr D and Billy have been forming quite an attachment. Mr D is exceedingly well read and he seems to have very similar tastes to the boy. They spent all afternoon talking about Long John Silver and David Copperfield. In the meantime, Julia has offered to help Tommy with his music and has added the violin to his repertoire. (A foundation only; I expect you to lend style to his substance.)

We spent much of the afternoon on the beach. Oh, I wish you could have been here. I have never heard Davenport laugh so hard. It is hard to reconcile the sprightly, energetic gentleman who played ball with the boys with the reserved, controlled butler of the manor. I teased him about it and he said, 'Do you know, Lady Beatrice, when I was fired from Rillington Manor I thought my life was over. Now I am a successful businessman and shall soon be a husband. I cannot believe it myself.'

I had a letter from Rivkah Solberg and she tells me she and David are to be married, too. I am so pleased he finally asked her. She is a lovely girl and I believe they shall do very well together. I hope you will be able to accompany me to the wedding.

As you can see, we are very well looked after. I hope you, Watson, and your brother are equally safe.

With all esteem and affection,
B.

Monday 23 May 1898

A letter from Stevens arrived in this morning's post. He waxes poetic about the delights of the seashore, but adds that B is becoming restless with country life. As if there is anything I can do about it.

Billy and Tommy are well and headed off to Bodiam Castle tomorrow. Mr and the future Mrs Davenport are delighted with the boys and spend hours with them. Tommy's fondness for B grows daily. They all join him in sending warm regards, etc. Bodiam Castle. I do hope they'll be careful.

2.00 pm
News from France that Zola's second trial has begun. The post brought a letter from Billy with a few words from Tommy:

Dear Mr Holmes,

I hope this letter finds you in good elf health as it does me and Tommy.

Lady B says we should send you a word to tell you we are well. We is are keeping busy. We help out with the horses, least, I do. Tom Tom prefers that bloomin pianer. All day long he's at it. Plink plink plink. Sounding good but don't tell him I said that.

We went to a castle today. A real castle. With a moat and everything. It was great fun pretending to be nites knights and have sword fights and such. Lady B says we can be her knights. Tommy – he isn't half wet sometimes – got all daft and said he'd defend her to the death. Lady B says she'd be happy if he'd just wash behind his ears. Oh, we did laugh.

Mr D is that nice. He says I can stay with him any time I like. Good to know for next time I can't find a bed. Oh, and get this me and Tom Tom have bin been invited to the wedding, his and Miss Simms. And Mr Stevens and Daisy say we can go to their nuptials and all.

Hi Mr H. Tommy here. Just wanted to say thanks a lot for everything. I ain't never had a holiday, Billy neither, and we ain't never even seen the sea. Don't know how I'll manage when I get home but her ladyship says I can visit her any time I like. She's a proper lady and no mistake.

Yours sincerely,
Tommy and Billy

I spent much of the day in Camden Town. That is to say Christy Day, an Irish labourer, spent his time there. He went from door to door offering to do odd jobs.

The first door was opened by a bronze-complexioned young man. I asked if he had any work for a poor Irishman who just wanted to earn an honest shilling.

"I'm afraid not, father," he said. "I do all my own jobs around the house. But here's tuppence so you can get yourself a cup of tea."

"Ah, now, I can't take charity, sir," I said. "There must be something I can do to earn it? I can sweep up or clean your windows…"

He laughed. His teeth were very white and even. He said, "I admire your principles, father. Well, the weather's not so good for window cleaning, but if you like you can help me pack up some things in the attic."

"Gladly," I said as I shuffled into the house behind him.

"Very Christian of you, sir. Though perhaps you're not a Christian? You're not from these parts, are you?"

"I'm from Egypt," he said. "My name is Amun. And yes, I am Christian."

I shook his hand. "Christy Day from Dublin City," I said. "I'm pleased to make your acquaintance."

I followed the man up the stairs into a low-ceilinged attic. There were trunks and boxes and all sorts of odds and ends.

"*Yarra*," I said. "I've never seen such treasures. Are you a rich man, Mr Amun?"

"Not I," he said with an easy laugh. "These were all my mother's things. She died a few months ago and I've been putting off sorting them out. I really cannot put it off any longer."

We sat together in the cramped space and he showed me how to pack the various statues, ornaments and other gewgaws.

"Ugly stuff, isn't it?" he said, laughing.

"Well, not my cup of tea, anyway," I said.

"Speaking of tea," said a soft voice at the door. A young woman stood there with a tray.

The man rose and helped her. "My wife, Mr Day," he said, introducing us.

"Your servant, ma'am," I said, rising and bowing stiffly. (I decided Day should be rather arthritic.)

"Sit, sir," she said. "How are things going, Abram?"

"Well, well," he replied. "With Mr Day's help we shall be done by this evening."

The woman nodded and left us. We sipped our tea and carried on with our work. In a very short time, I learned that Amun teaches Egyptian studies at University College London. He has been living in England for nearly twelve years, married for the last three, and is hoping his wife will soon give him a son.

I asked about his neighbours but, alas, he refused to speak ill of them. Still, reading between the lines I got the impression it was not easy to be a foreign man in London.

As he spoke, I was struck by how guileless he seemed. He was affable, kind, and considerate. He made sure I, as an old man, got the most comfortable chair and he kept me well supplied with food and tea. He inquired into my welfare. Did I live alone? I invented a daughter and a grandson. How did I manage? It was not idle curiosity, either. He gave me the distinct impression that he was genuinely concerned for the wellbeing of all his fellow man. Delightful as this was, it did nothing to advance my case.

I turned the conversation to Egyptian myths and legends. My host was delighted to tell me about those old tales and for the next hour, he spoke of Amun-Ra, the king of the gods, and of Anubis, the protector of the dead. He told me about Osiris, and Isis and Horus, and held me spellbound. Not only is he knowledgeable, but his enthusiasm for his subject is contagious. Indeed, I was so transfixed by his lesson that I almost forgot my purpose.

"Such stories you have, Mr Amun," I said. "I suppose all these things happened millions of years ago."

He shook his head and said gently, "Not at all; only a few thousand. Man wasn't even on this planet a million years ago."

"I suppose all these gods were forgotten when Our Saviour arrived?"

In this manner, I brought the conversation around to the Church in Egypt and within a few minutes, Amun himself brought up the subject of St Mark and the coins.

He related the tale as I had heard it but somehow imbued it with a new life.

"And what happened, Mr Amun? Where are the coins now?" I sounded like Billy wanting more stories, which is rather how I felt.

"The story is just a legend, Mr Day," he said. "The coins do not really exist."

"Ah, do they not? That's a shame."

"Oh, some people believe in them and have dedicated their lives to looking for them, but they are just a story."

It was evident he had no illusions about the story, anyway, and we returned to our packing.

After a very generous luncheon, I asked if there were other newcomers to the area. Perhaps they might have some work? He suggested Mrs Portnoy. She is a widow lady who moved into Camden Town only a few weeks after he and his wife. She has two small children and possibly would be glad of a man to help her with some chores. Of course, as a widow, she probably couldn't pay much, but he would supplement any wages she could give me. It would be our secret. "The best charity is done without show, Mr Day," he said.

I thanked him and ambled down the street. I knocked on Mrs Portnoy's door but there was no answer.

22

I am restless this evening and cannot sit still. Watson says I am anxious about Watteau's execution tomorrow. I am unsettled, certainly, but I do not think 'anxious' is the right word. I pointed out to Watson that as a writer he ought to be more precise in his language.

"I will come with you, if you wish, Holmes."

I shook my head. "It is a measure of your friendship that you would make such a suggestion," I said. "I know you loathe the idea at least as much as I."

He did not press the point.

In truth, I recoil from the idea of attending so ghastly an event, but I feel I owe it to Beatrice. The lady, of course, does not agree.

"You know I expect no such thing, Sherlock," she said some weeks ago when we discussed it. "I would attend the execution myself if an outcry at a gentlewoman's presence could be avoided."

How far less squeamish women are compared with the male of the species.

Lestrade stopped by for a drink after dinner and asked if I still meant to go ahead with my plan.

"Yes," I said, "I must."

He nodded, sipped his drink. After a few moments he said, "Well, I shall be there at your side, Mr Holmes. This isn't the sort of thing a man ought to do on his own."

"Thank you, Inspector," Watson said, smirking. "I'm sure Holmes is very relieved to have a friend with him."

"You do not mean to attend yourself, Doctor?" Lestrade said.

"Holmes will find you more than adequate support." Watson said. "My duty is to the living, not the dead. Frankly, I think executions are an abomination. 'Thou shalt not kill.'" He smiled ruefully. "It seems my religious upbringing has deeper roots than I sometimes credit."

After Lestrade left, Watson and I sat in a morose—on my part, certainly—silence for some time. At length my friend said,

"What is it that troubles you, Holmes? Is it just the execution? That would be a perfectly understandable cause for distress on its own, but is there something more?"

"I do not anticipate Watteau's execution with any great relish, Watson. I confess I am dreading it; but it is not that, not alone. I am troubled that there is still no sign of Rickman. Beatrice grows increasingly unsettled in Sussex and it seems unfair to have her stay there indefinitely. Stevens is due back in Hatton Garden on Friday and while Davenport will do his best to keep our friends safe, I cannot help but be anxious."

"No, I quite understand."

"It is one of your greatest gifts, friend Watson. You always do understand and you never try to pretend otherwise."

"I need to stop filling your glass if you're going to say such nice things to me, Holmes."

"Ha!"

We chuckled together and fell into our familiar, comfortable silence.

A short time later he said, "How is Beatrice?"

"She is well. She says she is well, but I sense her restlessness. I cannot say I blame her; I should loathe being forced away from London for an indefinite period, particularly if it were not my own choice." I rubbed my eyes with my knuckles. "She tells me I should do my job and not worry about her."

266

"Well then…"

"She is only telling me what she thinks I want to hear. She wants me to be able to focus on my work without fretting about her safety. Damnation! The whole marriage lark is of the very devil."

He laughed most unsympathetically.

"Poor Holmes. All these years of treating women with disdain, telling yourself they are inferior, and here you are as much at the mercy of one as any other husband."

My mouth could not decide whether to grimace or grin and I ended up with some bizarre mixture of both.

"It is not funny, Watson."

He rose, swigged the last of his whisky, and said, "It's a little bit funny, Holmes. Good night."

That was four hours ago. I have heard the chimes ring two o'clock and still I cannot sleep. My mind cannot settle.

I would have tomorrow over. Today, I should say.

It is today.

Tuesday 24 May 1898

I slept wretchedly, which is hardly surprising. Lestrade picked me up in his car and we travelled together to the gaol.

Time seemed to stretch out like a long piece of elastic and then suddenly it snapped back upon itself. We waited in the cold, a small group of us, until the chimes rang out the hour. Or did the chimes ring later? I cannot seem to recall.

For all the death and destruction I have looked upon over the years, nothing has ever seemed more grotesque than this state-sanctioned killing.

Lestrade introduced me to the hangman, Mr James Billington. "Tha' need have no apprehension, Mr Holmes," he said in his Yorkshire accent. "'T'will all be over as quick and easy as you please. 'Tis a matter of mathematical precision." Watteau, it must be said, was surprisingly calm. He nodded at me quite genially, and climbed the gallows. His hands were strapped down at his sides with leather handcuffs. Billington, incongruously, asked if he was comfortable. Watteau smiled and nodded. His collar was removed with exquisite gentleness and this was tucked into his waistband.

Only when the yellow bag was placed over his head did Watteau's chest start to heave and collapse under the weight of his fear. Still, he made no sound. Not even when the noose was placed around his neck and positioned with the knot beneath his ear. Then came the drop and the twitch and it was all over.

It was horrid.

Lestrade handed me a flask and I took a long mouthful of whisky. I handed it back to him and he took an equal measure.

"Come along, old friend," he said, gently. "Let's get you home."

Wednesday 25 May 1898

Beatrice telephoned this afternoon: the Queen has asked her to attend Gladstone's funeral this Saturday. "I cannot refuse Her Majesty," she says. She tries not to sound relieved.

I suggested she stay at Windsor while she is here and return to Sussex as soon as the Queen can release her.

"That is a dreadful idea, Sherlock," she said. "Who is to look after the boys while I am freezing and starving in that monstrous old castle? No, I shall stay in Wimpole Street and they shall stay with me. I will still have Davenport and Simms with me."

What can I say? Should I be truculent? Overly cautious? She will do whatever she wills, whether I like it or no.

"Well, then," I said. "Come home. London is dull without you."

Saturday May 28 1898

Gladstone's funeral. I did not attend. The boys, accompanied by Davenport and Simms, are confined to Wimpole Street for the moment. Beatrice is surrounded by royal and state officials. I must trust they will do their job. While the Queen had no great fondness for the late Prime Minister, I suppose at her age any death is a reminder of her own mortality. She likes to keep all her loved ones nearby at such times.

Beatrice telephoned from Windsor half an hour ago to say she is on her way back to Wimpole Street. The Queen has supplied her with a carriage so she has refused my offer of an escort. I shall call upon her this evening and we shall dine together.

Dear God. This is my fault. I should have done my job better.

How? Why?

I am incoherent with rage and grief.

I cannot write.

This death is my fault.

23

Monday 6 June 1898

There is one thing I have learned this year. Something there is that is worse than attending an execution: Attending the funeral of someone... Of someone one regards.

We gathered at the Kensal Green Cemetery. There was a spitting of snow in the air, even this late in the year, and the sky looked bruised.

The usual inanities ensued. Prayers and the like. No one wept, at least not overtly. I was conscious of eyes watching me, wanting to assess my reaction. I would not give them the satisfaction.

As soon as the coffin was lowered into the ground, I turned and left before anyone could speak to me.

Tuesday 7 June 1898

It was almost dawn before I fell asleep and so my response when Watson shook me awake at eight o'clock was less than cordial.

"The telephone, Holmes," he said. "It is urgent."

Glaser's voice crackled on the line. "Mr Holmes? Mr Holmes? Is that you? It's Rickman... Can you come?"

I dressed in a hurry and rushed to Hatton Garden. Watson, silent, anxious at my side.

We hurried up the steps into Schwartz's workshop. A small, silent group met us and parted to reveal Avery Rickman. The thing that had been Avery Rickman.

The monochromatic light turned the scene into a tableau. That bench, the bench where I sat when I first came here, was overturned on the floor. One of the man's shoes had fallen off and lay on the ground in a puddle of urine and faeces. Slivers of sunlight picked out the hairs on the rope and the knots in the stout wooden beam. There, amid the pouches of tobacco, hung a grotesque thing: the corpse. The neck was unnaturally stretched, the face livid.

Watson pulled over a chair and climbed up to examine the body.

"Dead for hours," he said.

"Is it all right if we cut him down?" Glaser asked.

I nodded.

The body was in full rigor and when they cut him from the beam, he toppled like a grotesque carved statue, like a monolith from Stonehenge. The men laid him on the floor. I examined his neck and the beam. "Suicide," I said. "He brought the rope with him. There are fibres under his coat around his shoulder and under his arm where he carried it.

"Who found the body?"

"Daniel."

Solberg was sitting on a chair in the back room. His face was the colour of sour milk. The rabbi held a cup of cherry-sweetened tea to his lips, but the jeweller shook his head.

I pulled up a chair and faced the man.

"I am sorry to trouble you, Mr Solberg," I said. "I have only a few questions."

He nodded.

"Were you alone when you found the body?"

"Yes."

"What time was it?"

"Around half-seven. I am always the first in. I like to work when it is quiet, before anyone else arrives."

"And you have a key?"

"Yes. I've always had one. I was *Reb* Mordechai's manager and Leah saw no reason to change anything after he died."

"Leah?"

"Mordechai's widow," Glaser said. "She took over the business when her husband died."

"When you arrived, was the door locked?"

Solberg frowned. "I don't remember... Yes, it must have been. I mean, I would have been surprised if it hadn't and I had no sense that anything was amiss until I came in and I..." He swallowed. "I saw him."

Watson took the man's pulse and said, "You've had a bad shock. If there's nothing else, Holmes, I think Mr Solberg should go home and rest."

"Yes. Yes, of course."

The rabbi led the shaken man out. A short while later the corpse was removed. There was nothing on the body. No identification, no letters, no suicide note.

His clothes were expensive but past their prime. They stank of cheap alcohol and tobacco. He was well nourished and his soft hands were without calluses. His shoes were two years old and had been re-heeled twice. They were long past needing to be done again.

"A man who was once affluent but has come down in the world. His change in fortune is recent: You can tell by the age of his clothes and his shoes. A man who can afford tailoring and footwear of this quality will buy new when fashions change or when the garments show signs of age. He has not done so. The cut of his coat is excellent and was tailored to fit him; the sleeves, you see, are the perfect length, and yet you see the tear in the lining was repaired by someone with very poor sewing skills."

"A wife?"

"Perhaps. A woman, anyway. She has some rudimentary skills. No man would manage half so well unless he were a tailor, and then he'd do far better."

"That is true," Watson said. "Most soldiers can sew, but they only have one basic stitch. This stitching assays a style of sorts."

"She is not accomplished though," I said. "The stitches are uneven and there are no less than three drops of blood on the seam. She pricked her fingers."

A quote from something I learned many years ago came back to me, "By the pricking of my thumbs something evil this way comes," I muttered.

"*Macbeth*?" Watson said, recognising it. "It's wicked, I think. Not 'evil'."

I shrugged. "Well, he is dead, and by his own hand. The timing is curious, don't you agree?"

"The timing?"

"The day after the funeral."

"You think he was driven by guilt?"

"Have you another theory?"

"No."

In the cab, shaking. Even now, hours later, I cannot seem to get warm.

Watson said, "At least the danger is past now. It's all over."

"Over?"

"We got our man. Or, I suppose, he got himself."

"What about the 'Patriarchs'?"

"He discovered they were fake. Perhaps one of the reasons why he took his own life."

"Perhaps." It was hard to think. There were things just out of my reach and I wanted quiet and seclusion, a chance to put my thoughts in order. After several minutes, I roused and said, "Where are we? This is not the way to Baker Street."

"We're not going to Baker Street." Watson waited a moment then said, "You know where we're going."

I swallowed back the protest and made myself nod.

24

"Mr Holmes?" Julia Simms gave me an anxious look. I suppose my appearance spoke for itself. "Come in. Sit here in the parlour. Let me bring you a pot of tea."

A moment later Davenport joined us. "How are you, Mr Holmes? Doctor?" he said shaking our hands.

"About as well as expected," Watson said.

"Has something happened? I see that it has." He motioned for us to sit. "Just a moment."

Watson and I sat in silence. Outside, Pimlico was rattling into life. Shadows from the street passed the green concave panes of glass, becoming misshapen and not quite human. The inn smelled of spirits and sawdust. Despite the early hour, the place was immaculate. It was odd to find so public a place so still. It felt as if the building were holding its breath, waiting for its customers. Or perhaps it was I who was waiting.

Soft footsteps, a familiar foot, hurried down the stairs. The door opened and there she stood.

Beatrice.

Watson and I rose.

"You have news?" she said. She did not sit. She did not smile or even acknowledge me at all. I was a stranger.

"That fellow Rickman," I said. "He's dead. He hanged himself in Schwartz's shop."

"I wish he was alive so I could kill him," Billy said, bursting into the room. I have known him since he was hardly able to reach my knees and that was the first time I ever saw him weep. His face was blotched and his eyes bloodshot. I thought he'd been weeping for hours, perhaps days. Was he weeping at the funeral yesterday? Was that only yesterday? I cannot remember.

I was so lost in my own grief and anger I had no room for anyone else.

"So it is over," Beatrice said. "A shame he did not kill himself before he murdered Tommy."

Billy was sobbing. Beatrice put her arm around him and said, "Thank you for letting us know." Then she turned and left us standing there. Dismissed.

25

Tuesday 19 July 1898

Zola has arrived in London after being found guilty in a second farcical trial. Better exile than imprisonment, I suppose. Rickman's death has left me with too many questions. Watson suggests that the man became fixated on the 'Patriarchs' and was determined to find them. Once he finally realised the coins were merely a myth he lost all hope and took his own life. It is reasonable enough as explanations go, so why can I not accept it? No, there are questions that remain without answers and it is these that haunt me. For instance:

How did Rickman first hear of the coins? What led him to Mrs Prentiss? Why did he never find her copy of the translation? Indeed, why bother with a translation when the original was of far greater worth? Why did he arrange the meeting with Schwartz and why kill him? Why kill Connie Kidwell? Was it merely because she could identify him or was there another reason?

I have no answers. I suspect, but cannot prove, that Rickman was no killer, not to begin with. Was it desperation that drove him to such extremes? What set him looking for the coins in the first place? Is there anything to suggest the coins really exist? All the experts say no and I share their scepticism. Then again, experts have been wrong before.

I have retraced my steps. I visited Bramley and Sons, the auction house that handled some of the late Sir Nicholas Fleming's Egyptian collection. They knew nothing about coins or documents. They showed me the catalogue of items they auctioned and their buyers. I have been working through the list, visiting or writing to everyone. The reply is the same: They always understood the coins were a myth but if I find evidence that they exist they would be extremely interested in that information. Assuming provenance can be established, of course.

Camden Town offers no help. The elusive widow Portnoy does not answer, though I have knocked upon her door several times, always in a variety of disguises. Neighbours believe she had to take a job as a governess and has sent her children to live with relatives. Probably there is no help to be had there, but I hate leaving some lead, however tenuous, unexplored.

So the matter seems to have stalled and I am out of avenues. I have resumed some of my scientific experiments.

4.00 pm

One new development: A telegram just arrived from Sir Jeremy Jeffrey, the late Sir Nicholas Fleming's friend and partner. He says he has only now received my letter and will be happy to assist in any way possible. He shall be back in England next week and shall call to Baker Street.

Perhaps it is foolish, but I retain hope he may know something about the peculiar document that ended up in Mrs Prentiss's document box.

Watson tells me Billy and B remain in Pimlico.

Wednesday 27 July 1898

A case. A veritable case.

I received a visit this morning from a gentleman by the name of Hilton Cubitt. He has been troubled by a series of messages comprised of hieroglyphic figures that Watson, in his poetic way, has called 'The Dancing Men'. Cubitt seems a decent, guileless man. He has, as the saying goes, 'No harm in him'. His worst failing is a distinct lack of imagination.

There is no doubt these messages are a simple substitution code. I cannot give the matter my full attention at present. I am most anxious to speak with Sir Jeffrey and see if he can finally solve the mystery of the Coptic Patriarchs. Nothing much to be done with Cubitt's case for the moment anyway. It does not appear to be pressing.

Thursday 28 July 1898

Watson is looking into another minor case that has come up. I cannot find the enthusiasm to participate. The case is not very interesting and I prefer not to be distracted. The curious hieroglyphs of Cubitt's case are intriguing. I make slow progress with it. Too much on my mind, Watson says, whatever that means.

Saturday 30 July 1898

Sir Jeremy Jeffrey arrived this morning and gave me a full and frank account of Sir Nicholas Fleming's affairs. Sir Jeremy is a tall, stately person who would not look amiss leading a cavalry charge. He strikes me as a man of intelligence and integrity.

"I was Sir Nicholas Fleming's business partner for eighteen years," he said. "And we were friends for twenty years before that. I think I know his property as well as he did himself."

"I understand the distribution of the estate was divided between Brahms Antiquities and Bramley and Sons. Can you explain why that was the case?"

"Well, Brahms prefers to handle the larger and most expensive items; objects of great historical significance. The smaller, cheaper things—clothing, costume jewellery, and Nicholas's coin collection—all went to Bramley and Sons for auction."

"Coin collection?"

"A very unprepossessing set of coins from around the Empire. Nothing of any great interest."

"What was the oldest coin in the collection?"

"A George the Third guinea dated 1799."

"Nothing older? From ancient Greece or Egypt, perhaps?"

"It was a schoolboy's collection, Mr Holmes. Perhaps worth slightly more than the collections of most boys, but really its value was almost entirely sentimental. If you gave me some idea what you were looking for I might be better able to help you."

"I am trying to trace a document that showed up in Sir Nicholas's documents that went to Brahms Antiquities. The page in question was in Greek. Ancient Greek. It may have something to do with ancient coins."

He frowned and scratched his chin. "Nicholas had a fondness for ancient Egypt but he was indifferent to the Greeks."

"The document was written in Greek," I explained. "I assume because the Christian Church in Egypt was established by the Greeks."

"Ah, I see." He was silent for some moments then said, "Nicholas owned a few sculptures and artefacts, but not much. There were no documents, nothing such as you describe."

"Is it possible," Watson said, "that he had such a document and you did not know about it?"

He thought about that for several minutes and then shook his head. "I'm sorry, no. Nicholas was not the sort of man to keep secrets. One of his greatest joys in collecting was showing off whatever he had acquired. A curiosity such as the one you're describing—no, he would have been very eager to show me."

He smiled, remembering. Then a look of sadness came into his eyes. "Poor old Nicholas, I do miss him."

As he rose to leave, he added, "There's another reason why Nicholas would have shown me that document, Mr Holmes: He knew no Greek."

"And you do?"

"Indeed. I am something of an expert."

I walked him to the door and shook his hand. I said, "By the by, did you send any documents to Brahms Antiquities?"

"Yes, there was the inventory, a letter from me, a copy of Sir Nicholas's will…"

"And how were they sent?"

"How?"

"Were they delivered personally in a valise? Sent by post?"

"Ah, I see what you mean." He frowned. "No," he said. "Brahms picked them up himself when he came to oversee the removal of the items. The catalogue was part of the documents. They were all in a leather satchel, I remember."

"And who was responsible for the documents?"

"I was. I mean, I had some assistants helping, but I had the primarily responsibility. Obviously, Nicholas's solicitor took care of the legal aspect of things, and Brahms himself made up the catalogue, but I oversaw all of it, and I was present when the documents were put together in that satchel."

"And no one else had access to it?"

"I kept it in a desk in Nicholas's study and the drawer was locked. I'm sorry I cannot help you further, Mr Holmes."

Wednesday 10 August 1898
A message from Hilton Cubitt: He will arrive this afternoon. His train gets into Liverpool Street Station at one-twenty. He sounds anxious.

Excellent!

7.00 pm
Cubitt has been. More messages that should help me crack this code, I hope. It has some peculiar inconsistencies that challenge the resolution. But it is a relief to have something real for my brains to work on. All the vagueness and the oddities of the Camden Town case lead nowhere. I spent the afternoon examining the various messages and I am satisfied, yes, I really am satisfied that I understand what is at the heart of this Norfolk mystery. I have sent off a telegram and if all goes well I should be able to resolve this matter tomorrow.

Thursday 11 August 1898
No reply yet. What is keeping them?

Friday 12 August 1898
Still nothing. I grow restless. All my decisions seem to have gone awry of late. I want to act, yet how can I when I have no confirmation? No, I must keep a cool head and wait.

Mycroft telephoned and asked me to dine with him this evening. He made it sound like royal command.

It is evident he has something to discuss. Something delicate. I am in no mood to dance to his tune and so I shall keep the conversation to the food and the weather.

11.00 pm

So much for keeping the conversation to trivialities. I began well enough; indeed, by the time the entrée arrived my dear brother was quite vexed. Well, I am pretty short of amusements at present.

Once the waiter left, however, there was no deterring him.

"Whether you would hear it or no, I have to tell you," he said. "I have news which I believe will interest you," he said. "It may even assist you in resolving one of your cases."

I cut my roast beef. "Nowhere in London manages to get the meat this perfect shade of pinkness," I said. "I do not understand why English cooks are so unkind to a perfectly fine cut of meat."

"It concerns Beatrice," Mycroft said.

I did not reply.

He placed his hand upon mine and I dropped my knife.

"Why do you insist on blaming yourself for that boy's death? You are not responsible for the actions of a murderer."

"I gave my word I would keep them safe." The rage was hiccuping out of me and Mycroft seemed startled by its intensity. "I gave my word, Mycroft, and I failed."

"You did everything you could. No one else blames you, you know."

"Beatrice does. How can she not? That day, the day he was shot, she could not even talk to me. And she has not spoken one word to me since."

"She was distraught, Sherlock, and in shock. You both were. The two of you so wracked with guilt and grief you cannot face each other. Oh yes, she has discussed it with me. She thinks you will never forgive her."

"It was not her fault. Not remotely. I was the one who said it was safe for her to return. It would have taken no more than one word to persuade her to stay in Windsor, but I am so punctilious about honouring our contract I let her take an unnecessary risk."

"Everyone agreed Rickman had fled the country. It was a perfectly reasonable conclusion under the circumstances. You could not keep Beatrice under guard forever, you know. She blames herself because she thinks she said or did something to encourage those boys to wait on the steps for her return. That lad, Billy, keeps telling her she did no such thing and they were just looking forward to seeing her, and in the Queen's carriage too. Childish exuberance. No one could have anticipated an assassin shooting from a passing cab."

"Please stop twisting that napkin. You will have it in shreds."

I dropped the napkin onto my lap. "How do you know so much about it?"

"My dear brother, I have more than a few acquaintances in Scotland Yard. I have dinner with Bradstreet from time to time. He says Lestrade and Glaser are full of self-reproach."

"They are not to blame. All the evidence suggested Rickman had fled."

"Why can you be so forgiving of them but torture yourself for making precisely the same error?"

"Because I hold myself to a higher standard. Please, let us talk of something else."

Mycroft cut his beef before saying, "Certainly. That was not what I wanted to discuss in any case. I loathe these emotional upheavals. Very bad for the digestion. I wanted to discuss Zola. You heard that he was found guilty in his second trial? He came to London on the nineteenth with nothing but the clothes on his back. He brought some very interesting information concerning that Austrian fellow, Ferdinand Walsin Esterhazy."

"Indeed? Esterhazy was the real forger of the documents that sent Dreyfus to Devil's Island, no matter what the courts say. How so many otherwise intelligent Frenchmen should continue to have faith in such a scoundrel is beyond my comprehension. I remember one of his letters was published last year and he was quoted as saying 'I would not harm a puppy, but I would with pleasure kill one hundred thousand Frenchmen.' Yet those same Frenchmen would rather put their trust in him than in a poor beggar like Dreyfus."

"Oh, he's a thoroughly bad lot. He was suspected of spying before, you know. In Tunis. He tells people he is a Count. Lord knows why."

"There must be money in it. Everything he does is for money," I said.

"That's true. Well, it seems Esterhazy has been receiving payments from Maximilian von Schwartzkoppen."

"Ah, another man whose name was on that list of possible Porlock associates. Though as I recall, there was never any proof. I thought you had men keeping an eye on these fellows?"

"I have." The expression that flashed across his face was so swift no one but a brother would have seen it. Someone has erred and will face my brother's wrath.

He leaned across the table and in hushed, urgent tones, said, "This situation in France can no longer be ignored. Initially I had hopes, high hopes that Colonel Picquart's investigation would resolve the matter, but as soon as he began to make progress the wretched man was himself arrested on a trumped-up charge. Whoever is behind this affair will not let anyone get too close to the truth. There is nothing they will not do to keep their secrets."

"Well? It is an internal French matter you said, and so it is."

"Sherlock, you cannot be so naïve. France is not the only country at risk. The world's stage has changed considerably in the past few months. If France falls to civil war, the repercussions will spread throughout the Empire and beyond. I need you to go to Paris and see what you can learn. My friends in the statistical section of the French military tell me unofficially they would welcome your assistance."

"No."

"Sherlock—"

"When I wanted to go to France in March you refused. In fact, you made a point of forbidding me. Now you expect me to drop everything and rush across the Channel to do your bidding? No, no, Mycroft. I am not your puppet. I have other obligations. Send that chap who's so good at such things, what's his name, Mansfield Smith-Cumming."

"This is important."

"So is what I am doing."

His expression of displeasure has not changed since our childhood. The only difference, in fact, is my ability to resist it.

"Is it important, this case?"

"It is to my client." I rose.

"There is more."

I focused on buttoning up my coat. Well, one should be deliberate about even minor tasks. "Well?" I said as I slid the last button into the buttonhole.

"Zola has identified the man who followed Beatrice from Paris as Émile Casonne."

"Casonne?" I whistled. "Another man I believe was involved with that gang, though I could never prove it. He is Austrian by birth, I think, but has a French mother. Who has his allegiance, I wonder?"

"The highest bidder."

I tied my scarf and said, "I thought it curious at the time that he should follow Beatrice all the way from Paris and then vanish as soon as he confirmed she was coming to see you. I assume he returned to France."

"He did." Mycroft rose and came around the table to face me. "I have a man keeping an eye on him."

"I hope this one is reliable. Thank you for dinner, Mycroft."

"Beatrice and Billy are staying at Davenport's Inn for the moment. I am to dine with them tomorrow. Would you like me to pass on some word from you, Sherlock?"

I shook my head. "One word is too much; a dictionary is inadequate. No. No word."

I returned home to find two messages. The first was a reply to my telegram confirming my suspicions. The second, a letter from Hilton Cubitt with yet more 'dancing men'. The content made me quake. I do not want another death on my conscience. We must hurry to North Walsham if we are to prevent a tragedy. Alas, we have missed the last train and must now wait until tomorrow morning.

26

Saturday 13 August 1898

It has been a long and miserable day.

I arrived too late at Riding Thorpe Manor to save my client. His wife still lives, no thanks to me. At least I was able to save her from the gallows by revealing the truth behind the mystery. The true killer, too, Abe Slaney has been identified and placed under arrest. I suspect he shall avoid the noose; there is little doubt he fired in self-defence...

Ah, I am rambling. A combination of fatigue and distress.

I will say the local constable and Inspector Martin, once they accepted I was there only to help, were very willing to hear what I had to say. There is something to be said for being the 'elder statesman', I suppose. Martin seemed singularly impressed by my deduction that the window had not been left open a long time because the candle had not guttered. A very simple observation, but in my experience it is these simple observations that most people miss.

In the end, it was a simple matter to copy the code of the 'dancing men' and send word to the farm where the gunman was staying. He came promptly enough, believing it was his former lover who beckoned, for who else knew the code? Once he arrived, he admitted the truth and that was that.

Watson and I took the train back to London a little later than I had hoped.

My friend is still exuberant about the case despite the tragic outcome. He reminds me that without my involvement, Mrs Cubitt would be under arrest, assuming she survives her injuries. As to that, he seems confident that she will, in time, make a full recovery. He has visions of her taking over the administration of her late husband's estate. When I seemed sceptical that a woman might do such a thing he replied, "Well, Mrs Schwartz seems to be doing very well running her late husband's jewellery business. In my opinion, women are just as capable as men of doing anything a man might do."

At that, I closed my eyes and went to sleep.

Monday 15 August 1898

With the greatest reluctance, I allowed Watson to help me dress for the first of this week's three weddings. My friend tutted as I lingered over my choice of necktie, he remonstrated when I said I had not thought about getting them a gift (he anticipated me and has already bought some trifle from both of us), and he became almost apoplectic when I suggested it would hardly end all civilization if I did not go.

"Not go?" he spluttered. "Not go? Of course you must go. Why on earth wouldn't you want to? You like Daisy; you have great respect for Stevens…"

"I dislike these events. Could you not go and represent me?"

"Absolutely not. Finish dressing."

By heaven, the man can be exceedingly tiresome at times.

At last, we were ready and climbed into a cab. My stomach churned and I focused on some mental techniques I learned in Tibet. By the time we reached the church, I was somewhat calmer.

I was surprised to see so many people I recognised in attendance: Lestrade and Hill with their wives, looking very smart. Glaser and Rivkah looking uneasy but brightening when they saw Watson and me enter.

"Oh, it is good to see you, Mr Holmes, Doctor Watson," Glaser said, shaking our hands. "I confess Rivkah and I are feeling a little strange. Neither of us has ever been in a church before. Still, young Maurice is a good man and we could hardly refuse."

"It will be your turn on Thursday," Watson said. "Are you ready?"

"Oh yes," Rivkah said. She gave her fiancé a look I can only describe as triumphant. He smiled at her. Love. Such a blasted toxin.

As if heralded by the thought, my wife entered the church. She looked resplendent in blue silk. Almost, she shimmered.

Billy was with her. Not the Billy I have known since his earliest days; this was a youth on the cusp of manhood. Such a transformation she has wrought in him. He wore a morning suit and a clean shirt and tie. He hovered at her side as if afraid to lose her.

Rivkah waved and called, "Beatrice."

Beatrice stopped and managed a smile. Almost managed. She joined us and said a generic hullo to no one in particular.

"You look lovely," Rivkah said, kissing her cheek.

Beatrice said, "Thank you, as do you. As do we all. Sherlock. Doctor." She acknowledged us. For a moment I thought she would shake hands, but she did not even do that much.

The music began and we all slid into the pew and waited for the bride to make her entrance.

I have erased the service from my mind. It was like any other wedding: sentimental, excruciating. I vow the only wedding I have ever enjoyed was my own. What a day that was.

This one followed the usual course and we made the usual responses and sang the usual hymns. Glaser and his fiancée only listened but they seemed enchanted. Now and then, they stole a look at one another, once her fingers curled around his hand and I saw him smile.

Milan... other hands, other smiles, an equal share of joy. At that stage, we had been married for several months. Our peculiar arrangement that allows for mutual respect and support but no imposition upon one another. Nor had we made any, not then. What a giddy, joyous thing that early marriage was. Truly a bliss. No, bliss did not come until Milan, two weeks into our holiday. The opera and the carriage ride, her hand in mine, and that sudden, utter surrender to my long-denied nature. Intoxicating.

No, toxic.

The vows exchanged, the parson droned on about duties of husbands to wives and vice versa. I amused myself by analysing Lestrade's bruised left index finger and calloused right palm. His wife was wearing a new hat and kept giving him coquettish looks. It was obvious: she has just had a birthday. He surprised her with that hat. But why the bruised finger? Ah, he also gave her a picture and tried to hammer a nail in the wall in order to hang it. I smiled. He would be vastly entertained when I congratulated his wife after the service.

The organist began to play a tune and we rose to sing. Then I recognised the melody. There was a sudden sharp intake of breath and I saw Beatrice blanch. Billy stifled a sob. The congregation began to sing:

Amazing grace, how sweet the sound,
That saved a wretch like me.
I once was lost, but now am found,
Was blind, but now I see...

My hand of its own volition reached out and grasped hers. Beatrice squeezed it and though we did not look at each other nor speak, I felt the old affection reassert itself and the despair that has engulfed me these past weeks suddenly lifted.

The wretched tune ended at last and the service moments later. We gathered outside, but Billy pulled away and ran off towards the cemetery. Beatrice gave me a helpless look. I hurried after the boy.

He was sitting on a gravestone sobbing.

I sat beside him and put my arm around him. For a moment, I thought he would shake me away, but he just buried his face in my shoulder and wept like the small boy he still is.

"It's not right," he said. "It's not right…"

"No."

"'e was just a kid. A year younger than me. You know? Why'd they 'ave to play that ruddy song?"

"I do not know. Probably the parson selected it. Stupid song to play at a wedding."

"Very stupid," he agreed. He stopped weeping and I offered him my handkerchief. He shook his head. I used it to wipe my own face.

Billy took a crisp white square from his pocket. "Aunt Julia has me all sorted," he said.

"Aunt Julia?"

"Mrs Davenport. She said I might call her Aunt Julia. And Mr Davenport is just 'pops'. I'm staying with them; well, me and Lady B. We couldn't go back to Wimpole Street. Not yet. Every time we go there I see it all again: the hand at that carriage window with that gun; Tommy screaming for us to get down, then blood all over the steps and Tommy lying in Lady B's arms.

Poor bugger. Mind you..." He managed a smile. "I reckon there's no place 'e'd have rather died than in 'er arms."

"I think you're right."

We sat in silence for a few minutes. He took a deep breath and said, "We ought to get back."

As we rose I said, "I am truly sorry, Billy. I should have protected Tommy better."

He looked surprised. "Ain't your fault, Mr H. Ain't no one's fault but that bastard what shot 'im. 'E better not let me get my 'ands on 'im. I'll swing for 'im."

Back at the church, people were milling about, talking to one another. Lestrade and his wife were having an animated conversation with Beatrice. She turned and smiled at us, at both of us.

Lestrade said, "Lady Beatrice will be putting you out of business, Mr Holmes. Just now she congratulated my wife on her birthday. And how did she know that—"

"Because of your left index finger," I said. "Obviously."

"Oh, you're a pair," he said. "You ought to get married."

Glaser's laughter was infectious and we all joined in.

Later, as I walked Beatrice to her carriage I said, "I should like to talk to you."

"I would like that, too, but can it wait? Julia and Edward are getting married tomorrow and I'm her matron—maid—of honour. It will be a very busy evening and I should prefer to give you my full attention. Tomorrow?"

"Tomorrow," I said.

I am a patient man. But I wish it were tomorrow.

27

It was still early when we returned to Baker Street. Watson was full of the service, the vows, and memories of his own wedding.

"Mrs Lestrade is not at all what I expected. They're a bit like Jack Spratt and his wife: He's small and thin, and she's… big."

"True," I said. "And there's no doubt who runs that household either."

"Not just the household, she also runs her own business."

"Does she indeed?"

"She's 'Mrs Legrand'."

"I thought she was Mrs Lestrade."

"Oh really, Holmes, you must have heard of Mrs Legrand. She makes cakes. You know, those little teacakes that Mrs Hudson serves from time to time. Yet another woman managing a business without a man's input. Well, not unlike Mrs Hudson herself. You see, it does happen. You are surrounded by adventuresome women and ignore them because they are not men."

I said nothing and he changed the subject. "How is Billy?" he asked. "Unfortunate the parson chose that song. I think it must always remind us of Tommy."

"Billy is still mourning his closest friend. They were all but inseparable, those two."

"Terrible for him to see his friend die in such a ghastly manner. I am glad the Davenports are looking after him. Mrs Davenport is past childbearing so it is good that they will have a more or less adopted son. Good for everyone."

He picked up the newspaper and said, "Beatrice looked well, I thought."

"Blue suits her," I said.

He gave me a look over the top of the paper. "I meant she looked happy to see you."

"Did she? I didn't notice."

He shook the newspaper and it crackled. "We've just come from church, Holmes," he said. "Do you think you should be lying?"

"Anything in the paper?" I said.

He smirked and said, "More about the Dreyfus Affair. That Esterhazy fellow seems a thoroughly bad character. The word 'debauchery' seems to be attached to his name quite a lot."

"Oh, he is a fiend of the highest order, but he has influential friends who protect him, as the unfortunate Colonel Picquart discovered to his cost."

Watson tutted. "It seems endless. You really would not think the whole affair could continue so long, and yet on it goes with no end in sight. I suppose that poor beggar Dreyfus does not even know what a hullabaloo has been going on in his name."

"Probably not." I would have said more, but was interrupted by Mrs Hudson.

"Sorry, Mr Holmes," she said. "A gentleman left this for you a short while ago."

I examined the letter. A curious thing it was. "No envelope?" I said.

"No, Mr Holmes," Mrs Hudson replied. "It was dropped off by that tall, distinguished-looking gentleman who was here the other day. Sir Jeremy. He said he was on his way to the railway station and he suddenly remembered something. He thought it might be of interest to you and jotted it down on a page from his notebook. He said he'll be in Dublin for a few days before he heads off to America, and you may contact him there if you have any further questions."

"Thank you, Mrs Hudson."

Watson folded the newspaper and said, "Well, it's a good thing for this Esterhazy person that you were not investigating the case. You'd have it sorted in a just a few hours and then where would he be?"

"Yes, indeed… Watson!"

"What? Holmes? What did I say?"

"You've solved the case."

"What, the Dreyfus Affair?"

"Watson! My dear fellow, you never cease to amaze me. You are really quite astounding. Get your coat."

It was late afternoon and all of London seemed bathed in an apricot-coloured glow. It was a day for weddings, I thought, or for picnics in the park, for holding hands with a lover. Not for confronting an insidious enemy.

Watson read Sir Jeremy's letter and handed it back. "I don't follow," he said.

"Read it again."

My dear Mr Holmes, I just now remembered something that happened while I was putting Nicholas's estate in order. It was quite a small, fleeting thing, so I hope you will not think less of me that I forgot it until now.

I was finalising all the details for the auction, the sale, and so forth. It had been a long day and I was thinking about going home. There was a knock on the door and I was surprised to find a woman there. She was dressed in mourning and said she had

296

met Nicholas briefly and he had done her a great favour. She gave her name as Mrs Poole. She said she had only just heard of my friend's death and wanted to know the funeral arrangements.

It is only now, months later, I find myself wondering why she had not gleaned that information in the papers, but at the time it did not occur to me.

In any event, the woman seemed very distressed and for a moment, I thought she would faint. I left her in the study while I went to fetch her a glass of water. By the time I returned, she was much improved and she departed. I should add that the satchel and Nicholas's papers were on the desk.

Probably this trifle is nothing at all, but since you asked particularly about Nicholas's papers, I thought I should tell you.

I am afraid I cannot identify the woman. She was dressed all in black from head to toe, with a heavy veil. Oh yes, she wore an exquisite sapphire ring on her wedding finger.

You can reach me in Dublin at the Grafton Hotel until Saturday the 20th inst, when I depart for New York.

With sincere regards,
J. Jeffrey

"I'm still not following," Watson said. "This woman would seem to be Mrs Portnoy, the widow in Mornington Crescent. And I gather you think she took the opportunity to slip that paper into Mrs Prentiss's files. But why?"

"Why indeed?" I smiled at him. "Let me ask you something: When you saw her how was she dressed?"

"All in black."

"You said she'd been weeping."

"Yes."

"Did you see it? Did you see her tears?"

"Well, no… she wore a veil, a widow's veil. It's not unusual, especially if a woman is trying to hide her grief."

"Or hide her face."

I sat back and closed my eyes. We would be in Camden Town in a just a few minutes and I wanted to gather my thoughts. Watson, sensitive to my mood as always, fell silent.

We arrived at Mornington Crescent and I followed him up the stairs.

I knocked and called, "You will speak to me this time, Mrs Porlock."

A moment later, the door opened.

"Mr Sherlock Holmes," she said, "And his cretin of a friend."

"May we come in?" I was determined to be civil. There were still things I did not know and I hoped to beguile her into revealing all. I was hideously conscious of the fact that we have no evidence, not one jot, to incriminate her.

"Come in," she said. She stood aside and we entered a cramped room. There was a bed, a table and two ramshackle chairs. Through the uncurtained window beyond, I could see across the park and had a direct view of the Prentiss house.

The woman stood with her arms folded. Waiting. She reeked of malevolence and hate.

"Where are your children?" Watson said.

"Abroad."

"In Munich with your family?" I said.

"My only family was my beloved Albrecht, whom you sent to the gallows. My mother died because I could not care for her, since I had to flee with my poor husband. All that I had left was my brother and you drove him to suicide."

I heard Watson's intake of breath. "Rickman," he said. "Avery Rickman was your brother?"

"Albert," she corrected. "Albert Richman. He was a gentle boy, an innocent. Wounded to the very marrow by his sister's loss. There's nothing he would not do for me."

"Even murder?" I said.

Her smile was an evil thing to behold. "He wasn't a killer, not by nature. He had a good and sweet heart. Even as a small boy he adored his big sister."

"You wanted vengeance," I said. "You knew Gillespie's daughter was a translator; you knew she lived here."

"And once you discovered the Amuns had moved into this area you thought you could throw suspicion on them if Holmes came asking questions," Watson added.

"Well trained, isn't he?" she said.

"Animals are trained. People are educated," Watson snapped.

"Like I said, well-trained."

"Your brother was well-trained, Mrs Porlock," I said. "You had him court that unfortunate Kidwell girl so he could gain access to the Prentiss house and pull pranks that would draw my attention. You planned it so I would wait there in the dark for him. He was supposed to kill me that night, only his courage failed him."

"Not courage," she snapped. "He never wanted for courage did Albert. He was decent. More decent than an interfering busybody like you could ever understand."

"And when he failed you needed to make another plan. You could still make use of those fake Greek documents and the story of the Coptic Patriarchs so you had Albert contact Schwartz and arrange a meeting. You deliberately let your brother walk into a trap hoping it would end as it did, with him killing Schwartz."

299

"Ghastly woman," Watson said. "You gave your own brother a weapon and told him he must be prepared to defend himself. You set the whole thing in motion so he would become a killer."

"You needed Albert to overcome his natural revulsion of murder if he was to do your bidding," I added.

"That old Jew was a liar," she said. "He deserved to die. Him and all his kind."

The ugly plan was falling into place now: She had lived in Bavaria for years with her monstrous husband. She knew the story of the fake coins; knew about the Greek documents that supposedly confirmed their *bona fides*. Perhaps Porlock, himself, was behind the original scheme; or his friend and mentor Professor Moriarty before him. What a legacy of evil.

Frau Porlock could have simply shot me at any time, but that did not appeal to her sense of the theatrical. This whole charade was a plot to manipulate me. It was a game of chess that deprived me of half my pieces.

Zugzwang. Just like Mycroft's telegraph that drew me back from Italy, Frau Porlock forced me to act with no good options. But she did not do it alone.

"This time," I continued, "Your brother did not botch the job. At point blank range he could hardly miss, and fear of capture meant he would not fail. Was it easier for Albert to kill this time because Schwartz was a Jew?

"But he did not have a killer's temperament, did he? He had to fortify himself with alcohol. Then, in his panic, he murdered a policeman. This was unplanned and he was so affected that he vomited."

"Started drinking heavily, poor lad," she said. "That's on you, too."

I could not afford to bait her, not yet. I let the condemnation pass.

"The fellow's nerves were shattered and you could not depend on him, so you contacted your old friend Michel Watteau to assist. You promised him diamonds. Albert was supposed to rob Schwartz's workshop, wasn't he?"

"Damned fool," she snapped. "He panicked and fled."

"Watteau was willing and was efficient, but he was dying. You could not be sure he would live long enough to do the job. So you told Albert he had to redeem himself by killing anyone who might be a witness against you. He killed Demosthenes Jones, and attacked Watson. He must have been in such terror of you, that young man. 'Not very bright,' Connie said. He was no more than a tool for your use."

"If my brother ever did anything it was to protect me."

"From my blameless friend?"

"He's not blameless because he is your friend."

"What of Connie Kidwell?"

"He never laid a hand on her," she snapped.

The butcher's shop. All women. A man would stand out…

"No, that was you. You killed her."

Her eyes gleamed. The apricot light was turning to plum and long shadows turned her angular face into a mask. Her blonde hair seemed like flame. The entire conversation felt unreal.

I took a shuddering breath and said, "It was you who killed the boy. Tommy."

She smirked. Never in all my life have I so wanted to strike a woman.

"It would be better if it had been you," she said. "But hurting you works, too. A shame that gunman, whoever it was, didn't

301

kill her, that snooty bluestocking bitch. Oh, there would be tears aplenty then, wouldn't there, my dear?"

My fist was iron and would have flown, but Watson grabbed me and all but dragged me from the room.

"Come away, now," he said. "Come, Holmes. She's quite mad."

As he dragged me down the stairs, her voice echoed and ricocheted through the building. "You think we don't know about the two of you? You think we didn't see her spying for you in France? Jew-loving strumpet…"

"Holmes, come on. Don't listen." Watson had a firm grip on me, which was as well, or I would have throttled her and the devil take the consequences.

"She'd better watch herself," the harpy shrieked. "Next time someone goes looking for her they won't miss… And you had better stay out of my way or I'll make sure the whole world knows about the two of you. No corner of the world will be able to hide you then."

Watson half-dragged, half-carried me down the stairs. I had no idea of his strength.

That was four hours ago and I have not yet stopped shaking with fury. I despise these passions. Nothing destroys reason more thoroughly than pure—or impure—passion.

It was Watson who thought to call Lestrade and have two officers keep watch on the woman. No, not *the* woman. Irene Adler woman was a creature of integrity and possessed a certain nobility. This other woman is a monster of madness, of spite and of malice.

For most of the evening, I sat staring into nothingness as my mind sorted through the labyrinthine events since Beatrice and I returned from Europe. Yes, that is where it began. For all our attempts at circumspection, there are those who sense the bond between my wife and myself, even if they do not know we are married. Watteau, of all people, had dropped me that hint: *You should not have gone to France. You make people nervous.* That creature who followed B back from Paris and who vanished after seeing her arrive at Mycroft's office. What was that Mrs Porlock said: *you think we did not see her spying for you in France?*

Mycroft was right—at least I know he will not gloat over the fact—my presence in France and, later, Beatrice's sojourn in Paris did attract attention. Esterhazy, von Schwartzkoppen, and Casonne all had ties to Porlock and all were involved in the Dreyfus Affair. What terrors they must have endured when they saw B and me arrive in France. They assumed we were there to spy for the British government. They had B followed and saw her arrival at Mycroft's office as confirmation of their suspicions. They were happy to assist Frau Porlock with anything she needed so long as it meant I could be distracted from the Dreyfus Affair.

I see from my notes that matters became more desperate in May, presumably because Zola's second trial was pending. The spies feared that I would intervene. Fools! As if there are no men of intelligence in France.

When all the men around her failed, Mariah Porlock took matters into her own hands. She planned to kill Beatrice as a way of injuring me. Her notion of tit-for-tat: You cause the death of my husband; I kill your wife. But Tommy saw the gun and flung himself in front of Beatrice an instant before the weapon was fired. I doubt Mrs Porlock gave the boy's death a second thought, but it was the final straw for her brother. I do not believe it is a coincidence that he hanged himself on the same day as Tommy's funeral. And he hanged himself in Schwartz's shop in almost exactly the same spot where he committed his first murder.

Watson brought me a nightcap. "I do not want to interrupt your thought, Holmes," he said. "But it's been a stressful day and I think a single-malt might help you sleep. You can keep it until you are ready to retire," he added, anticipating my usual lecture about alcohol and its effects on the human brain.

I took the glass and nodded for him to sit down. I reviewed the results of my ratiocination. I find explaining things to Watson often helps me to clarify my thought. His knack for asking the right questions amounts almost to genius.

"I think you are right," he said when I finished. "But why did Watteau come back? He knew he was dying. Surely he wasn't driven by malice?"

"He was deployed by Esterhazy and the others, I think. They could not risk Frau Porlock would fail. He was their insurance. But Watteau knew he was dying; that is why he did not bother offering any defence at his trial. Perhaps he thought killing me would be his crowning achievement. Besides, he expected to be paid in diamonds. Rickman, Richman, I should say, was supposed to steal whatever gems and gold from Schwartz' workshop as he could get his hands on."

"But he didn't realise the jewels would have been locked up in the vault?"

"There were a number of things Richman did not consider: he did not realise Schwartz wouldn't put the light on. He did not anticipate the difficulties of getting around so confusing a building, particularly in the dark. What with the uneven floors, the irregular ceiling heights, and the labyrinthine layout, it is challenging enough in daylight. In the dark, in a state of panic, it was almost impossible. So much misery would have been avoided if Schwartz's plan had worked. It would have worked if de Vine were not such an indolent fool."

"One thing I don't quite follow," Watson said as we sipped our drinks. "How did Mrs Porlock know about Gillespie?"

"Her husband had me followed much of last year, as you recall. Very likely, his wretched organisation had a file on every one of my associates. Gillespie attended Porlock's trial; he had lunch with us during one of the adjournments. He is pretty well known in his circle. It would not have taken much effort to learn about his daughter. Mariah Porlock was looking for something outré, something that was guaranteed to lure me in. Alice Prentiss's translations, the arrival of the innocent Mr Amun in Harrington Square, and those old stories about the Coptic Patriarchs all came together in her terrible mind. It is curious, you know, that Tommy gave me one of my biggest clues, but I did not realise it at the time."

"He did? What clue?"

"When we had dinner in Sussex I was talking about the case and said I came to investigate it because Gillespie asked me. Tommy said, 'Good thing he knew you, Mr Holmes. If you had to look into every haunting in London you'd never have a day off.' He was absolutely right: It was my acquaintance with Gillespie that led me into this case. Without that relationship I would never have known about Mrs Prentiss or been drawn to that particular investigation."

We sipped in silence for several minutes, enjoying the quiet of the evening. Then Watson said, "What sort of a man could this Albert Richman have been? How could his sister manipulate him to commit murder?"

"There was a fairly large age-gap between Mariah Porlock and her brother; I suspect she abused and harassed him for years.

He was too cowed, too unintelligent to defy her, but he was not murderous by nature, not like Mariah or Watteau.

"By the by, after Watteau's discussion about diamonds I did some checking and I am fairly certain he was involved in a number of jewellery thefts in London last year. If you recall, Lady Dalrymple's rose diamond was one."

"Oh, I remember that case." He smiled. "You were outraged you could not look into it because you were so ill. I was seriously worried for your health."

"Thank goodness for Cornwall and—"

"—Healthy air."

"—Interesting murder." We spoke at the same time and I laughed. "We shall never take the same view of things, my dear fellow. And thank goodness. Who else would put up with me?"

"Well, Beatrice, for one. You made up your quarrel, I see."

"It was never a quarrel… I just felt so wracked with guilt, so sure she must blame me for Tommy's death. It transpires she thought I blamed her. What fools we mortals be."

"None more so than the unfortunate Richman. And it is a good thing for Mariah Porlock that Watteau died. He was expecting to be paid for his troubles and she's as poor as a church mouse."

"Oh come, Watson. Do you really believe she is destitute?"

"Well, her husband's estate was confiscated by the government. You saw how she lives."

"My dear fellow! Yes, Porlock's British property was confiscated, but he had a vast estate in Munich and assets hidden in many other places. Mariah Porlock does not live in Mornington Crescent because she cannot afford better."

"She picked it for the view. Oh, I am a dunce."

"You are nothing of the sort, my dear Watson. I have no doubt it suited her purpose to appear impoverished to her brother; it would inspire his sympathy. She even went so far as to sew up his jacket. You know, I am very grateful to you for getting me away from her before I committed some dreadful act."

"You're welcome." He rubbed his chin and said, "It was what she wanted, isn't it? To goad you into killing her."

"Good God," I exclaimed. "I had not thought of that. You are quite right, Watson, that is exactly what she was doing. What a revenge that would have been: to see me follow her husband to the gallows, my name disgraced. I am exceedingly grateful to you, my dear chap."

He looked embarrassed. He always does when I praise him, which is why I do not do it too often. He laughed and said, "Oh, my dear Holmes. It was surely very elementary."

I laughed. "Mock all you wish, my dear fellow. You have earned it."

"Do you think you will be able to gather enough evidence to bring her to trial?" he said, after a moment.

"I doubt it. She covered her tracks very well. Sir Jeremy might recognise her voice or that ring. Even if he could identify her, there is no proof that she placed those papers with the rest of Sir Nicholas Fleming's documents."

"But she is a menace, Holmes. Neither you nor Beatrice are safe while she lives."

"All we can do is watch her for the moment."

He nodded and rose. "You should get to bed. We have another wedding tomorrow."

I groaned. "Yes." I downed the rest of the scotch. "Goodnight, Watson."

"Goodnight, my dear fellow. Hang on; something has been nagging at me: The veil. You seemed to think there was some significance in the fact that Mrs Porlock kept her face covered, but that is not unusual for widows. What did I miss?"

"Think about how she was described to you by the locals in Camden Town."

"As a pretty blonde... Oh, how did they know what she looked like if she always wore a veil? So she only wore it so I wouldn't recognise her and Sir Jeremy wouldn't be able to identify her."

"Exactly."

"Wicked woman," Watson said. And he closed the door behind him.

28

Tuesday 16 August 1898

Edward Davenport and Miss Julia Simms are now Mr and Mrs Davenport. It was a very small, very quiet ceremony, at least in comparison with Daisy and Maurice Stevens' event yesterday. Most of the attendees were staff from Rillington Manor and I must say they gave Watson and me a charming welcome. This was nothing to the greeting my wife received. There is no doubt they hold her in the very highest esteem.

The ceremony was blessedly brief. B sat at my side and though she neither looked at me nor touched my hand, I had a profound sense of connection to her that bypasses all laws of reason.

After the ceremony, I took her aside and told her about Mariah Porlock.

"Good God," she exclaimed. "What an odious woman. She killed Tommy?"

"I believe she did," I said. "But I have no proof. You need not worry for the moment: She is under close watch. Not only are the police standing guard, but I have Kevin and some of the other Irregulars keeping an eye on her, too."

"It is not my safety I am concerned about, as you well know." She bit her lip then said, "Forgive me. I seem to be irascible of late."

"Under so much strain, the loss of Tommy, it is hardly surprising."

"You may be right. Or perhaps I just miss you."

"Then perhaps I might have the pleasure of your company this evening? If you are not otherwise engaged?"

"I am at your disposal," she said.

"Excellent. Are you planning on returning to Wimpole Street?"

"Yes, I must. Now my friends are married they should have some time alone, I think."

"And Billy?"

"Billy will stay with the Davenports. They have become a family. It was for Billy's sake I stayed in Pimlico as long as I did. I think now it is time I resumed my usual routine."

"Then may I escort you home?"

"I should like that."

Thursday 18 August 1898

There has been such a confusion these past few days as all our questions and riddles have found resolution.

I should review the events in the order they occurred. Then, perhaps, I can determine what they mean. Perhaps my suspicions are unfounded.

Beatrice and I dined together and renewed our old—I was about to say friendship, but of course it is rather more than that. Our old acquaintance? In any event, whatever word fits, we had a frank and complete discussion about the events of the past few months.

I thought she blamed me for Tommy's death, for not keeping her and the boys safe. She, in turn, thought I blamed her. She should not have returned to town, should have stayed at Windsor, etc., etc. Both of us so full of self-reproach and guilt.

In any event, we have both granted and received absolution for crimes real or imagined. Our night was all I had hoped and quite fulfilled the promises of Milan.

We discussed Mariah Porlock at length. B said, "So that creature is responsible for Tommy's death. She has made your life a misery and I assume she plans continue to do so."

"So I surmise."

"It's intolerable. She must be stopped, Sherlock."

"She will be. She will make a mistake and in time we shall have her."

"In time? Meanwhile, you must live under such a shadow."

"I am well able to look after myself. I am more concerned for your safety. Yours and Watson's. I think she has decided that torturing me is far more entertaining than killing me outright. The safety of my friends is my primary concern."

I was trying to lift her spirits but she is too wise to be beguiled by easy comfort, and too honourable to pretend to believe a lie. At last, she said, "Well, I will not let her malice spoil our night. And who knows, perhaps she will have a fatal accident."

As we ate breakfast I said, "I need to return to Baker Street to change. Will you come with me? I shall not take long."

"Thank you, my dear, but I have an errand to run," she said. "I shall meet you at the synagogue. Oh, I am so looking forward to seeing you wear a yarmulke."

I returned to Baker Street and changed, and went on to Holborn with Watson. The rabbi and his wife greeted us with great warmth. As Watson observed, we shook more hands than the Prime Minister greeting his public.

"Where is our friend Beatrice?" the rabbi said. "Miriam and Esther have been asking for her."

"She had an errand to run. She should be here soon."

Watson said, "Mr Solberg has something to tell you, Holmes."

Glaser's friend was serving as best man. He looked fit and healthy, his appearance vastly improved since the last time we met. But then, finding a hanging corpse would make anyone ill.

He took Watson and me outside the synagogue. "Some things should not be spoken in the presence of the Torah," he said. Then he explained how a woman had come to him last night to seek advice. "With my friend Glaser being properly focused on the wedding, she was reluctant to bother him. A little afraid, too, perhaps."

"Afraid? Of what?"

"Well, that man you had been looking for, the one I found… it seems she gave him lodgings. She is not religious, though she is Jewish, and she doesn't have much to do with us. Anyway, she often takes in lodgers to supplement her earnings."

"And this fellow, Richman, was one of her lodgers?"

"Yes. She said she tried three times to approach my friend David. She thought of speaking with the rabbi, too, but she feels intimidated by him. Goodness knows why, no one could be kinder. Anyway, the reason she came to me is this fellow, Rickman, left behind some belongings and she didn't know what to do with them."

"She could have sold them," Watson said. "If she's that hard up, I wonder she didn't try."

"I suspect his leavings were not particularly valuable," I said. "But she might have destroyed them."

"She might. In fact, I think she planned to, but some superstition prevented her. In the end, she came to me. I know her slightly and I flatter myself I have always treated her respectfully. She wanted my advice."

"And what did he leave behind?"

"I do not know."

A crowd of people, laughing, celebrating, passed us and entered the synagogue. Solberg dropped his voice and said, "David ordered the room sealed until you could examine it."

"Daniel," the rabbi said. "David is looking for you."

"I'm coming, Rabbi."

We all went into the synagogue together and took our seats. The service began. Still Beatrice did not arrive.

The service was like nothing I have ever experienced before. It was lively, noisy. There was a great deal of discussion amongst the congregation, with cheers and applause greeting the bride, the groom, and many of the rabbi's comments. I should have been vastly entertained.

"What's the matter with you, Holmes?" Watson hissed. "You're like a cat on hot coals."

"I cannot understand where Beatrice could have got to."

"I am sure she's perfectly safe. Look, here she is."

Looking unusually flustered, my wife hurried into the seat beside me.

"Are you all right?" I asked her.

"Yes, yes, I'm fine," she said. She seemed out of sorts but she gave me a smile and seemed to relax.

The service continued. Glaser stamped on a glass and everyone shouted *Mazel Tov!* It was quite delightful.

The reception was to take place in the hall attached to the synagogue but Glaser excused himself and joined me.

"Congratulations, Glaser," I said, shaking his hand. "It was a charming ceremony."

"It was indeed. Mr Holmes, Daniel told you about Netta Appleby? That she's been providing lodging for that Rickman fellow?"

"Yes he has. I should very much like to examine the room."

313

"As would I. If we leave now, I can be back in half an hour."

"What, leave your wedding?" Solberg sounded aghast.

"Only for half an hour. Rivkah understands."

Solberg rolled his eyes. "Oy, oy, oy," he said. "Well, come on, let's go."

In the corner of my eye, I saw Rivkah and Beatrice engaged in earnest conversation. B caught my eye and nodded. So she knew and approved. I am not sure why, but that gave me some comfort.

Appleby was full of apologies. Glaser cut her short. "You're very lucky I'm in too good a mood to scold you, Netta. But this is a serious matter. You knew we were looking for this fellow. I spoke to you myself, in fact."

"You did, Inspector," she said, tearfully. "It was very wrong. But he was such a sweet young boy. Simple. There didn't seem any harm in him. I know he must have family; he spoke of a sister… Between ourselves, I think he was terrified of her. But I couldn't just get rid of all his things…"

The room was a jumble of confusion. Clothes, once good but now soiled and frayed, were strewn around the bed and the floor. There were dozens of empty whisky bottles. No drinking glass.

Curiously, the surface of the table was empty except for a letter. The paper was cheap stationery available anywhere, and the note was written in pencil. It was a disjointed, sometimes incoherent account of the thoughts of a man about to take his own life.

My dear Mariah, it said,

I cannot live with the wicked things I have done. I have become a monster. I have failed you and myself.

Do not be angry with me. Please, please... I know what a wretch I am. A fool, just as you always said. But, Mariah, I cannot live with the things I have done. You tell me these things are right, are just, but what if we're wrong, Mariah? Dear God, what if we're wrong?

Your quarrel you should have kept to yourself. I have sins enough of my own without needing to add yours.

I would go to the police but I cannot bear what they must do to you. And what of your dear children? They would forever hate their Uncle Albert.

I cannot sleep. I lie in the dark and those faces haunt me. They say I am accursed.

A boy, Mariah. Just a child. How could you? Oh God.

I did not find the diamonds. I did not find the coins. I have failed in everything as I always do.

I beg you take care of Connie and my child. Give them what money you can spare, I know it cannot be much.

May you and God forgive me.

Your devoted brother,

Albert.

I felt Watson shudder. "Poor wretch," he said. "What a terror his sister must have been. A shame he did not admit his guilt and let justice be served."

The letter was not surprising, nor was it particularly helpful.

"Nothing that specifically inculpates his sister," I said. "We shall have to find our own evidence. As you say, Watson, a pity this fellow did not admit his crimes and do penance.

"You and Solberg should return to the wedding, Glaser. I would like to examine this room more thoroughly. Watson and I shall join you shortly."

"Be sure you do," Glaser said. "My wife will never forgive either of us if you do not."

The two friends left, leaving Watson and me to examine the room. A half an hour was sufficient. Truthfully, the job was done in a matter of minutes but I wanted to be thorough.

The only thing of even slight interest was a floor plan of a building. After a moment's study, I was able to identify it as Schwartz's workshop.

"What do you make of it, Holmes?" Watson said.

"He was trying to discover the entrance to the vault. A useless endeavour for it is beneath the building and not on these plans. I studied every inch of that establishment, Watson, and it took me almost an hour to find it. That was in daylight with my eyes and my wits. This proves conclusively he was hoping to get to the gems and precious metals that are hidden away in there. Yes… I think, apart from his guilt and his shame, he was afraid to tell his sister he failed. How she must have bullied and vexed him to make him so terrified of her. Harridan!"

"He asked her to look after Connie and his child. He didn't know they were dead," Watson said. "She did it. By heaven, Holmes, we have met scoundrels before: Moriarty and Porlock; Grimesby Roylott and Milverton, but this woman is their equal in wickedness."

We kept the letter and sealed up the room, reminding the landlady it was not to be entered until Inspector Glaser gave permission. We returned to the wedding and the festivities. Around two o'clock I was surprised to see Lestrade beckon me from the doorway.

"Forgive me, Mr Holmes," he said. "But something has happened and I wanted to tell you at once."

Beatrice and Watson joined me. "What is it, Inspector?" Beatrice said. She seemed to be holding her breath.

"That woman you asked us to watch—"

"Oh, for heavens' sake, Lestrade, surely you have not lost her already?"

"No, Mr Holmes. She is dead."

I cannot say what feelings coursed through me: elation, relief, and deep, ugly suspicion. I did not dare to look at my wife.

"How?" Watson asked. "Did she take her own life?"

"Well, that's possible, though I doubt it. She left her lodgings around noon and went to the railway station. To Euston, that is. It was busy on the platform with a sudden surge of crowds as happens sometimes. Anyway, somehow she fell onto the tracks. Fell, or was pushed. She is badly... I mean, identifying her wasn't easy, but my men recovered this."

He handed me a blood-stained sapphire ring.

"I see," I said. "I appreciate you letting me know."

"I understand you are busy, but if you wanted to investigate...?"

"Why should I want to do such a thing?" I said. "No, Lestrade. As far as I am concerned, she met with an unfortunate accident. I am happy to leave it at that."

Wednesday 31 August 1898

Beatrice is quiet and very gentle in her dealings with me, but her sleep is troubled and once I heard her call out. I held her and she stopped trembling at last. "You are safe," I said. "Hush, you are safe. I'll never let anyone harm you."

Nor shall I. No matter what sacrifice I must make. This I vow.

Background Notes

I was very young when I began reading the Sherlock Holmes stories, and for a while I was convinced he had really lived. Well, I was only seven years old.

Later, I started to wonder: what if he *had* really lived? What would his life have been like? What did he get up to between cases? Watson hints that Holmes was consulted on matters of international importance. What were they? These questions and hundreds more inspired me to write my first Holmes novel, *A Biased Judgement: The Sherlock Holmes Diaries 1897*. In the book, I combined the canonical stories of Sir Arthur Conan Doyle with the historical events of that year. Writing it was so much fun and reader response so positive I knew I had to write a sequel. So, *Sherlock Holmes and the Other Woman.*

I wanted this book to follow immediately after the first, so I started researching 1898. As before, I began with Doyle: what happened in the Sherlock Holmes canon that year? Watson shares only two cases, though he teases us with hints of others. *The Adventure of the Dancing Men* began in July and *The Adventure of the Retired Colourman* took place in July or August, depending on which chronology expert you believe. I wondered what Holmes was doing in the months prior. Well, one event dominated the world's newspapers in the last decade of the nineteenth century: the so-called Dreyfus Affair.

My novel is fiction and cannot do justice to such a convoluted tale, but I hope I have included enough detail to capture the essence of those events. My research included reading a large number of books, in particular Ruth Harris's definitive book, *The Man on Devil's Island* (2010) published by Allen Lane. I also read a number of contemporary newspapers and on-line articles.

Here are some of the undisputed facts about the Affair: Captain Alfred Dreyfus (1859 – 1935) was born in Alsace to a Jewish textile manufacturer. His family moved to France and he later joined the French army. Dreyfus was considered a good soldier until 1894 when the French became aware that military secrets were being passed to the Germans. Suspicion fell on Dreyfus because, as a Jew and an Alsatian, he was deemed an outsider. Despite a case built on little more than badly forged documents and anti-Semitism, Dreyfus was found guilty in a secret court. He was publicly disgraced, stripped of his rank, and sentenced to life imprisonment in the notorious French penal colony on Devil's Island.

In 1899, Dreyfus was pardoned by the French president and released, but he was not fully exonerated until 1906. He was then readmitted to the army with the rank of major. A week later, he was made a Knight of the Legion of Honour.

Dreyfus died in 1935, 29 years to the day after his official exoneration.

The supporters of Captain Dreyfus were called the 'Dreyfusards'. These included members of the literati and the most brilliant intellectuals of the day such as Jean Jaurès, editor of *La Petite Republique*; Émile Duclaux, a microbiologist and chemist who was an associate of Louis Pasteur's; and Émile Zola.

Zola (1840 – 1902) was a renowned novelist who was nominated for the first and second Nobel Prize for Literature in 1901 and 1902. He put his career and indeed, his life in jeopardy when he published *J'Accuse*, an indictment of the French military and government's anti-Semitism and hypocrisy, and a demand for justice for Dreyfus. This stance shattered Zola's reputation. He was convicted of libel in 1898 and was removed from the Legion of Honour. He fled to England and remained there until June 1899 when he returned to France.

In September 1902, Zola died of carbon monoxide poisoning. There were rumours that he was murdered. Indeed, a chimney sweep by the name of Henri Buronfosse allegedly claimed he deliberately blocked Zola's chimney in order to kill him.

Zola was honoured with re-interment in the Panthéon in 1908. He shares a tomb with fellow literary giants Victor Hugo and Alexandre Dumas.

Marie-Georges Picquart (1854 – 1914) was the youngest Lieutenant-Colonel in the French army and chief of its intelligence bureau. His investigation into the Dreyfus Affair led to the discovery of the real traitor, Ferdinand Walsin Esterhazy. Picquart was cautioned to keep his discovery to himself, but continued his investigation despite considerable opposition. One of the people who tried to hinder him was Hubert-Joseph Henry (more on him shortly). Picquart was himself arrested on a trumped-up forgery charge when he seemed likely to exonerate Dreyfus. He subsequently resigned from the military. However, Dreyfus's exoneration also exonerated Picquart, and he returned to the army in 1906 with the rank of Brigadier-General.

Ferdinand Walsin Esterhazy (1847 – 1923) was an officer in the French Army. He was a spy for the German Empire and committed the act of treason for which Dreyfus was convicted. One of his letters fell into the hands of Picquart, and the investigator realised at once the handwriting was identical to the documents that had sent Dreyfus to Devil's Island.

Despite overwhelming evidence against him, Esterhazy was acquitted by a French military tribunal in January 1898. The judgement led to riots in the streets and, ultimately, to Zola publishing *J'Accuse*. In September 1898, Esterhazy fled France. He made his way to Belgium before settling in England.

Hubert-Joseph Henry (1846 – 1898) was a French Lieutenant-Colonel who admitted to forging two documents known as the 'faux Henry' that had helped convict Dreyfus of treason. He was sent to French military prison at Fort Mont-Valérien. The next day he sent a letter in which he admitted his guilt and added, cryptically, "You know in whose interests I acted." He was later found dead in his cell. His throat had been cut. Although no razor was found at the scene, the French police pronounced his death a suicide.

The prevailing air of conspiracy was intensified by the unexplained death of one of Henry's agents who went by the name Lemercier-Picard (real name Moses Lehmann). His death by hanging was never fully explained. Indeed, when Lieutenant-Colonel Picquart was arrested he said, "To-night perhaps I shall go to the Cherche-Midi, and this is probably the last time that I will be able to speak in public. I would have the world know that if the rope of Lemercier-Picard or the razor of Henry is found in my cell, I shall have been assassinated. No man like myself can for a moment think of suicide."

I'll leave the Dreyfus there and move on to Sherlock Holmes and the world in 1898.

The 'Coptic Patriarchs' will be familiar to Holmes's readers as one of those cases Doctor Watson mentions only in passing (*The Adventure of the Retired Colourman*). For more than a century, Sherlockians have wondered who these 'Patriarchs' were. I'd like to think Dr Doyle would have approved my interpretation. The myth of the coins is an entire fiction, although the history of the Coptic Church is real. The City of Akhetaten (Tell el-Amarna) was founded and deserted just as Bazalgette describes to Holmes.

The term 'zugzwang' will be familiar to chess players as meaning a forced move with no good options. It wasn't introduced to England until 1905, but it had been in common use in Germany since 1858. It derives from the German *zug* meaning move, and *zwang* meaning compulsion. While Sir Arthur Conan Doyle never mentioned Holmes playing chess, it seems reasonable to assume he was familiar with both the game and the term.

In October 1859, the steam clipper *Royal Charter* was wrecked in a storm off the coast of Anglesey and some 450 people died. As a result, Vice-Admiral Robert FitzRoy introduced a warning service for shipping in February 1861 using telegraph communications. While the system was managed by the Met Office, it's likely Mycroft would have kept an eye on the forecast while he was expecting his brother's return.

Hatton Garden had, and has, an international reputation as the centre of London's jewellery industry. While David Glaser and the other inhabitants are entirely my own creation, the neighbourhood and the Jewish community are mostly real. Like much of London, it has changed considerably over the past century. I hope readers will forgive my filling some of factual gaps with supposition and, on occasion, complete fabrication. For instance, although there were several synagogues within a mile or two of Hatton Garden, there wasn't one in the immediate vicinity. However, for the sake of the story, I played with the geography a little. The district was much more ethnically diverse, too.

The nearby Saffron Hill where the unfortunate Constable Bing meets his end, was notorious as one of the most dangerous places in the city. Conan Doyle mentions it in *The Adventure of the Six Napoleons* as the home of the Venucci family. Although that story is set in 1902, I paid homage to it by putting a bust of Napoleon in Demosthenes Jones's shop and have Holmes threaten to break it as he actually does in Doyle's tale.

Much of my information about London during this period comes from the extraordinary work of philanthropist and social researcher Charles Booth. He mapped out the entire city according to crime and poverty rates in 1898. His maps and notes are available on-line at http://booth.lse.ac.uk/ and make compelling reading.

My descriptions of Mrs Prentiss's neighbourhood owe much to the paintings of The Camden Town Group. The group included Walter Sickert, Spencer Gore, Augustus John and many others. The artists painted various scenes around Mornington Crescent and Harrington Square at the turn of the century. It was fascinating to see what Camden Town looked like during this period.

While the Home for Unfortunate Women in Holloway is my own creation, many establishments of this sort existed at the time and were very unpleasant places.

Telephones were in use by 1898, though they were hardly commonplace. Sir Arthur Conan Doyle mentions them in several stories, including *The Sign of Four* and *The Adventure of the Dancing Men*. While only the wealthiest or most important members of society had their own telephone at this time, it's probable Holmes arranged for one to be installed in 221B Baker Street. Perhaps Mycroft insisted upon it. I speculated Holmes's telephone was kept in the downstairs hallway, so Mrs Hudson, bless her, could take messages when Holmes and Watson were out.

James Billington (1847 – 1901) was the executioner for London and the Home Counties from 1892. He hanged 24 men and three women in Newgate Prison.

Mrs Prentiss keeps carbon copies of her translations. Carbon paper was widely produced since the 1820s.

Captain Sir George Mansfield Smith-Cumming, KCMG, CB (1859-1923) was the first director of the Secret Intelligence Service (SIS), later known as MI6. I'd like to think he was influenced by Mycroft, wouldn't you?

Fans of the Granada television series might recognise 'Peter Huggins' as the real name of the late, much-missed Jeremy Brett.

While I was writing this novel, and shortly after I completed it, a number of events happened that echoed my fiction: anti-Semitic attacks in France (some would say they never stopped), and a major jewel robbery in Hatton Garden. The more things change...

Acknowledgements

This book would not exist without Sir Arthur Conan Doyle's extraordinary creation of Sherlock Holmes, nor without the readers, publishers, editors, and filmmakers who keep him alive.

I would like to thank my daughter Cara and her partner Chris for their unfailing support, and my family and friends for their encouragement.

Special thanks to Jane, Patty, Ellie and Sherrill for their tireless readings, suggestions, and corrections.

Thanks to Steve Emecz and everyone at MX Publishing for all their help with this manuscript.

Finally, much love and gratitude to my readers and to Sherlock Holmes fans everywhere. I'll see you in the bookshop.

Also from MX Publishing

MX Publishing is the world's largest specialist Sherlock Holmes publisher, with over a hundred titles and fifty authors creating the latest in Sherlock Holmes fiction and non-fiction.

From traditional short stories and novels to travel guides and quiz books, MX Publishing cater for all Holmes fans.

The collection includes leading titles such as *Benedict Cumberbatch In Transition* and *The Norwood Author* which won the 2011 Howlett Award (Sherlock Holmes Book of the Year).

MX Publishing also has one of the largest communities of Holmes fans on Facebook with regular contributions from dozens of authors.

www.mxpublishing.com

Also from MX Publishing

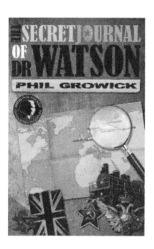

"Phil Growick's, 'The Secret Journal of Dr Watson', is an adventure which takes place in the latter part of Holmes and Watson's lives. They are entrusted by HM Government (although not officially) and the King no less to undertake a rescue mission to save the Romanovs, Russia's Royal family from a grisly end at the hand of the Bolsheviks. There is a wealth of detail in the story but not so much as would detract us from the enjoyment of the story. Espionage, counter-espionage, the ace of spies himself, double-agents, double-crossers...all these flit across the pages in a realistic and exciting way. All the characters are extremely well-drawn and Mr Growick, most importantly, does not falter with a very good ear for Holmesian dialogue indeed. Highly recommended. A five-star effort."

The Baker Street Society

www.mxpublishing.com

Lightning Source UK Ltd.
Milton Keynes UK
UKOW06f1618211015

261112UK00001B/14/P